ONE PEOPLE

"The vibes of modern Jamaica are captured perfectly in this gloriously candid book. In-your-face and utterly authentic, its pages are saturated with humour and humanity – this is the next best thing to jumping on a plane and going there."
Steve Barrow, co-author of the *Rough Guide to Reggae*

"Any vignette out of the gorgeous thousands which lope and bustle through [*One People*] might suffice to give an image of Jamaican spirituality, humanity and fecklessness ... a great book."
The Herald

"an explanation of how storytelling constitutes life itself in this village – reputations are forged as these tales become the stuff of local legend."
The Times

"an extremely well-written, highly entertaining and often very funny read ... Guy Kennaway has a deft way with a tale."
Echoes

"turns every trick to bring local flavours into his prose."
The Observer

"This year's funniest, most thoroughly likeable novel ... a fantastical yet believable microcosm of life ... Kennaway has succeeded in following in the footsteps of his acknowledged model – Garrison Keillor."
GQ

ONE PEOPLE

Guy Kennaway

CANONGATE

First published in 1997 by Payback Press, an imprint of Canongate
Books Ltd, 14 High Street, Edinburgh EH1 1TE. Second edition 1999.
This edition published in the United States and Canada in 2001.

10 9 8 7 6 5 4 3 2 1

Publisher's Note
This is a work of fiction. Names, characters, places and incidents either
are the product of the author's imagination or are used fictitiously, and
any resemblance to actual persons, living or dead, events, or places is
entirely coincidental.

British Library Cataloguing-in-Publication Data
A catalogue record for this book is available upon request from the
British Library

ISBN 0 86241 829 1

Typeset by Carnegie Publishing, Lancaster, Lancashire
Printed and bound in Finland by W. S. Bookwell

www.canongate.net

OUT OF MANY, ONE PEOPLE
(Jamaican national motto)

CONTENTS

THE BIRTH OF JAMAICA

One moonless night a whole 'eap o' year ago, the vast equatorial ocean stirred, and boiling black volcanic lava bubbled from its depths to explode onto the surface. Relatively quickly, within ten thousand years, the molten rock cooled and solidified. Over the next couple 'ondred tousan' year it was reshaped by earthquakes, and sculpted by wind and sea. The island was a terrible place: tempests blew for fifty years at a time, bolts of lightning cratered the earth, and peals of thunder sent massive boulders hurtling into the sea, crushing everything in their path. A drought lasted eighty years, and was only broken by downpours of sulphurous rain. Earthquakes shook the ground for weeks at a time, and rent great fissures in the hills that opened and then closed like abominable mouths. From one bottomless chasm, a scalding geyser shot steam hundreds of feet into the air with no warning, while another devoured with a gulp a river which flowed into its throat and was never seen again. Twice, the island dropped out of view entirely, once for over a century, before being catapulted up through the depths to break the surface again.

Millions of years later the storms ease back, the ocean cool out, aftershocks became infrequent, the land finally settled, and the sun, one bright day, rose on the newly born island of Jamaica. Compared to what was to come, it was an uneventful and easy birth.

One hundred and fifty miles from west to east, and fifty miles from north to south, its silhouette on the map was amorphous, though at either end of the island the shape of two heads was clearly discernible, each pointing purposefully in a different direction.

The north coast of the island was a necklace of windswept cliffs, sheltered bays, little inlets and white talcum sand beaches. Reflected in the clear turquoise water were the hills that rose a little inland; hills the shape of good size wuman dem lying asleep on their sides, or fronts, or even their backs, their mounds and curves thrusting into the sky.

From the rock, mysteriously, came plant life: lichens and strange mosses quite extinct today, that thrived in the tropical heat and humidity. Seasons carved themselves out of the year: a dry winter, a cool wet spring, a hot and rainy summer and a windy, stormy autumn, and not long behind them came leafed plants, flowers, trees, and animal life. A jungle grew up, covering the highest misty hill and the deepest shady valley, but conditions were so fertile that a second jungle soon grew on top of the first: whole gardens, including large bushes and trees, took seed and thrived on the upper branches of big trees, and plants which entwined themselves around others were themselves soon covered in a third growth. In places the forest collapsed under its own weight before picking itself off its knees and forcing its way once more through the suffocating blanket of broken branches, wist and creeper.

Off the coast, in the warm, sunny shallows, microscopic life patiently weaved pink and green reefs that kept the deep sea predators out of the sandy bays, making a sanctuary for the striped and spotted fish which dwelt there.

* * *

The only scientific fact known about early human beings on Jamaica is that they were created fully formed by Jah and one day walked out of a cave to begin life on the island. Everything else was disputed. Some people said the first Jamaicans were descendents of monkeys and apes through an unlikely process known as evolution, and others that they were 'Mesticans' who arrived by canoe from Guatemala and Belize, but these two theories were considered far-fetched because they presupposed Jamaicans to be in some way the same as other people, which of course stretched credibility too far.

However humans got there, Jamaica proved to be so beautiful and bountiful that they thrived, and soon after the first people appeared, there were settlements dotted around the coast of the island, many of which are still in existence today. An interesting example of this is the ancient community of Firefly Bay, in the parish of St John.

FIREFLY BAY

Firefly Bay was the prettiest village on the north coast of Jamaica, with the exception of Negril, whose picture post-card beauty was to damn it. It had the benefit of a sheltered beach, a breezy promontory, a fresh-water river, fertile, easily turned soil, and productive fishing grounds. But it was the people of Firefly Bay who were really remarkable. A tight-knit, determined community from the very beginning, they passed the desire for their village to prosper and grow from one generation to another. For this laudable ambition they suffered the derision of other less progressive villages on the coast, like their immediate neighbours, Angel Beach, but were never deflected from their purpose by the criticism of the unenlightened.

In Firefly Bay they learnt early the civilised art of enjoying themselves with moderation. They alone could meet in the wooden bar by the bend in the road, enjoy a few drinks, put the cork back in the rum, and go to bed sober. In other villages, like Angel Beach, when a cork was removed from a bottle of alcohol, it was flung into the sea. But the next night, when the improvident drunks of Angel Beach had nottin fi drink, the men of Firefly Bay still had nearly three-quarters of their bottle of rum left. And not only were they clever in Firefly Bay, but they were kind. If one of them began to lose more than he could afford to, playing dominoes, his friends refused to play any more with him, and more often than not escorted him to his yard to prevent him finding anyone else to whom to lose money. That was the behaviour of a community that really cared. In Angel Beach, if a man hit a losing streak at poker, word quickly got round, and friends would get out of bed and hurry to the game so they could strip him of his last dollar.

Unfortunately, Firefly Bay people got an undeserved reputation for being priggish and self-important. When a Royal Tour of the West Indies was made in 1984, the foolish people dem of Angel Beach joked that Mrs Queen was only coming to the Caribbean to see Firefly Bay. Firefly Bay easily rose above the criticism; they knew Angel Beach people to be lazy, irresponsible and incapable of taking the important things in life, like being a little mindful of what others thought of you, at all seriously. It is the lazy and irresponsible men, women and picknee of Angel Beach whose stories are told here.

✳   ✳   ✳

Angel Beach stood around a sandy inlet twenty miles east of the western tip of Jamaica, under some forested hills the shape of a good size wuman lying curled up asleep on her side. The sun rose behind her knees, and set on the sea in front of her. The moon travelled the same felicitous arc, burning as it came up through the trees and throbbing directly overhead at midnight when it was full, so bright that one night half the village got up at two in the morning thinking the day had started. A river flowed from the woman's belly into the cove, duning the sand as it crossed the beach, and mixed in a filmy way with the warm water of the sea. The ocean, held in the cove by overhanging jungle, was invariably as flat as a pond, and always warm. It wasn't dangerous or frightening, like on the point at Firefly Bay where it boomed onto rocks, but comforting and reassuring, as if, like the sun and moon, it had singled out Angel Beach to be its friend. It made the village seem a blessed place, a little Eden made more interesting by the Fall.

The first people to dwell in Angel Beach were the Arawaks over 5000 years ago, but little remains of their occupation because the corrosive effects of heat, humidity and tropical rain, not to mention the devastation of rare but regular hurricanes, left so little of the past on the ground. What few historical sites there are in Jamaica are suspect; Rose Hall, a slave plantation Great House, and one of the nation's premier tourist attractions, was built in 1975. The Arawaks were not the kind to build large monuments, mainly because cutting and hauling stone in that heat was punishing work, something the Arawak was careful to avoid. Their legacy can be found in the language and character of the modern Angel as a person from Angel Beach is known. Words they coined which are still in use evoke the Arawaks' easy life: tobacco, hammock and barbecue. From time to time they fished from canoes dug out from the abundance of towering cotton trees, but otherwise, at least in Angel Beach, they did pretty well nothing but lie about. Up at dawn, have a smoke, put your feet up and wait for some barbecued snapper – that about summed their life up. They were way ahead of the field in refining the art of leisure, and it was still only the fifth century, when everyone else's life was nasty, brutish and short. The Arawak Heaven (they had no Hell) comprised intermittent feasting and sleeping, with sex thrown in whenever they wanted it. It was the sort of place Christians went to Hell for, for even thinking about.

Jamaica has always been the most fertile island on earth. If you snap a twig off a tree and ram it into the ground, a couple of weeks later leaves shoot from its top. Centuries after the Arawaks, when the first fence posts were hammered into the land, they regularly sprouted into crooked lines of trees. The forest was full of fruit; in Beach the Arawaks didn't have to plant a thing, they probably didn't even go to the trouble of picking it, but waited in their hammocks for it to drop fully ripe into their open palms. Most of all, the Arawaks loved harmony, and rarely fought amongst themselves. Disputes were settled by one side (the weaker) backing down just before they were beaten up. Nowadays, you can tell a Beach man by the way, when he has a ratchet knife pulled on him, he'll reach quickly into his own pocket, pull out a packet of Craven A cigarettes and offer the assailant one. The Arawaks were good carpenters, fishermen and cooks, but they were most highly skilled in chat, which unfortunately was a talent not in demand when the man-eating Caribs began to make attacks on the islands of the Caribbean.

In all military history, there cannot have been an easier race to surprise than the Arawaks, and the Caribs made swift work of them. Big meat-eaters, the Caribs moved up from South America through the Leeward and Antilles. After a one hundred and fifty mile row from Cuba, they arrived, famished, at Firefly Bay, three miles down the coast from Angel Beach, and devoured the first eight people they saw, who happened to be the official reception committee. They were still laughing about this a few days later in Angel Beach, when Carib canoes rounded the rocky promontory and headed into the calm inlet, where the village huts stood on the beach. The Caribs splashed ashore, raped and killed a number of women and children, and chased the men into the bush as far as they could be bothered to. They argued that people so cowardly couldn't possibly put up a decent fight, and anyway, after years of carnage, a feeling was growing amongst the middle-class Caribs that they should eat more vegetables, and hunt only for the pot, and the plump Angel Beach picknee were quite sufficient for a good light meal.

The Caribs liked to fight, and they liked to party. They made noise all night, and torched vast tracts of forest for a laugh. Their songs were not noted for their melodies, harmonies or lyrics, but for their volume. Arawaks hiding miles into the jungle heard them and said, 'Mi kiant believe dem listen a dis fart.' Carib blood has given the modern Covite the ability to sleep soundly inches from immense speaker boxes. They were always beating each other up, and the men carried knives in their belts at all times, causing a number of accidental suicides when they tripped over rocks in the dark.

The Caribs were just beginning to feel happily settled in Beach when the white man turned up. There was nothing superhuman about the white man, but when it came to fighting (which it always did with the Caribs), they had the edge because of things called muskets. The Arawaks came down the hill specially to watch the Spaniards slaughtering Caribs. Then the Spaniards turned their attention to the Arawaks, who gave themselves away by laughing too loudly.

The common enemy drove the Caribs and Arawaks into each other's arms. The Caribs swore they were really sorry for everything, and the Arawaks, in their usual way, forgave them, and introduced them to the delights of eating things that didn't walk around on two legs or talk. They lived deep inna de bush, coming occasionally to the top of the hill to gaze longingly down on the creek that cupped the calm sea at their beloved Beach. Their grandchildren saw the Spaniards replaced by the British, and, finally, their grandchildren got to live back down in the village, though in somewhat less than desirable conditions, for by then slavery days had begun.

In the autumn of 1690 two hundred and ten black Africans, the property of an English adventurer called Edwin Fairfax, arrived at Angel Beach after a one hundred and eighty mile march manacled at the neck, blinking with confusion, fear and loneliness. It had not been their year: captured in battle, taken from their lands, tribes and families, imprisoned under purgatorial conditions in boats which left a trail of corpses floating on the Atlantic, they were split into new groups, stripped of their language, religion and remaining friends, and sold to a man who genuinely believed he was doing them a favour feeding and sheltering them in return for a brief life of back-breaking toil.

Once in Angel Beach they were quick to notice how fertile the red soil looked, how sweet the water in the river tasted, and how plump and plentiful were the fish in the transparent sea. In many ways it was a better land than the one they had left – but that only made them hate it more. On the first night one proud man escaped, and waded into the moonlit water to commit suicide.

They were set to work under a ginger-haired overseer called Swing, the offspring of a brief but sweet union between a Carib woman and a Scotsman, to build a sugar mill and slave accommodation. By the time the task was completed forty-eight had died from disease or accident.

Within twelve months the estate was milling sugar worth £25,000, though that of course was a gross figure from which annual running costs of £26. 11s. 6d. had to be deducted. Edwin's son, Thomas (Eton College and Oxford), visited his plantation for the first time aged twenty-one, and was shocked by the conditions his slaves endured. He immediately put some proposals for reforms to old Swing concerning diet, sanitation and hours of work, but when Swing explained how they would eat into profits (which were by then £128,000 per annum, £1.8 million in today's money), Thomas saw that the issue was more complex than he first realised. The problem was that his income was fully committed on a new ornamental lake, grotto and classical ruin on his Gloucestershire estate, so there was nothing for it but to put off the reforms until he could afford them.

There were many courageous attempts to throw off the yoke of slavery, but none emanated from Angel Beach, where they directed their energy to skiving work and minor acts of sabotage like peeing in the sugar mill and adulterating Swing's flour with salt.

Priding themselves on their bravery, the men and women of Angel Beach responded enthusiastically when a Coramantee slave called Tiger Taylor in Lemon Grove, a village ten miles to the west, asked them to join a revolt he was going to start. For a few days they talked excitedly in whispers of butchering old Swing and Fairfax's agent, Knibb the attorney, simultaneously thinking that if the revolt looked shaky they could always not come out to support Taylor.

A rumour of the plot reached the authorities – from the goody-goodies in Firefly Bay, everyone said – and on the day before the revolt a detachment of soldiers was posted to Lemon Grove. When the platoon marched through Beach the sight of the muskets and bayonets made everyone's blood run cold. A ten year old boy ran the ten miles from Tiger Taylor to Beach with a message: because of the soldiers, the uprising would now have to be started by Angel Beach.

There wasn't a coward in Angel Beach, of course, but the idea of starting a revolt, rather than joining one that was already going well, did not have quite the same attraction, and everyone was subsequently subdued by the prospect. A deputation went to Maas Wellington, the obeah man, to ask for magical powers of protection against musket balls. After throwing a handful of animal teeth and chanting some ancient African incantations he gave the assurance that not a single man from Beach would die. To ensure this science would work, he went secretly to Swing and said he feared a revolt. Within three hours a second platoon of soldiers arrived in Beach. The brave people of Beach agreed, reluctantly of course, that this ruled them out from starting any revolt. The baton was passed again, this time to Firefly Bay, who declined to grasp it, declaring that reform, not revolution, was the way to ease the burden of slavery. With some satisfaction, Angel Beach branded Firefly Bay cowards, and the whole affair has been remembered ever since as one of the many heroic episodes in the history of the village.

Edwin Fairfax's great great grand-nephew, Sir Somerset Webb, sold the plantation in the late eighteenth century for a colossal sum. His daughter Jane inherited his money and diverted it into her pet hobbyhorse: the fight for the abolition of slavery. Her generous contributions to the cause helped bring slavery days to an end in Angel Beach.

When news of emancipation reached Angel Beach (some months after everywhere else), the new owner of the plantation, an uncouth Yorkshireman called Hogg, asked the slaves to continue to work for a wage. But by then they'd had enough of working for the white man, and argued that after two hundred years of slavery they were owed some time off, about forty years each man, not to mention back pay. So Hogg, like other owners, imported indentured labourers from India. In Firefly Bay the Indians were resented because they took all the work, but in Beach they were loved for that, and one other reason: they brought with them the ganja plant, the leaves of which, when smoked, tasted sweet and minty, and took all your troubles and cares away. Possibly as a consequence of this development, the next one hundred and fifty years in Angel Beach were somewhat uneventful. In an average life of sixty-five years, a Angel Beach man spent twenty-one years dozing, a decade working on his appearance, eight years flirting, a month having sex, five years boasting about it, six years generally showing off, four years laughing and the balance in idle chat.

To Angel Beach the twentieth century was very much like
the nineteenth and eighteenth, and for that matter the seven-
teenth and sixteenth too. While the rest of the world strived
to invent and use cars, planes, computers and the other
paraphernalia of twentieth-century life, Angel Beach got by
fine with the wheel, the wood saw, the hammer, the machete,
and a single slightly broken screwdriver which was always
left lying in the dirt where the last person used it. The village
did not prosper and expand like the towns and cities of the
south coast, but stayed pretty much the size it was when
Hogg, the owner of the plantation, went bust in 1878, blam-
ing the uselessness of the local work force, and left to seek
his fortune in America. The sugar mill and slave accommodation fell apart with neglect, and soon melted into the rising
foliage.

For many years, the village stood on the beach and along
the rocks just above the sea, but a tidal wave in the autumn
of 1909 swept everyone back onto the flat pasture between
the sea and the hills, where they felt out of reach of an angry
ocean.

'It dangerous fi live too close to de sea,' they told one
another.

'Ya man, we nuh gonna make dat mistake two time.'

The coast road, or track as it then was, followed the curve
of the bay and then climbed a little hill and left Angel Beach
for Byng River, Sandy Island, Lemon Grove and the Morass,
where it petered out due to lack of interest in any place
further west. An even rougher track led to the symmetry,
where the village dead were buried. The track then bent right
into the Back Street, where about ten wooden houses, raised
at each corner on rocks to avoid flooding and deter ants,
stood in yards worn to dust by children's bare feet, each
about fifty yards apart in the dense foliage.

In 1939, the population of thirty-nine supported one shop, two bars, and eight churches. A year later, six men left to fight a distant war for the white man inna foreign, and the loss of business closed one of the bars down. Three of them returned in 1945, with paler skins and exciting tales of life outside Beach.

Even in the 1960s travel was rare. Montego Bay, fifty miles to the east, was considered a long way away, and some people only got that far once in their lives. At Christmas and Easter people walked the seven miles to Content, the nearest town, to get drunk and find someone new to have sex with. Otherwise they stayed in the village and had sex with the same old people. In 1971 a primary school was built, where subjects were taught in English, a language no-one spoke, so only a handful of exceptionally gifted pupils learnt to read and write.

In the 1970s, political rivalries made metropolitan Jamaica a genuinely terrifying place, with murder many men's preferred form of self-expression. Elections were blood baths in Kingston. In Beach they liked to believe they too could produce political violence, but somehow no-one ever got round to it. A gun did enter the village at one stage in 1971, but only for a couple of months, while its owner, a Kingston gunman, was in the lock-up waiting for someone to buy him out. Fortunately, it had no ammunition, so the men of Beach were free to make big boasts about who they'd use it on if only they had the bullets. When the gunman returned to pick up his piece, he brought with him six bullets, loaded the gun, and let the yout of Beach feel it in their hands. Gucci, a facetious twenty year old farmer's boy, twirling the revolver on his forefinger, accidentally let off a shot which passed under his friend, Wilbert's arm, making two neat holes in his shirt sleeve. Wilbert, thirty, quick-tempered, touchy, and strongly built, was a man who wasn't afraid to get into a fight. Fortunately for Gucci, who was a weakling with stick-like legs and tiny fists, Wilbert was stone deaf, and didn't notice the gun going off a few feet behind him, and although he asked what all the commotion in the room was about, no-one ever told him that he'd been shot by Gucci until years later, when Gucci had moved to Kingston.

It was during these years of ferocious political turmoil that the government decided tourism would play a leading role in the economy. It was a desperate plan, but there seemed nothing else left for the government to try. The country was bankrupt. Sugar cane was no longer a jackpot commodity in a world where a billion people were on low-sugar diets, and bauxite hadn't developed into the big winner the mineral companies assured the government it would be when they demanded the compulsory purchase of large tracts of fertile land in the '60s.

Everyone knew, even the government, that tourism in the capital was a non-starter. Kingston was, after all, the gun capital of the world, and proclaimed itself the baddest city on the globe, not without some pride. So in its time of need, the City of Kingston, once preeminent in the Caribbean, had to call upon the rural parishes for help. It was a national act of faith in the obscure towns and fishing villages of the sandy north coast, which were instructed to play host to the white man and his dollar.

Far to the west, tarmac was laid across the twenty-mile swamp called the Morass, to Negril, an isolated hamlet on a seven-mile white sand beach, whose entire population of twenty-six came out to watch when the first bulldozer crashed through the mangrove, all wondering why anyone wanted to connect them by road to Montego Bay. They soon found out.

The smugglers' airstrip at Mo-Bay was swallowed up by the Donald Sangster International Airport, and wide-bodied jets were soon releasing, on each touchdown, enough tourists to fill four big hotels. Within a few years Negril underwent a crazy, uncontrolled expansion. Wave upon wave of tourists broke on its delicate shore. It was a village cursed by a win on the lottery. They soon had to call it a town, but it actually had all the features of a Third World city: dereliction at its centre, grotesquely opulent and heavily guarded suburbs around its middle, and a shanty town multiplying on its boundaries. It developed chronic water, power and traffic problems, and a sewage crisis so serious that when rain farl Negril was virtually marooned on a lake of ordure.

While the big people dem built hotels in Negril fast, the little people dem slowly erected bamboo sheds along the Main (as the coast road was called), and enthusiastically painted signs that read ONE STOP BEER JOINT FRY FISH, with a few even going as far as getting some beer and frying some fish, though these were invariably consumed by the owners of the sheds and their bredren, while they watched the tourists pass by, in air-conditioned coaches, speeding directly between the airport and the hotel lobbies. The white faces gazed back at them through the windows with varying degrees of boldness, the way they'd later gaze into the deep water under the hotel's glass-bottomed boat.

Angel Beach was no longer out on a long limb, far from the rest of the world, but near the centre of the action, on the road between the airport and Negril, and the inhabitants began to think ambitiously about expansion and prosperity. If it could happen to Negril, whose transformation everyone envied, why not to Angel Beach? Leroy, known as Busta, a bandy-legged, diminutive dreadlock, led the way. He was the head of the Wellington family, considered, in Angel

Beach, one of the most important dynasties in Jamaica, though outside Beach no-one had heard of it.

Busta worked as a mason at Coconut Grove Hotel in Negril, and had seen tourists close up. He was particularly impressed by their behaviour in bars. In Angel Beach the little people dem went regularly to Zapo Bar on the Back Street, sometimes hanging out there all day long, but it didn't mean they actually had a drink. Mostly they just stared at the dusty Red Stripe and Dragon Stout bottles sitting on the shelf behind the bar.

'De whitey go inna bar and him buy one Red Stripe or one Appleton and him drink it fast, man, fast,' Busta reported to his friends, a damp and stained spliff resting impassively on his bottom lip. 'Ya kiant believe how fast dem drink it. And dem alway tip de barman. For sure, man. Dem just say keep de change, buddy, an' leave maybe twelve dallar or twenty or even one US.'

On the rare occasion a bokkle o Red Stripe was bought in Beach, it was far too prestigious an object to drink swiftly. On average a bottle lasted an hour, though Vash Crooks, the village show-off, once eked out a Red Stripe for two days, carrying it with him wherever he went fi brandish it at his friends who couldn't afford a drink. 'And when dem want a smoke,' Busta continued, 'dem nuh buy one cigarette, dem buy twenty! Ya man. Mi gonna capture a piece o land and build one shed for de tourist dem bus fi stop at.'

So Busta picked a spot beside the Main on a slither of pretty land that ran down to the sea. Capturing land was a game of grandmother's footsteps. One sleepy afternoon when no-one seemed to be about, you surreptitiously framed up a little shed with ten pieces of wood and then laid low to see what the owner of the land did about it. If no-one complained you then gradually improved the structure until you had a proper house and a yard marked off around it, by which time it was too late for the landowner to get you off the land. The Police only threw people off during the first stage of squatting, before a yard was established, before the people could say, 'Afficer, dis a fi mi yard, man. Mi live ere, mi likkle son and darter born an' raise ere.'

When capturing land the trick was to do very little work on the shed each day – which suited Busta – in the hope that the landlord wouldn't notice the house going up. Usually it was pretty easy. Most of the land was owned by middle-class people who lived miles away, because no-one with money stayed in Beach any longer than they had to. Their land in Beach was pretty well worthless, and yielded nothing but problems; it certainly never produced any rent, and it was only the difficulty of getting rid of the land that made the owners keep it.

The bit of land Busta picked was owned by Mulgi, a successful Asian businessman who lived in Vancouver. Mulgi paid Maas Percival, a calm and dignified fisherman distantly related to the Wellington's, to keep squatters off his estate. Because the land lay between the seashore where the fishermen drew up their canoes, and Maas Percival's yard on the Back Street, Maas Percival walked past it every morning and evening. Busta therefore worked in the afternoons when he knew Percival was sleeping before his night's fishing, and sat with his friends in the shade of a baseda tree across the road to watch him pass by on his way to his boat. Each day the same thing happened: Maas Percival walked by, his trim figure as erect as a soldier's, his gaze fixed straight ahead of him, never even glancing at the logwood and bamboo shed which was slowly appearing beside the road.

'Yes, Busta,' he would say, without looking at Busta.

'Maas Percival,' Busta would reply.

No-one knew how much Mulgi paid Maas Percival, but the bonds of community proved stronger than the bonds of commerce, and he turned a blind eye. And out of respect for Percival, Busta worked particularly slowly so as not to seem too brazen and put him in a difficult position.

Three weeks after Busta started, Gucci began building on another piece of Mulgi's land. Before his second timber was nailed onto his first, Maas Percival went and found him where he was skulking in Zapo's and told him to stop building or he'd call the Police.

While Busta built, the coaches swept by, back and forth between Negril and the airport. The drivers knew the road so well they drove hard an fast, hard an fast, only keeping themselves interested in the run by trying to trim minutes off the time it took, and duelling with other vehicles on the road. Hopton, from Angel Beach, achieved widespread fame and respect for piloting his thirty-four seater past the Mo-Bay Fire Engine, going flat out to a fire, on the tight, blind bend in Hopewell.

At the airport the coach drivers group up to exchange stories about driving other unit off the road and to laugh about how many goats and fowl they bounce. When the jets landed and passengers emerged blinking from customs looking anxiously for their tour reps, the drivers said goodbye to each other and prepared for the race to Negril in the customary fashion: with a large swig of rum, 'fi clear de eyes fi de road'.

THE FIRST STRANGER

The only tourists who stopped in Angel Beach were those with a flat tyre, or those who lick dem car, which is why the bridge over the river was so useful. It had a vicious reverse camber and was built slightly out of line with the bend so that unless you knew the road well you had suddenly to correct the car's direction to prevent it ploughing into the river bed. Beach's first tourist entrepreneurs were the yout dem who sat under the almond tree on the seashore waiting to help whities out of the swamp in the hope of getting a few dollars' tip. American college boys on rental motorbikes were the most reliable crashers. Driving too fast on the wrong side of the road, high on a spliff, they didn't stand a chance on the Beach Bridge.

Three of the yout dem were from the Wellington family, and one, Garnett, known as Mooney, was a Crooks, one of the other noble houses of Beach. They were all present one windy autumn afternoon in 1978 when Billy, a black American man of about forty, stepped off a minibus. He was the first stranger any of them had ever seen voluntarily stop in the village. Up until then, strangers swept straight through without stopping on their way to Negril. Once or twice someone had engine trouble, or a flat tyre, but coming to Angel Beach was an act of volition for Billy, and for this reason alone, everyone liked him.

Billy came to Beach on a search for 'native dancers' which he said there was demand for on the cruise ships and in the hotels.

'Most of the guys on the boats right now are dancers from the States,' he informed a rapt audience who'd assembled to watch Busta and his business partner Blender argue over a hammer they were sharing while they banged a bamboo extension onto Busta's shed.

It was thought an extension might make whities stop; after all, Rick's Cafe in Negril, which was always full of tourists, had a massive extension. They only had two-inch screws for the job, but the single slightly broken screwdriver that had served Beach for so many years had finally broken, so they were banging the screws in with a hammer.

'The dancers on the ships pretend to be Caribbean, right?' explained Billy. 'But they have to learn all the moves, and are paid one hell of a lot for it, plus they're all joining a union which the operators don't like one bit, I can tell you. I figured you guys must know all the dances already, kinda have them in your blood, and would be prepared to undercut the market – though still make a packet by your standards,' he added quickly. 'But I musta been in twenty villages so far and nobody knows the traditional African stuff in any of them. You know, old tribal dances like limbo and such like. You don't seem to do them these days.'

It was true – although billed as a 'native' activity, the only limbo in Jamaica took place in front of white people at the hotels. To everyone in Angel Beach it was a new dance.

'It's one helluva pity, cos there's some money in this, believe me,' sighed Billy.

'Mi can limbo,' Vinton piped up. Vinton was the gangly, gummy-eyed thirteen year old nephew of Busta Wellington. He got his younger brother Maxwell, and Mooney, to hold up a stick of cane which he edged towards and collapsed under, getting up quickly to tomp Trevor and say, 'Fool. Nuh drop it, nuh drop it. Mi can do it. Watch.' The second time he succeeded.

'You don't know how to do the wheel dance, or fire dance?' asked Billy.

'Ya man. For sure. Dem mainly hotel style dance,' Vinton answered. 'Dem easy. Fi mi oncle know dem.' Uncle Tom had played banjo in a bright shirt provided by the hotel at Round Hill in the '60s, and told stories about the goings on there. 'He can tell we how dem run.'

Billy looked at Vinton sceptically.

'Fi sure man,' Vinton said, with a bright confident smile. 'No problem. Trost mi.'

The Jungle Rhythms, as Billy named the troupe, was made up of eleven guys – almost every available man in Beach – but dwindled by the third rehearsal to four: Vinton, Maxwell, Mooney, and Trouble. Billy produced a bit of paper which guaranteed each of them $2 US whenever they performed, which they painstakingly signed to prevent him backing out of the agreement. Even a single US dollar was an immense sum to the boys. The year before, Vinton changed a flat tyre for a tourist who mistakenly gave a greenback to Barrington, his cousin, who was standing by, giving Vinton instructions, most of which had been wrong. It was the first dollar bill they had touched. It was such a curiosity it was worth more, in a way, than the eight Jamaican dollars it would fetch in the Bank of Nova Scotia in Content, so Barrington kept it to show anyone who wanted a look.

Uncle Tom was no help with the choreography; he roared with laughter when they told him what they were up to, so the boys told Billy he'd taught them how the dances went in one intense session, and enthusiastically invented all the traditional dances themselves.

They should have been at school, but Vinton hadn't been for years. Originally, his reason for not attending was that he didn't have a school uniform or shoes, and was too proud to go in the rags he'd grown up in, but when, at nine years old he was thrown out of his mother's yard, an old lady of forty called Miss Liza, who needed the help of a picknee for things like moving the goat and fi ketch water, lured him to her yard with the promise of a shoes and a khaki. Life wasn't as easy as he'd anticipated at Miss Liza's but it was too late to move back in with Momma, so instead he spent hours dawdling on errands ignoring the faint shouts of VIN-TAN that wafted across the village from Miss Liza's yard. She did give him the shoes and uniform, but he didn't waste them on school. He was so proud of the outfit he brandish it all day long up and down the Main.

One day, Billy didn't turn up for rehearsals, and couldn't be found anywhere. Vash, Mooney's elder brother, was quick to laugh and say it was the last they'd seen of him. With his off-the-peg American clothes, Billy had displaced Vash as the village's criss dresser, and Vash didn't like him. But the boys were familiar enough with disappointment to have spent many hours boasting about their imminent fame and prosperity, so that if (or when, in the case of Angel Beach) everything fell through they knew they had been admired, or more importantly, envied, by the rest of the village for a short time at least.

But Billy did return after a few days with a black eye, some revealing stage clothes and the news of an audition in Montego Bay. The fake leopard-skin loincloths were too small, but Billy said that that made them better, and with only Billy and a white man in the audience for the audition, the boys didn't get nervous, and put on their best performance.

But Billy, who would hear nothing said against the Jungle Rhythms, had to admit, to himself, that his group looked unlikely to pass the audition. In Angel Beach the foursome seemed athletic and appealing, but with the critical eye of the white man beside him Billy suddenly saw how tall and spindly Mooney really was, how spherical Trouble looked, and how enormous Vinton's feet were. Maxwell, at least, was perfectly proportioned, and handsome by anyone's standards, but his problem was that he was minuscule.

They were quite unaware of their glaring shortcomings as professional dancers. Billy was so moved by their naïve belief in themselves, and by extension him, that after one particularly clumsy sequence (executed without an iota of embarrassment), he had to wipe a tear from his eye.

After the audition, Billy introduced them to the white man, whom he informed that all the dances were 'totally authennic', and were passed down to the Jungle Rhythms by a 'village elder'. In accordance with Billy's instructions they agreed with everything he said to the white man, and answered 'seventeen' when the white man asked their ages.

A week later, after spending an hour and a half at the public telephone in Content, five minutes of which was in conversation, Billy came away with the news that the Jungle Rhythms had passed the audition and were booked for a four-week cruise around Cuba on a Yugoslav shipping line. Carried by the conductor of a crammed minibus, the news got to Beach before Billy, where it swept through the population, though by the time it got to Fozzy, who lived in the last yard on the ball ground, the engagement was a residency in a Miami nightclub and lasted not four weeks but two years, and included a house, car and white girls.

When Billy turned up, the boys were pon de street exulting in their success. The first person he buck up on was Vash who, thinking Billy might not have heard the news, asked him if he could rejoin the Rhythms, for he'd dropped out at the second rehearsal. Billy shrugged him off, found the others, and got them all drunk on one Red Stripe each at Busta's shed. He was genuinely elated, and for the first time expressed surprise at their success.

'I never really believed this would happen, you know? I never really thought we'd get our shit together enough to make it to a professional gig. I mean when I first set eyes on you guys I thought Billy, forget it, this aint gonna work. But I was so goddam desperate ...'

Vinton was hurt by this. 'Nuh say dat, man,' he said. 'When you find we, ya buck up on a whole heap a talent.'

'Ya man,' insisted Maxwell.

'I know, I know,' said Billy, with tears of happiness welling up in his eyes. 'Well now I know. Hey Busta.'

'Ya Billy.'

'Another beer for everyone.'

'Irie.'

The boys were astonished. They'd never seen anyone buy someone two beers. Those who weren't in the Rhythms hung about in the darkness outside the shed, and had not shifted off when Billy, by then in a state of euphoria, left the bar with his arms around his boys. When they were past the fishermen pushing out their canoes he said, 'Isn't this the greatest feeling in the world? We're all here in this beautiful place about to begin a new chapter in our lives which we're all going to be in on together. Yeah? You know what I mean?'

'Ya man,' said Maxwell, who did.

'Ya man,' said Mooney hesitantly, because he didn't.

'And I gotta feeling we're going a good distance in each other's company,' said Billy, staring up at the stars.

'Just gimme mi passport and let we go,' Maxwell laughed.

'Passports. You guys got passports, right?'

'No man,' they told him.

'No problem. We'll get onto that tomorrow morning. But maybe tonight would be a good moment to get the haemorrhoids test over and done with.'

'What haemorrhoid?' Trouble asked.

'You know, piles.' There was a pause. 'They're a complaint every dancer has to keep a watch for. They've ruined many a career, I can tell you. Quite a few great dancers who coulda made a fortune had to throw the towel in on account of them. You ever heard of Baryshnikov?'

'No. Him fram Montego Bay?'

'No. He's American. A great dancer. Made a mint. Now he damn near lost his career to piles. But it's a simple enough test. Nothing to worry about. If you get on top of the problem early they're a cinch to eliminate. I just run my forefinger up your anus to check if you're likely to get any trouble. Trouble, you look a little tight in that region. I may be able to do a little work relaxing you down there at the same time.'

Trouble said nothing.

'Nobady put dem finger inna mi botty,' Vinton said.

'Nuh man,' added Maxwell.

'Cho,' said Mooney dismissively. 'Dat nuh sound right.'

'Who touch dat mi tomp im,' stated Vinton.

'Look, it's not that important, right? If anything crops up on board I guess the ship's doctor can handle it. Hey, check that out!'

Billy pointed to the distant glistening cruise ship inching across the black sea and sky. 'That's where we're headed, guys.'

'Ya man,' said Maxwell softly.

Trouble, Mooney and Vinton nodded, but said nothing. The ship looked a long, long way away to them. The prospect of leaving Beach suddenly seemed scary. They were to be away four weeks. The longest any of them had been out of the village was for the audition, nine hours. Each had their own gnawing worry: Trouble that he had no criss clothes, Mooney that he had no shoes, and Vinton that he wouldn't be able to use a flush toilet, for he, like everyone else, had always used the bush.

Mooney wisely waited for his father to be in a good mood before he asked for his birth certificate, so when he heard Mr Crooks bragging that he'd sold the Sandy Island Police station a load of sea sand as salt-free river sand, to build the new cell block with, he put his request to him.

'What ya need age paper for, picknee?' Mr Crooks snapped back. He looked so aggressive, like a boxer dog, and had once almost killed a bad boy with a tin of mackerel in a lada bag when he jumped out of the bush to rob Mr Crooks.

'Mi gawn a foreign fi dance wid Billy, and mi need one passport, sah,' Mooney told his father.

'Ya tink Billy want mi fi go a foreign fi dance too?' Mr Crooks asked.

'No, sir. Billy want ongle Vinton, Trouble, Maxwell an' mi,' replied Mooney apologetically.

'Well ya nuh de go, annerstan? Until mi go, nobady in this family reach up inna foreign. Ya tink picknee take first place to him farder? No sah. No sah. Tek up de rake and work, boy. You nuh go nowhere till ya pay ya farder the debt fi raise you. Gwaan! Tek it up.'

And Mr Crooks in his turn took up a stick and set to work whipping his son's long thin legs as he raked the yard.

Later, Miss Myrtle, Mooney's mother, gave him the birth

certificate. 'Nuh tell ya farder. An' carry back com gimmi soon.'

'Ya Mamma. Tank ya.'

When Trouble, who was a year and a half junior to Mooney, asked the mountainous Miss Dahlia, his granny, for his birth surfaceticket, she lumbered swiftly across the creaking wooden room, lifted her mattress and slid out the family heirlooms: a couple of disintegrating official letters relating to her brother Wilbert's deafness, some blurred photographs, one or two of people she didn't know, yet treasured nevertheless simply because they were photographs, all the documents relating to her favourite son-in-law's conviction for assault and rape of two different women, and a couple of his painful letters from Spanish Town Gaol, a 1972 Jamaica Labour Party calendar, two prescriptions she couldn't afford to fill, and birth certificates of two of the six minors in her care.

'Ya send mi money each mont, y'annerstan?' she shouted at Trouble, even though he was just across the room. 'An' send down one bedcover and one cooker. Tek this.' She thrust the bit of paper in his hand.

When Maxwell and Vinton asked for their birth certificates, people heard Flossie's laugh on the other side of the ballground, actually only an average distance for Flossie, whose laugh was one of the Seven Wonders of Angel Beach. She once laughed so loudly, a solitary fisherman working out of sight of land in his canoe heard her disembodied guffaws coming over the horizon.

Before she ceased laughing she went at her sons with the flat side of her machete, a surface which had more than once made high-speed contact with their flesh. But that Sunday eveling, when Flossie walked up and down pon de street in her finery, Trevor, as agile as he was naughty, slithered over the room partition through the nine-inch gap, and found Momma's papers. He climbed back with one birth certificate between his teeth – Dalton Wedderburn's – his own in the formal name no-one ever used.

Mooney, Maxwell and Trouble toiled over the first line of the passport application form until Billy took over and answered all the questions at an astonishing speed, which confirmed the idea they had that he was very clever, for he'd known the answer to the Kool-Aid radio quiz question that had foxed the whole of Jamaica for six weeks – Mr Moneyman asked, 'Eighteen King of France share de same name. What is dat name?'

When a caller said, 'Is de answer Dwight?' Billy laughed.

'What de right name, den?' Vash, who looked in through the window of Busta's shed, where a radio played on the bar, asked Billy.

'Louis,' Billy replied.

'Dat nat true,' Vash said, but a week later a caller said 'Louis' and won the accumulated jackpot of 600 J, which most people felt was at least partially owed to Billy.

Billy explained to Vinton that he had to go to the government office in Mo-Bay to get a duplicate certificate. 'Tell them your parents' names, place and date of birth, all that shit, and you'll get it easy.'

'But mi nuh know mi father name,' said Vinton shamefully.

'Ask your mother.'

'Mi ask fi mi mudder, but she nuh tell mi.'

'Why?'

'Mi sit down and tink about dat all day, Billy.'

Eight hours after Vinton was born in the Content hospital in 1966, Flossie, his mother, went back to her yard to wait for Aubrey, the baby farder, to come and acknowledge his son. She knew better than to walk to his yard with the infant. Her friend Carlene had confronted her baby farder with his daughter when she was three days old and he had licked them down in front of his friends with a hax hangle. After waiting four days, Flossie's father, a drinker and a fighter called Seymour, shook Flossie in the night and demanded with overproof rum on his breath the name of the infant's father. She didn't tell him, or anyone else, and the next day tore up the birth certificate with Aubrey's name on it and gave her own surname – Wellington – to the child. From that time on, she swore never to business with Aubrey again, however much he sweet up her mout wid words. This was why she never told Vinton who his father was, despite the fact that Aubrey lived on the Back Street and Vinton passed his yard practically every day.

'They'll give you the birth certificate with just your mother's name. Sure they will. And you know it might even have the name of your father on it.'

With criss clothes borrowed from around the village, Vinton waited for the minibus in the short, still, smoky dawn before the sun exploded over the top of the hill. He saw Vash, Con, Mooney and a group of little boys walking up the slope from the seashore.

'Boggy,' called Vash, using one of Vinton's names.

'Ya man.'

'Con hear from Boydie cousin in Mo-Bay dat Billy is one botty man.'

'Dem gonna dance pon one ship wid a botty man,' piped Con in his high-pitched voice, making everyone but Mooney and Vinton roar with laughter. They looked sick.

The thud of a bass line heralded a minibus called Dutchman, which came off the long straight and around the corner listing heavily with the G-force. Vinton didn't stop it. Nor did he stop Pomp Action, which careered by a minute later. He had to find out more about this.

He and Mooney found Maxwell bouncing barefoot down the back street slopping water from a bucket he was carrying, and singing at the top of his voice: 'Mi no more move cow dem, mi no more ketch water, mi no more rake de yard dem ...'

'Vash say Billy one botty man,' Vinton told his brother.

'Raas claat Vash is a idiot, fool. Him nuh like Billy. Everybady know dat,' stated Maxwell, adding, 'blaad claat.'

'Boydie cousin hear in Mo-Bay, Billy try fi interfere wid one boy.'

There was a pause while Maxwell ruminated on this. Then he suck teeth and said, 'Cho.'

'Mi nah go pon no boat wid no botty man,' said Vinton.

'Nuh sah,' said Maxwell ambivalently, then added with more conviction, 'Ya kiant business wid no botty man.'

Mooney gravely agreed, relieved that this would mean he could return his age paper to Miss Myrtle before Mr Crooks found it was missing and beat her bad.

Shouts could be heard from Miss Dahlia's yard, where Billy stayed, so the boys hurried towards them. Miss Dahlia had moved the infant Kermit, Dwight and Nerine into the octogenarian Miss Amy's bed in order to rent a room to Billy for a couple dallar a week.

The boundaries of the various yards in Angel Beach were by and large invisible, but known and respected by all. They operated like a force field around either one, or a group of houses. Those whose yard it was could wander in and out from the street, but all outsiders had to stop on the border line – which often only someone from Beach could recognise – and hail up whoever they wanted to see in the house by calling out their name. It was on the boundary of Miss

Dahlia's yard that a growing crowd of curious people stood. Vash shouted abuse at Billy, who cowered inside. 'Botty man!' he called, 'move from here, botty boy …'

An elderly woman, the usually kind and helpful Miss Joly, threw a stone, and a boy with an unbroken voice yelled, 'Pussy claat!'

Inside, Billy sat on the bed trembling with terror, occasionally peering through a gap in the louvred shutters, and jumping whenever a stone cracked against the thin wood clapboarding of the wall.

'Oh my God,' he uttered, crossing himself feverishly.

A minibus drew up, momentarily diverting attention. The door slid back, and after a moment Miss Dahlia hobbled out, dressed in her best clothes. She looked almost uphol-stered, as though she were padded with springs and might even possess a pair of ball and claw feet. A visit to Dr Bury in Sandy Island, made on the expectation of the funds Trouble was going to mail her from the ports he'd visit on the cruise, necessitated wearing the finery.

'Faggot!' screamed Vash at the house. 'Ya one faggot, Billy.'

'Let 'im pass out. Let 'im pass out,' shouted Miss Dahlia, parting the crowd before her. Inside, she said, 'Pack up ya tings in ya suitcase, Billy, an' jump trough dat back window, an' run off a back street.' Billy frenetically pulled his glad rags together. Another rock cracked against the side of the house. 'Gwaan,' she urged, 'ron now, ron now …' But as he squeezed out of the back window she said, 'Hol' on now. De rent. Ya owe mi for mi rent.'

With one leg out the window, Billy dug into his pocket.

'How much is it? Three dollars?' He winced as another stone struck the house. The crowd was now a mob, and it was getting angry; Miss Dahlia saw the strength of her nego-tiating position.

'Gimme ten dallar.'

'Ten?' cried Billy.

'Tree rent. Seven for cancellation.'

'Jesus,' Billy said under his breath, reaching for his wallet.

While he clambered out the back of the shack, Miss Dahlia went to the front to pacify the mob. 'Hol' on. Im just com. Let im pass out fram mi yard, annerstan?'

Afterwards, when the story of Billy and the Jungle Rhythms was told in the sheds and on the porches of Angel Beach, no-one ever blamed Miss Dahlia for this little deception, because everyone, with perhaps the exception of Vash, saw it for the simple act of kindness it was.

When the cry, 'Him roun' a back street!' finally went up, most people were glad that the three-minute start Billy got meant that he was pretty well out of the village before anyone could catch up with him. The Angel Beach mob liked to make a lot of noise, but had little taste for blood, and had been known in the past to catch up with and run right past a culprit rather than attack him. At the ballground Billy's suitcase burst open, and a trail of bright clothes was laid across the bumpy cricket pitch curtailing in an empty case with a broken catch. The mob chased him around Bubbles' yard, parted into two around the primary school and met again on the other side to see Billy sprinting down the middle of the tarmacked Main in the direction of what the government had recently rather optimistically named Industry Beach. It was not a name that stuck. By then the Angel Beach mob had run out of both venomous jibes and, more importantly, puff. Chasing Billy all the way down the hill would only mean walking back up in the increasing heat of the morning, so they slowed to a trot and then a standstill and laughingly congratulated each other on a good morning's work.

One night, over a year later, Trevor, Mooney and Vinton were scanning the shallows near the canoes with paraffin-soaked rag torches hoping to find swimp. Vinton and Mooney looked up to see a glistening, silent cruise liner hanging in the dark out to sea. Both were about to resume their search of the sandy shallows when Maxwell, a little way off, said, 'Remember Billy?'

'Ya man,' said Vinton.

'Billy cool,' Maxwell said.

'Ya man. Mi know,' answered Vinton.

'Remember when him buy we two Red Stripe?'

'Ya man. Billy kinda nice.'

'But him a wah botty man,' Maxwell stated, to stop himself recalling more good things about Billy.

'Ya man,' agreed Mooney.

'And ya kiant business wid dat,' Maxwell sighed. And all three bent back over the water to look for swimp, happy to think about something else.

NAMES AND ALIASES

Babies came into the world of Angel Beach at the hospital on the windswept point at Content, where mothers nursed their newborn infants looking out at the white-capped ocean, while the Caribbean breeze billowed the curtains, and wafted the nurses' paperwork across the lino floors. The papers once got so muddled that Wilbert, a Beach farmer, visiting hospital because he woke up stone deaf one morning, was given an enema and discharged, while a man who hadn't been to the tilet for twelve days had his ears syringed; both men were satisfied with their treatment and pronounced themselves cured.

No man from Beach ever went near the maternity ward. The subject of childbirth made men nervous in Beach. When a girl got off the minibus from the hospital with her newborn baby in her arms, every Beach man felt anxious until one of them acknowledged the child as his. An unclaimed baby put them all under suspicion, and it was years before a physical resemblance could unquestionably clear up the matter.

During her short stay in hospital a new mother named her child, and the doctor filled in the birth certificate. Baby mudders felt that as they'd given birth without assistance from the baby farder, they could probably manage to name it on their own, as well. In the feminine atmosphere of the maternity ward, far away from the dust and squalor of a Angel Beach yard, the women picked romantic and impractical names. While lying in the sweet luxury of a bed not only to herself, but with a mattress and pillows covered in crisp, clean linen, Nerine conjured up the name Nakissia for her first daughter and Najia for her second. Venezia and Tamara were named in the same fashion by their mother, Miss Rung, and other Angel Beach products of the Content maternity ward were Doreenia, Hyacinth, Adolphus, Beresford, Viviena, Euphemia, Estella, Bevlie and Weeville.

They were not names that lasted long in the roffness of a back-street childhood, yet neither were they worn down into diminutives, but stored away in one piece, like something treasured, and replaced by a tougher name for everyday use. The name on the birth certificate was often never seen again except on an electoral roll, if they were lucky, a Police charge sheet, if they weren't, and a concrete headstone in the symmetry if they were rich.

New names, or aliases, sometimes grew out of the way you looked. Blackie was the blackest woman in Beach. Biggar, as a child, was biggar dan de nex one, though when he stopped growing, and his friends shot past him, his name changed to Likkle Biggar. Barrington Wellington, Vinton's big and talkative uncle, inherited the Wellington voice which jumped from deep rounded bass to falsetto and back again sometimes twice in one sentence. Like most physical abnormalities, it was considered special, and often Barrington would be stopped by someone who'd heard about his voice and asked to say a few words. He always obliged, being singularly proud of his vocal peculiarity. He first got called Piano by Biggar, during a game of dominoes, 'cas im voice sound sweet like one piana'. It was adopted by the other players, and became a kind of password for the Barrington posse – the guys he hung out with inna Back Street. But it soon spread outwards from Barrington's closest ring of friends, first to everyone in his yard, girls included, and then to the Back Street, and finally the whole village hail up the man as Piano. It was around about then that the men he played dominoes with began to call him Voices, which they pronounced Vices. This caught on too, so a new nickname emerged to mark out the initiates from the rest. Some said Vinton thought it up, others Maxwell. They called him Bird, 'cas im sing so sweet'. This, months later, was developed into Blackbird. Everyone could tell, by the name someone used to address Barrington, how long they had known him, and how close was the friendship.

More commonly, names were pinned on a person by events in their life, and in this way the contemporary history of Jamaica was recorded in the aliases of its people. Usually, only important events were commemorated, but in Beach nothing important happened, so they commemorated the insignificant instead.

Garnett got the name Mooney on a strange fishing exped-ition in 1981. A man from inna de hills had come down to the seashore and asked Mooney if he could use his bamboo raft to fish from. Mooney took the stranger out into the cove and they dropped their lines into the coral reef. Their fishing tackle comprised a baited hook on a length of thick nylon wound round an empty bleach bottle. A float wasn't needed because the fish were so plentiful and tame, and the water so clear, they could be watched taking the bait from the raft.

Suddenly, the stranger pointed at something on the end of the raft.

'Go way fram mi! Go way ... Go way. Mi know you Mooney. Leave mi, leave mi!' he shouted feverishly.

Garnett looked but saw nothing, yet the stranger grew more vex and confused, eventually hurling himself off the raft into the water, which was only a few inches deep because in places the coral grew from the sea floor right to the surface. He tried to stand up, but slipped over, gashing his hands and feet badly on the coral (when recounted later, that bit always made everyone laugh), all the time shouting, 'Go way Mooney, go way Mooney!'

Mental illness was considered so hilarious in Beach, that the story soon became popular, and lest anyone should forget it, the name Mooney was given to Garnett. He was honoured by this, knowing the high status any association with the insane gave a young man, and was proud to have it conferred on him.

If you asked, 'Why dem call Maxwell Maxwell?', an inhabitant of Beach would answer, 'Cas him see one show pon television,' and leave it at that, as if it required no further explanation. Few pressed for more information for fear of appearing ignorant of the magical and powerful world of television.

What had happened was this: Trevor, on a trip to Sav to buy DDT with his father for their ganja plantation, saw a television in the hardware shop. Only Shepherd Bush George in Angel Beach had a TV, a 36″ 1974 Grundig which he brought with him from Shepherd Bush inna London. It was one of the seven wonders of Angel Beach. It was only black and white, but no-one except Shepherd Bush George knew. People came from all over the village to gaze at it from the settee in the lounge of his much-envied concrete house. Shepherd Bush George always explained how it would be even more exciting when the Jamaica Public Service company brought electricity to the village.

The television in the Savannah La Mar hardware store was different: it was switched on and showing a programme. The programme happened to be Hart to Hart, in which

Robert Wagner and Stephanie Powers have a butler called Maxwell. The one line of dialogue Trevor could remember, when a rapt audience outside Busta's shed quizzed him on his experience was 'Maxwell, take my coat', and it was from this gem of American TV that the name came which remained with Trevor for years.

WHY DEM CALL U-ROY, U-ROY

Rayon get a idea to promote a music show when Gucci told stories about the times he party wid Bob Marley inna Kingston, and all the Beach girls loved to listen and did friend wid Gucci. Gucci had returned from the capital to claim his late father's estate. The first thing he did was sell a plot of valuable seaside land and buy a Lada car, a transaction considered shrewd by the entire village and which made him even sexier to the gal dem.

Rayon Fairfax was a slim, high colour man with darting eyes and lecherous hands which gave him a reputation amongst Beach men for being attractive to women. His old friendship with the singer U-Roy paled beside Gucci's with Marley, a global star and prophet to black people everywhere. Questions had begun to be asked about just how well Rayon knew U-Roy before Gucci turned up, and now they were asked again, louder. Why, for instance, did U-Roy never come to check Rayon if they were such buddies? It was a question that Gucci need never fear, knowing that his friend Bob was lying safely in a St Ann symmetry. Rayon therefore decided to stop the gossip and big up his status by getting U-Roy down to St John for a show.

Angel Beach didn't have a venue for shows, but Firefly Bay didn't either, so that was all right. The nearest place was Parkins Lawn in Lemon Grove, a rubble strewn slope enclosed by concrete sheds and corrugated zinc. The lighting rig was a single 60 watt bulb and the moon, but these could evoke magic. A big DJ, capable of drawing a crowd of 10,000 in New York, drew about 75 in Lemon Grove, 'though there were always another 100 listening for free on the other side of the zinc. The dancehall stars played the little villages for pocket money, for girls, and to keep their acts sharp. If they could hold the audience in Lemon Grove, New York was a breeze.

But Rayon booked a new venue in Bulls Bay, owned by an effusive dreadlock who'd come back to live in Jamaica in 1987 with a whitey girlfriend from England who people believed was a cousin of Mrs Queen, the British monarch. When they got married, Lord Locks, as he was soon dubbed, invited the press and TV as a surprise for his bride; but she had to tell reporters that there had been a misunderstanding about her relationship with Mrs Queen, and that people used the term 'cousin' in England rather more loosely than in Jamaica. The local guests felt that if there had been a misunderstanding, it was not one that they would have corrected. The ceremony nevertheless made the RJR News, the JBC television news (second item, ahead of the fall of the Berlin Wall), and the Western Mirror printed a photo of the white suited Lord Locks and his delightful bride under the headline NOT THE COUSIN OF THE QUEEN WEDS IN ST JOHN.

Rayon booked Lord Locks' brand new venue, called Zion House, for a Saturday night, after negotiating a deal over much bokkle o' Dragon Stout with the dread. Both men were pleased with the agreement: the Lord Locks because he got Rayon to pay an exorbitant rent for the venue, and Rayon because he had no intention of actually handing over a single cent.

Rayon commissioned four posters, and the week before
the gig persuaded the easily-bullied Devon to drive him up
and down the Main and into the hills and valleys in Bessie,
Devon's Hillman, with a megaphone strapped to the roof,
announcing that U-Roy was going to play in Bulls Bay that
Saturday. It was a euphoric few days. He sold, from a book
of obsolete Seventh Day Adventist church raffle tickets,
twenty-eight advance tickets, the money from which he
immediately invested in Appleton Estate Special White
Rum. The car, the megaphone, and the importance of his
position as promoter, attracted countless women, all of
whom, after telling Devon to take a walk, he had sex with
in the back of Bessie, once forgetting to plug out the megaphone and attracting a crowd of curious little picknee. But
while he enjoyed himself on the back seat he was aware of
a growing sense of unease, attributable only to the fact that
it was four days before the show and he still hadn't got in
touch with U-Roy. He had been meaning to check a girl in
Blenheim who did friend wid U-Roy in the old days, and
who knew a mechanic who fixed U-Roy's Benz on Hope
Road, Kingston, and he finally went up on Wednesday, but
Euphoria's yard was empty except for tree picknee.

'Momma reach up a Mo-Bay fi look fi work,' a little girl
who was cooking a pan of dumplings over a fire told Rayon.

'Tell her he must check fi her friend who know U-Roy
mechanic, and tell her dat U-Roy must com a Bulls Bay
Saturday night fi play one show for Rayon Fairfax.'

Rayon drove back down to the Level enjoying the feeling
of relief that at last he'd done what he'd been putting off
for so long. 'De job of de promoter easy!' he told Devon.
'Easy! Everyting gonna be all right.' This cheered Devon who
was anxious about the money Rayon owed for gas.

Rayon celebrated with a couple of shots of Appleton Estate

Special and a spliff, and told Devon to turn Bessie towards Salt Spring, a place sufficiently far from the Main that a man with a car was still an exciting, exotic rarity.

On the day of the show Lord Locks preened his locks in his large mirror in preparation for his encounter with U-Roy. 'Mirror mirror 'pon de wall, who is the most beautifulest rasta of dem all?' he purred, flashing his locks with a laugh. It was an important meeting for Lord Locks, who wanted to get his career off to a cracking start in Jamaica. Things in London had not gone well for him. He'd wound up forty years old with two ex-wives and eight kids on his tail for money, and a stalled career as a rhythm guitarist looking increasingly incapable of providing it. To get himself out of a rut he'd started to friend with a delicious looking white girl whom he met in Notting Hill Gate who wanted to scandalise her family. In England a man was made to feel guilty about going out with a rich girl, so he took her to Jamaica where he got the respect he deserved for pulling her. His wife took an interest in his career, and to ensure he could always get a gig she thoughtfully bought him a music venue: stage, auditorium, bar, the lot. He named it Zion House. His policy was to book the big names in reggae, Dennis Brown, Gregory Isaacs, Freddie Macgregor, then form a band and invite himself onto the bill as support act. When you had the kind of financial backing he had, it was easy to make it. That was the way Lord Locks saw it.

He loved to perform in front of an audience, and loved an adoring crowd, and had already decided to get to the microphone to introduce U-Roy himself, using a lot of echo and superlatives. He might have to push the likkle bald 'ead Rayon Fairfax out of the way, but he was a nobody from the middle of nowhere, fit only to be stepped on by the likes of Lord Locks. His text of the day from the good book was He who loves to exalt himself shall be obeyed – a favourite with many rastas. Quite where it appeared in the Bible Lord Locks was unclear, but no-one else knew either, so it was safe to make up a fictitious reference when he quoted it in conversation. He lit a spliff and meditated on Jah for a minute or two and then began to daydream about discussing future projects after the show with U-Roy over a couple Dragon Stout.

The night before the show Rayon got a message down the line from Euphoria in Blenheim that U-Roy could do the engagement, but needed a whole heap o dallar brought to him in Kingston before he'd reach up inna Bulls Bay. Rayon's good friend Gaddaffi, drawn down from the bush where he'd been thieving ganja by the pleasure of breaking bad news, brought the information. He stipulated the precise sum U-Roy demanded, but Rayon didn't listen because although he had a lot of money, 125 crumpled and damp J in all, he knew U-Roy would want more.

Gaddaffi suggested during the long moonless night the two spent in each other's company that it was time to use obeah – black magic.

'Mi can set one curse 'pon U-Roy,' Gaddaffi told Rayon.

'To make him com to Bulls Bay?'

'No man, fi kill him nex baby.'

This was Gaddaffi's speciality. He used obeah to kill Marva Crooks's newborn child because of a dispute he'd had with her father, and his sister Carlene's fourth baby died because she once dis Gaddaffi. Rayon was tempted by it, but knew Gaddaffi would charge a lot of money, and knew also that it would not solve the central problem of what was going to happen when everybody went to Zion House to see U-Roy, and U-Roy didn't turn up.

'Dat no good, Gaddaffi. Mi need U-Roy a com, or mi dead man.'

'Ya man,' agreed Gaddaffi warmly. 'For sure you will dead. Mi tell ya what can save ya from dead: if ya can find one man who favour U-Roy ...' by which he meant someone who resembled U-Roy, '... but nobady know how U-Roy look so ya gonna dead.'

'Nobady know? Somebady moss know.'

'All dem know is de same as we. U-Roy always wear one felt 'at, a bellfoot pants and a big boots.'

'... And de felt always have one fedder in it.'

'Ya man, one fedder in him felt 'at. But dat all mi know. Dat all anybady know, dat's de problem.'

'If nobady don't know what him look like, den all mi need is one felt, one boots and one bellfoot pants, and mi can be U-Roy said way 'pon de stage, and nobady kiant know it nat U-Roy,' said Rayon.

A smile, expressive of Gaddaffi's deep love of deception, spread upon his lupine features. 'And nobady kiant know cos dem never see U-Roy 'pon TV or in newspaper photo.'

'Ya man,' said Rayon, 'cas dem illiterate.'

'And dem kiant read,' added Gaddaffi, laughing, 'cas dem ignorant.' Then he looked serious. 'What bout de lyrics, man? Ya kiant sing,' he pointed out.

'Cho!' chided Rayon. 'Mi can sing so. Mi can sing fast, man, and hard. Ya man. Ya nuh hear mi pon de microphone in Bessie?'

'Ya man?' said Gaddaffi.

'Ya man,' insisted Rayon. 'True one gal up a Dias say mi voice sweet.'

'Even if ya voice sweet, ya nah know any of U-Roy song dem.'

'Mi do so. What bout "Cheek a bow, cheek a bow, cheek a bow wow wow"?' he sang tunelessly.

'Everybady know dat one. Dat one ole song. Ya nah know U-Roy new song dem.'

'When U-Roy play him show him sing one ole hit, and den showcase new material.'

'But ya nah know him new material.'

'Nobady don't know it. U-Roy just mek it up inna de studio. It nat even out on record. Nobady don't hear it. So mi can mek it up miself. Gaddaffi, de entertainer like we fi tink it difficult fi write song. It nat difficult. It easy. Ya man. Mi could be one DJ if mi had de time. Serious. If mi nah had so much pressing ting fi do mi could be one top DJ.'

By the time Rayon returned from Mo-Bay later that day with a felt hat, platform heel boots and flared trousers concealed in a lada bag (called lada because they, like the Czech car, suddenly flooded the island after the government made a bulk purchase), Rayon felt things had turned out better without U-Roy. For a start he no longer had to pay the entertainer, or rather think of a way of avoiding paying him, and second he could forget that the last time he saw U-Roy he tried to tief his girl from him and made him vex bad.

At Zion House the road disappeared under a crowd which pressed at the turnstile. Lots of people held up church raffle tickets which Rayon had instructed Gaddaffi, in the box office, not to accept. When Rayon hurriedly got out of Bessie to avoid paying Devon his debt for gas, the crowd recognised him and surged in his direction.

'Security! Security!' he shouted, desperately, although when a bouncer elbowed his way through the crowd and held Rayon protectively by the arm, he changed his tune to, 'Mek way for de promoter. Mek way! Move! Gwaan boy!'

He was propelled to a side door, but before going in turned to address the crowd: 'De management regret dem kiant accept no responsibility for illegal sale of forge ticket,' and with that he disappeared from view.

So few could afford a ticket, the inside of the venue was virtually empty. Rayon headed for the gloomy box office where Gaddaffi was deep in the long and arduous process of deducting forty from one hundred to give an anxious white couple their change. The boy, a U-Roy enthusiast from Dortmund, said, 'I sink it is sixti,' so many times Gaddaffi was sure it was a trick. Eventually the girl, clinging to her boyfriend, said in German, 'For goodness sake, Helmut, forget it. It's only a few Marks, and he's going to get heavy if we don't go in. Come on.'

After they had left, without their change but with effusive thanks, Gaddaffi said to Rayon: 'Ya kiant do dis, man. It kiant work.'

'Mi can do i', and mi will do i',' replied Rayon. 'Go on troo ladies,' he added, freeing the turnstile to admit two pretty girls.

'But dem will kill ya if dem find out. You want fi dead wid bokkle an' machete?'

'Mi nuh gwine dead. Trust mi. Dem will never recognise mi. Never.'

'Ya can run now easy, man,' Gaddaffi whispered. 'Look. We 'ave four ondred dallar. Go on. Excape before it too late.'

'No Gaddaffi. Mi gonna do it.'

'Why, man?'

'Cas mi want fi do it.'

'Ya wan fi do i'?'

'Ya man.'

'Ya crazy, Rayon. Ya crazy. Why ya want fi do i'?'

'Cas dis hat, pants and boots,' he said holding up the lada

bag, 'pull gal like magnet pull nail. Serious. When mi put dem on, dem mash op all de gal dem inna de place. Big entertainer like U-Roy have all de gal dem him can hangle. And tonight mi gonna be U-Roy, and tonight U-Roy gonna have trailer load of gal dem. Mi kiant wait fi start. Now. Listen. Mi gonna have couple Dragon. Come and find mi in a likker while and say, so dat people hear, U-Roy inna de place and want fi see mi backstage. All right? And bring all de money. Cool?'

'Ya man.'

'Then go a back of the building to the likkle window and wait.'

'Ya man.'

'Nuh worry, Gaddaffi. Everyting gonna be smooth and cool. Believe mi, smooth and cool.'

Rayon spent the next two hours drinking hot Dragon stout and asking girls if they liked U-Roy. Those who replied in the affirmative he made a mental note to seduce later. He was interrupted by the designer who appeared with two of the four hand-painted posters advertising the show. They were delivered an hour after they announced U-Roy would be on stage, but Rayon pronounced them criss.

'The other two I and I deliver nex week for definite,' the designer said. 'An' ya owe I tree ondred dallar for de four.'

'No problem,' replied Rayon. 'Check mi tomorrow or the day after and mi give it to you. Respect.' To Lord Locks, who was sitting close by with his wife and friends, Rayon added, 'De same fi de rent fi de venue. Check mi nex week for it, man.'

'No Rayon, mi mus haffi tonight,' Lord Locks insisted. 'Dat's what us agree.'

'Easy man, easy. Mi head nah feel too good,' Rayon said feigning illness. 'Mi will see what mi can do.'

The audience was growing restless. A Dandy shandy bottle, favoured projectile of Jamaican mobs, spun out of the crowd onto the stage.

'Oh my God darling, did you see that?' Lord Locks's alarmed wife shrieked.

'Nuh worry wuman,' he reassured her (and himself), 'mi know dese people. It only fun. Dey mean no harm. It all for show. After all, dey nat gonna mash op de one place dat provide top class entertainment in de whole parish, are dem? Anyway, U-Roy soon come.'

'Him inna de place now, boss,' Gaddaffi announced to Rayon. 'Him inna de dressing-room an' he aks fi see you, Rayon. And here de money,' he gave Rayon the wad.

'Give mi what ya owe mi now,' said Lord Locks.

'After de show,' said Rayon, 'like us agree.' He stood up. 'Likker while,' he said with a knowing smile, and walked backstage. But when he got to the dressing-room – a small concrete room full of crates of empties with one high, barred window – he found Lord Locks loping along behind him.

'Rayon. Mi want mi money, man. Serious. Nuh give mi nuh bullshit.'

'Hol' on. Let mi first hail op U-Roy.'

'Ya tink it possible for mi to meet the man?' asked Lord Locks.

Rayon's hand rested on the door handle. 'Can be,' he said, 'first him and mi have a likker business fi settle, and den mi will call ya. Wait a couple minute. Cool?'

'Ya man. Mi wait here.'

Rayon opened the door a little and slipped in, crying out, 'U-Roy! Respect, mi friend!' to the empty room. After shoving some crates against the door he began his metamorphosis from insignificant fisherman to top entertainer. Holding his old clothes and the money, he climbed up to the window and softly called Gaddaffi's name.

'Ya man,' came a voice. 'U-Roy a com, Rayon?'

'Fool, Gaddaffi. Course him nuh com.'

'Ya man. Mi hear ya talk wid him.'

'Idiot. Take dese. Go back a mi yard and wait fi mi. Okay?'

He pushed the bundle through the bars into Gaddaffi's outstretched hands. There was a knock at the door.

'Hol' an,' he called out. 'Mi deh com.'

He took a last look at himself in the broken mirror, pulled the felt trilby over his eyes, gave a pelvic thrust and flashed a wicked smile. Reaching for the door hangle he said loudly, 'All right, Rayon mi friend, if ya nah feel so good, ya stay here and chill out. Mi check ya after de show, man,' then slipped out of the door, closing it behind him.

'Rastafari! King of Kings! Conquering Lion of de tribe of Judah. Jah! Welcome a Zion House, brudder,' boomed Lord Locks, slapping palms and locking his fist around Rayon's limp hand. Lord Locks was thrilled. He was now on personal terms with the great U-Roy, who stood before him in his trademark felt, bell-bottom trousers and platform heel boots.

'Yes mi friend,' said Rayon warmly.

'Mi de proprietor,' explained Lord Locks, 'everyting cool?'

'Kinda cool, but,' continued Rayon, lowering his voice to a whisper and putting his arm around the rasta's bony shoulders, 'mi nah trust de promoter. Mi know him since lang time, and him a friend, true, but mi nah trust him all de same, annerstan? Im say im have fever and want fi chill out, but mi tink im gonna run off without pay mi, and me afraid mi nuh get mi money.'

'He have de money in der. Ask him for it,' urged the Dread.

'No man, a performer get pay after im sing, nat before. Mi kiant disrespect de man like dat.'

'Brudder, can mi do anyting to help you, cas mi tink him try fi run off widout pay mi too.'

'Mi kiant believe dis! Dat man one bad boy for true, eh?' laughed Rayon. 'But look, man, dis room have one lock. Ya have de key?'

'Ya man, right here,' Lord Locks took a key ring from his pocket with a twinkle in his eye.

'Well let we lock im in till mi finish sing, den im kiant leave wid de money before im pay we. Rayon try fi jinall ya, but ya cleverer dan him.'

'True,' laughed Lord Locks. This was excellent. U-Roy must have felt an instinctive bond to trust him so. Lord Locks turned the key in the lock. 'Now we know he is safe.'

'Ya man,' laughed Rayon, 'now us know im safe and sound.'

The Jamaican entertainer never toured with a band. He couldn't afford the cost of transporting men and equipment whenever he performed, so, instead he sung to the rhythm tracks which local dee-jays played on their turntables. Because every performer had to use the same few backing tracks, each of which had a name, like Salt 'n' Pepper, and the evocative Corduroy, he was judged not so much on his music but his lyrics. It was out of this economy that the lucrative dancehall music, which spread so successfully in the States and Europe, was born.

Few preparations were therefore necessary before Rayon took to the stage, though one was that Lord Locks had to waddle to the microphone to make his introduction. His text for the day echoed in his mind: He that loves to exalt himself shall be obeyed. On stage he exalted himself: he raised his arms above his head as if everyone had come to see only him, and shouted, 'Yo!'

'Yo!' the audience thundered back, for by then the place had filled out with all the boys who had vaulted the wall and those from Beach whom Gaddaffi, drunk on power, let in for free.

'Ya man,' he purred indulgently, and then intoned the rastafarian incantation, 'Selassie I, Rastafari, Conquering Lion of Judah, King of Kings, Jah!' In response to this a bokkle spun through the air and splintered on something behind him. Bald 'ead people, by which was meant anyone without dreadlocks, did not hold rastamen in the high esteem they did themselves. Scared of what else might come out of the darkness Lord Locks got on with it.

'People! Let mi introduce the greatest, the number one, the one and only, mi good friend U-Roy!'

The rhythm track started, the bass so loud it tomp you in the chest, and after a short pause, while Rayon tried to extract a promise out of a girl he buck up on backstage a minute earlier, he strutted on. Lord Locks retreated to the edge of the stage where he still felt sufficiently close to the centre of attention to satisfy his vanity. He was a happy man. His venue was buzzing. The rent he was due, which he had worried he would not see, was now safely locked up with Rayon backstage. A star, albeit one a little on the wane, was only feet away from him. He could henceforth tell people he'd been onstage with U-Roy without lying. His large, well shod foot tapped out the beat. In the audience his gorgeous and beloved wife clapped her hands pretty well in time. The rest of the crowd moved more subtly, skanking and wining to the rhythm, their mood mollified by the appearance of the man holding the microphone. He held up his hand to stop the rhythm and make an announcement.

'Dis number,' Rayon called out, 'is for mi good friend Rayon Fairfax of Angel Beach. Big up Rayon! Big up Beach!'

The Beach contingent blushed with pride – with the exception of Gucci, who suck teeth with jealousy.

The music kicked in again, and Rayon began to sing.

'Put on your best dress, baby, we're going out tonight. I'm going to let you wear my crown, I'm going to make you the talk of the town …' It was recognisably U-Roy's greatest hit, and with its rousing chorus, 'Cheek a bow, cheek a bow, cheek a bow wow wow', was a big crowd pleaser. All those with cigarette lighters (two in a crowd of 190) held them in the air.

To people's surprise, U-Roy's second song didn't seem to have any lyrics. Emboldened by the success of the first number, Rayon decided to make the next one up, but unusually for Rayon, words suddenly failed him. He had begun, 'All right mi friends mi could sing all night,' but couldn't think of a rhyme with night, so mumbled and hummed for a bit, and then, thinking of 'all right' struggled to get it onto the end of another phrase, but unable to do that, he began to panic as his mind emptied of any ideas except utterly irrelevant and useless ones. There was only one thing for it: a reprise of 'Put on your best dress, baby, we're going out tonight'. This got the crowd going again, so he scanned the faces at the front for any of the girls he'd checked out earlier.

When he sang the same lyrics for the third song, everyone knew there was something wrong. Lord Locks said to the person beside him, 'Not a vintage performance, I grant you, but a good one all the same. Ya man.'

Gaddaffi, listening outside the venue, grimaced, turned, and began to walk briskly into the safety of darkness.

In the audience, the Beach posse, like everyone else, fell silent and stopped dancing. Rayon leant down to shake a girl's hand, but she recoiled. Most of the crowd began to wonder if it wasn't U-Roy, but for those from Beach it was not a question of who it wasn't, but of who it was, for the moment U-Roy's hat slipped back on his head, throwing light on Rayon Fairfax's desperate grin, Vinton said, quietly to those around him, 'Jeeeezus, dat Rayon. Dat Rayon. Mi kiant believe it.'

Rayon froze when he heard his name being yelled from the audience during the fourth number (a song entitled 'Cheek a bow cheek a bow cheek a bow wow wow'). The game was up, but he had enough time to pull off his hat, flaunt his true identity to the masses and dance a triumphal jig centre stage before being driven off by a hail of bottles. He sped past Lord Locks who called out, 'Hey U-Roy, maybe we can drink a couple Dragon and talk 'bout management.' But an instant later Lord Locks was fully occupied on stage trying to save his expensive equipment from annihilation. Like the overwhelmed goalkeeper of Beach's football team he leapt one way, then the other, with his arms wide apart as bottles crashed and splintered against his amps and boxes. This horrible spectacle only ended when a bottle bounced off his head and forced him, to loud cheers, to totter off the stage. The undefended equipment was mash op by the crowd which, when it ran out of ammunition, turned its attention to the bar and looted that. Vinton and the other Beach yout dem were at the fore of the mob, though Vinton was never so prominent he couldn't slip away quickly if the Police suddenly turned up. The crowd then fanned out onto the Main and gave chase to Rayon, who had grabbed a girl by the hand and was sprinting as fast as his high-heeled boots and flapping bell-bottoms would allow.

Rayon made it safely back to Beach where he lived a hero's

life, revered by the entire village as the man who jinall the whole of Bulls Bay, for at least a month, though the story was kept alive for much longer by the addition of U-Roy to the list of Rayon's aliases. People noticed that for a while Gucci stayed in his own yard, and when he did come out and walk up and down 'pon the street, he spoke much less about Bob Marley in case someone brought up U-Roy's great triumph.

By the time Rayon caught up with Gaddaffi, Gaddaffi had spend down all the money, but to a man from Beach, glory was more important than material gain, and Rayon had a whole heap o' glory. He carefully kept the hat, boots and pants, and from time to time, when he heard U-Roy was playing a show, he'd bring them out and wear them to bars near the venue, and they rarely failed to get him a girl.

FOR THE BRAVE MAY FALL
BUT NEVER YIELD

Shepherd Bush George chat noff. He started stories and only stopped when nobody was listening anymore. As people liked Shepherd Bush George, and didn't want to disrespect him, they were often caught for hours by his tales of life at the wheel of a No. 22 bus from Putney to Piccadilly Circus for twenty-three years. If you met him in the Back Street, it could take you forty minutes to get past him, and if he came into your yard he could trap you for an entire afternoon. People, seeing him coming, plunged into the bush to hide, or vaulted corrugated zinc fences to avoid him, and eventually the only audience he could find was the village picknee.

When Cedric, the captain of the football team asked Shepherd Bush George to be a linesman in a match against the Police, Shepherd Bush George was honoured, and after a fifteen-minute speech, accepted. He had been looking for an opportunity to put something back into the village where he born an raise, and which he left in 1954 for work in Britain.

Touring Beach each day, trilby on his head, furled umbrella on his bony wrist, he liked to feel he was reintegrating himself into the community. When he had thought about retirement in Jamaica, while in gloomy Shepherds Bush, he envisaged himself being in demand as a school governor, or

magistrate, or in some other important role. He was prepared to be called on for advice on weighty village matters.
But that was not the way things turned out. People in Beach
did not seem to realise that he had mixed in Britain with
the very highest in the land. Twice he had shaken hands
with Sir Marcus Bromley, chairman of London Transport.
His next door neighbour in Shepherds Bush, with whom he
was on excellent terms, was the daughter of a cabinet minister, whom he'd said good evening to on more than one
occasion.

Angel Beach, it seemed to him, could little afford to ignore
the talents of a man like him, who could boast (and frequently did) thirty-two years experience in one of the world's
greatest cities working for a massive organisation like London Transport.

But there was something appropriate, Shepherd Bush
George felt, about being asked to be linesman. It showed he
was respected, and could be relied on to make sound, even-
handed judgements. A match official; it was the start of his
career as community leader. He knew little enough about
football, it was true, and had never played a full match, far
less officiated over one, but he watched football on teevee
in England, and it looked pretty easy to him.

The team had actually only asked Shepherd Bush George
because Rayon U-Roy Fairfax, the regular linesman, had
been beaten up by opposition supporters after the Dias game
for a dubious off-side decision against a Dias striker who
had chipped the ball over Busta, the sleepy Beach keeper.
Everybody had the idea that because Shepherd Bush George
boasted incessantly about the English football squad, particularly the World Cup winners of 1966, he actually knew
something about the game.

The year 1987 had not been a good season for the Angel

Beach football team. So far they had played seven matches, drawn none, won none and lost seven. And 1986 had been worse: beaten nine times out of nine (as well as a 5–1 thrashing by their own reserves, a team with an average age of about fourteen, with two girls in it.) Their best result in recent times was the draw against Blenheim in 1984, and that was only because Rayon disallowed four Blenheim goals on one pretext or another. The other clubs in the Westmorland and St John Senior Football League said that if Beach lost every match of the '87 season they'd be thrown out of the league. With only one game left, it was time for some soul-searching.

Football had only recently come to Beach. Cricket had been the big game in the village, and the cricket team 'de best inna St John, serious …' usually won as many as two games a season. But cricket seemed like a game from the past. The organisation it required, the gears, the pitch, the stumps and the scorers were all so much more easy to organise in the orderly colonial era. And cricket came from England, an exhausted source. Football was invented by the English, but that wasn't who brought it to Jamaica. For years England never let black people play football. Football came to Jamaica via teevee from places like Colombia, which was fast establishing itself, with its drug production, love of guns and constant provocation of America, as a nation of consequence enjoying a status equivalent to Iraq and Libya, (Saddam and Gaddafi being Angel Beach's favourite foreign leaders). Football was something which Jamaica could conceivably beat the USA at, and it wasn't outlawed by the Americans, like the only other thing they were better at than them – growing ganje. It was a sport for the likkle country dem; a place like Cameroon could get to the World Cup Finals. Those last three words were a phrase that when uttered brought a dreamy longing to all Jamaicans. 'Can be one day de national side will rise up and tek its rightful place amongst de big football nation dem at de worl' cop finals.'

Beach loved football because football was democratic. Nobody could stop you playing football. Anyone could play it anywhere. You didn't need gears, you didn't need a pitch, you didn't need to be white or even high colour, you didn't even need a ball. If cricket had been colonialism at leisure, then football was independence at play.

The weekly team meeting of the Angel Beach Football Club was held in Beach Primary School on Thursday evenings. They found that they had to wait for at least five days after each match to allow inflamed passions to die down. If they met too early, fights always broke out amongst the guys as they blamed each other for the latest disaster. Squeezed into the tiny classroom furniture it was the only place the team ever looked like giants. The first item each week was Cedric's captaincy.

'Answer me dis,' said Vices before the captain turned up. 'If a animal have no head it kiant live, it kiant go up an' down, can it?'

'No man,' answered some grave voices.

' ... Cas de head control de body. We is de body and Cedric is de head. If we go to lose football game it cas de head lead us der. If we miss de pass, or shoot wide, it cas de head place we in de wrang formation, or put we in de wrang part on de pitch. It Cedric fault.' This was possibly a reference to Cedric's abandonment of the 4–4–2 formation and the team's reversion to the classic Jamaican 1–1–8 formation, but the growl of Cedric's motorbike foreshortened the discussion.

Vices continued 'Bot, bot we moss support our captain,' he said as Cedric walked in looking apologetic. Everybody knew that any idea of deposing Cedric was unworkable, since only Cedric, who had a job at Grand Lido, the biggest hotel in Negril, could afford to fund ball and team food. Grand Lido had its own football team which was also in the league, but Cedric wasn't good enough to be selected for it, so he had to make do with captaining Angel Beach.

'Last Saturday we win a moral victory,' Cedric declared. 'Dem only win cas dem change de ball.'

The club couldn't afford a new football every season, let alone every match, and those they played with often had worn patches and rotten stitching that burst or split during the game.

'Nobady kiant play wid dat ball,' said Vices, who had missed two penalties in the second half, after the first ball was replaced by a newer one. 'Nobady.'

'Ya kiant score no goal wid ball dat obeah man deal wid.'

'Dat one duppy ball. Mi swear. It 'ate Angel Beach,' Cedric stated. 'It nat we fault we nuh win.'

'Ya man,' agreed the guys. 'It nat we fault. It de ball fault.'

'Bot dis Saturday ...' started Cedric, who was aware that the men, after seventeen matches and nearly two seasons without a victory, needed a morale boosting speech, 'tomorrer we gonna play like de champion team we really is. Ya know? And we gonna mash op de Police and win every game nex season ...'

'If we nah win gainst de Police der nat gonna be no next season, cas dem gonna trow we outta de league,' pointed out Bell, so called because he had once been sent a bell for a bicycle by an uncle in Wolverhampton. As he didn't have a bike, he mounted it on the broom he swept out his momma's yard with.

'David slew Goliat,' Vices said.

'And Samson slew de Philistine.'

'Bot de Police alway slew Angel Beach,' added Vinton.

'Wordswort must get healty and hearty,' said Biggar. 'We need Wordswort.'

Wordswort's debut hat-trick against Sandals Hotel in 1987 had looked like changing the course of Angel Beach football, and was a frequently recalled rare moment of sporting glory for the village. Wordswort's hat-trick became one of the seven wonders of Angel Beach. But that was Wordswort's last game, for the following week he fell seriously ill.

Vices examined his older, quieter brother, and declared Wordswort had one worm in him stomach dat make him maaga. His skin grew sallow and hung from his bones, his eyes lacklustre and bloodshot, and he hardly had the strength to kick a ball, though nothing could stop him, every Saturday during the season, dragging himself from his bed to watch Angel Beach play football. It was not much of a tonic for his spirits.

For over a year Wordswort fought the illness. Miss Dahlia and Vices, the top medical brains in the whole of Angel Beach, worked unceasingly on the case. Wordswort was made to drink rum and sea water, lime and Epsom salts, gallons of bicarbonate of soda, Breeze soap powder ('fi wash out de worm' Vices explained), and many many bush teas, picked and prepared by all the well-wishers in the village. He'd applied poultices of logwood ash, seaweed and hog doo-doo, but nothing worked. Wordswort, once a handsome, athletic and industrious fisherman, was a husk of a man, with pale, yellowish skin, assaulted by horrible stomach aches, and forced to live on his bed periodically vomiting blood and spume.

It was agreed that Wordswort had to play on Saturday against the Police, so football club funds were voted to pay for a visit to Dr Bury in Sandy Island. His friends helped him dress up in his best clothes, which were a necessity for even a dying man to wear on a visit to the doctor.

Dr Bury took two minutes to diagnose the problem.

'In my opinion, young man, you are afflicted with what is known as Bellicium Piritis Stupendum.'

'Dat what worm call, den?' asked Wordswort.

Dr Bury shot him a panicked look. 'You don't know anything about medicine, do you?'

'Mi ongle know dis 'bout medicine: if you have one fi cure mi, please gi' it mi soon, dactar, cas mi belly hurt bud.'

'I will endeavour to do the very best I can,' said Dr Bury, looking relieved. 'Now,' he explained confidently, 'you see Bellicium Piritis affects the gerundive fibulator ...'

'Dat some kind of worm?'

'In a manner of speaking.'

'It can wash out?'

'I'm afraid not entirely. You see the problem is, the gerundive fibulator is a tenacious little fellow, and very difficult to budge with only medicine.'

'It have claw like crab?'

'Quite like that. Look, I'll give you some pills that will prevent it growing further and give you some relief, but an impacted gerund can only really be cured by a surgical procedure.'

'Inna de 'ospital?'

'Most certainly.'

'Dat expensive?'

'Not really, not when set against your life. I can probably arrange to have it done by the estimable Dr Canute Asquith, M.D. M.S.C. Cantab and Cambridge. It will only cost five thousand dollars or maybe four thousand eight hundred ...'

'Bot mi nuh have monny like dat.'

'How much do you have?'

'Mebbe five 'ondred J.'

'Well for that I can do an excellent wart removal or maybe two ingrowing toenails. Have you got any unsightly warts that want removing? They're three hundred J each ...'

Wordswort stepped off the minibus where the football squad waited on the roadside. He showed them a bottle of pills.

'Dr Bury say mi need one cut inna de 'ospital, bot mi can tek one pill and it will hold back de worm.'

'Bot ya moss play tomorrer,' said Cedric, desperately.

Barrington said, 'Him will play, Cedric, him will play. If one pill stop de worm grow, all de pill moss kill de worm, so tek all de pill at one time. Den ya can play wid ease, man.'

'If dat true, why Dr Bury say only a surgeon cut can cure Wordswort?' asked Miss Dahlia, who swore by Dr Bury and spent every available cent she had on visits to his surgery.

'Ya man, why?'

'Cas him want monny, fool.'

'No man,' protested Miss Dahlia. 'Surgeon Canute Asquith at Bulls Bay 'ospital tek dat monny.'

'Bot him give som a Dr Bury. Cho!'

'No. No. De reason Dr Bury nat want fi cure Byron is dis,' Barrington said. 'Tell mi. Wishart de dactar in Sandy Island?' By which he meant, where is the doctor's surgery?

'Before de Police Station,' Maxwell said, and everybody suddenly fell silent. The plot was thus revealed.

'Right,' said Barrington, his eyes glistening with the insight. 'And it true Dr Bury Police doctor?'

'Ya man, ya man ...'

'And it true we play de Police Saturday? Dat why him nuh cure Wordswort. Cas de Police feart dat Wordswort play in de match, cas him one wickid strika. Wordswort.'

'Ya man,' came Wordswort's weak voice from where he'd gone to sit in the shade.

'If one pill hold back de worm, all de pill gwine kill it. Tross mi ...'

This seemed to make sense, so Wordswort took all the pills in the bottle. He was bed-ridden within hours, and couldn't stand for a week after that, so everybody said Dr Bury deliberately poisoned Wordswort to keep him out of the match. It was a comfort to go into a game armed with a good excuse for losing it.

Despite the certainty of defeat, there was the usual fierce competition to get on the team, not out of hunger for sport, but because the Police always attracted plenty of female supporters.

On the morning of the game the squad emerged from their yards with their usual self-confidence, and set off to the sloping and pitted Angel Beach ballground, with the glad hearts of the doomed but brave.

The match referee was an unknown schoolmaster from the other side of Mo-Bay, but the Police linesman was a lawyer called Charles Brown, referred to by everybody as Liar Brown, who did the job as a favour to the Police, in return for which bail was always forthcoming for his criminal clients. Shepherd Bush George, Liar Brown and the referee took the captains out to the centre spot where Cedric typically lost the toss. Beach did possess a newish, only one season old, football, which they tief after a match up inna de hills against Kendal, but it was felt wise not to parade it in front of the Police unnecessarily. They played instead with a ball that had spent a season or two in dusty Beach yards, and whose colour and stitching was faded and worn.

As soon as the match started, Shepherd Bush George began to relax. He loved officiating, and found he was good at it, better, certainly, than Liar Brown, who kept his flag down despite a blatant offside run by the Police striker that resulted in the ball being struck through the Beach keeper's legs and into the net.

'De linesman one tief!' the Beach supporters shouted. But Shepherd Bush George was impressed that the Beach players accepted Liar Brown's decision so compliantly. It showed sportsmanship and character which he thought they didn't possess. In fact, they didn't complain because they were so accustomed to the bias of the opposition linesman, who more or less counted as a twelfth member of the team, that they fully expected Shepherd Bush George to do the same thing for Beach when he got the chance, which he did, ten minutes later, when Barrington, doubled up and groaning with exhaustion after a fruitless run at the Police goal, and unable to sprint back onside, suddenly found himself on the end of a long ball that sailed over the Police back four, and which, almost incredibly, he blasted past the Police keeper who stood motionless in the goalmouth, shouting 'Aff-side linesman!'

Vices smiled to himself. He knew he was offside, but with the ref stranded up the other end of the pitch, he knew that it was Shepherd Bush George who had to make the decision. With little hesitation, Shepherd Bush George raised his flag and disallowed the goal.

The Police goalie smugly set the ball down for a free kick. An outburst of abuse erupted from the Beach players. 'Ya fool, Shepherd Bush George. Ya nuh remember where ya live? Ya idiot, man.' All of which Shepherd Bush George rose above.

Play continued, the action never moving far from the Beach goalmouth. Things went pretty well for the boys, they only conceded three more goals in the next quarter of an hour. The Police hardly broke into a sweat as they kicked the ball confidently from one to another through the legs or over the heads of the huddle of Beach players trying to get in on the game, and made it seem more like a session of piggy in the middle than a football match.

Flossie paced the touchline shouting abuse. 'Ya useless' she laughed, 'ya kiant attack and ya kiant defend.'

At half-time, Cedric, Barrington and Bell sought out Shepherd Bush George, while the rest of the players sat in a circle being abused by Beach supporters, led by Flossie, who easily drowned out Cedric's well-meaning attempts to rally his men. They found Shepherd Bush George mingling with the Police players.

'Wha ya do, ya fool? Ya want we fi lose?'

Shepherd Bush George lowered his voice. 'Are you asking me to help you win the game?'

'Course we blaad claat are, ya raas claat Shepherd Bush George,' shouted Barrington.

'In that case you leave me no option but to make an official complaint in writing about Angel Beach Football Club to the Football Association Headquarters in Lancaster Gate London S.W.7.' As the relief driver on the 119 bus, Shepherd Bush George had stopped many times and stared at the impressive doors of the F.A. Headquarters, and had once seen Bobby Charlton emerging from them – though he hailed a taxi rather than getting on Shepherd George's bus. 'If this country was run by men half as dedicated to fair play as the English Football Association, then we would not be in the boat we are currently in vis a vis corruption and immorality. Have you never heard the saying,' he hissed furiously, 'It is not whether you win or lose but how you play the game? In England we were proud of that saying.'

'Bot Chicken George, ya not in England no more. Ya back

a yard. And we moss win dis match or dem trow we outa de league, an' if we trow outa de league den nobady gonna play de game gainst we, and football gonna stop in Angel Beach,' explained Biggar.

'From what I have seen of this club, I think that would be a very good idea.'

'Ya blaad claat,' Barrington cursed as Shepherd Bush George walked away.

It was twenty minutes into the second-half, during a stoppage caused by two Beach defenders running into each other and cracking their skulls, that the news came through. A Police car tore off the Main, bumping onto the ballground and drew up in a cloud of dust. Sergeant Dickinson from Sandy Island was at the wheel.

'Natty Morgan hold up de drinks truck wid one gun at Lemon Grove,' he shouted, 'and tief farty-one tousand dallar. Every afficer is needed fi de manhunt.'

The drinks truck was a noisy open-sided lorry piled high with crates of Red Stripe, Dragon Stout and saff drink, on top of which three men perched. It hammered up and down the Main ignoring the shouted requests from the likkle people dem for it to stop and trade with the bamboo sheds and bars, on its way to the big hotels in Negril.

'Nobady kiant come now, man. We gonna finish this game first,' shouted one of the Police defenders, leaning against the goal post with his arms folded.

'Dat gotta wait. Every man gotta com.'

'Who say dat?'

'Sergeant Pinnock.'

'Dis match gonna finish anudder day,' announced Afficer Barnett, the captain, who'd once trialed for a Brazilian club side and gained considerable fame by meeting a player in Brazil who'd met Pele.

'No sah!' roared the redoutable Flossie, striding towards the Police. 'Dis fixture a go finish today. Dat what de rule is. Mi wait tree year for one win and no Police a go tief it now.'

'Bot we haffi hunt fi Natty Morgan.'

'So ya lose de match den,' shouted Flossie.

'We are not going on no manhunt,' said two of the Policemen, Afficers Nini Hibbert and Cop Holt, who were suspended on full pay pending an inquiry into their robbing the bank at Sav. 'We can play.'

'Ya kiant play wid two men,' laughed Flossie. 'Dat kiant work.'

'Dat kiant work wid some,' agreed the Police skipper, 'but 'gainst Angel Beach, ref, how much minutes left?'

'Farteen minute to play.'

''Gainst Angel Beach,' the skipper laughed, 'for farteen minute, wid a four goal lead, can be it will work. Hibbert, Holt, you have the honour of the Force to play for.'

'Yah sah.'

There was screeching of tyres and revving of engines as the Police jumped into cars and headed up the Main to Lemon Grove. Hibbert threw Holt the goalkeeping gloves and said 'Let play begin.'

Cedric said, 'Alright team, gadder roun, hey, everybody gadder roun.' Five men responded to his order, and to them he said, 'We must score five goal gainst a two man opposition, and we win dis game.'

'Unless Pinnock catch Natty quick,' said Bell, 'and dem all come back fi finish we off.'

'Dat kiant happen,' laughed Vinton. 'Natty nuh gonna catch easy. Tross mi.'

'Dat right,' said Cedric. 'Now come now. Let we do it.'

'And God bless Natty Morgan,' said Vinton.

When the Beach team spread out across the pitch, leaving Hibbert stranded in midfield and Holt looking very lonely in goal it seemed as though nothing could go wrong for Beach. The problem was, that keeping possession and scoring goals were not regarded by Beach footballers as the real purpose of football. Making and receiving passes was something that only likkle people did. Football was barely a team game in Beach. It was a gladiatorial encounter between two men: the man with the ball, and the man trying to tackle him. Nothing else counted. The only glory and therefore the greatest glory was not to win, or even to score, but to salad a defender, that is, to tap it through his legs, or dummy him and make him fall over, or to bounce it off his body in a quick 1–2. It was stories of these incidents that were told after matches in Flossie's bar, or in a group of men standing smoking on the roadside in the gloaming. The fact that the player was finally surrounded and lost the ball, and the opposition passed it down the field and scored a goal, was not permitted to spoil the sweetness of the time a Beach man salad a defender. In pre-match strategy talks at Beach Primary the team did agree to pass the ball, and during the match some players stayed wide in the hope of receiving a long ball, but one never came, because passing was for wimps. The only time you passed the ball was the moment before you were overwhelmed trying to weave it through a wall of players. Other acceptable moves were scissor kicks, back heels and possibly back headers, but they were a bit run-of-the-mill for a Beach player whose head was filled only with dreams of personal glory. They cared more about entertainment than victory, and for that, as everybody knows, they stayed stuck to the bottom of the table. But they didn't care, so long as once a match or once every two matches, they saw and savoured a Beach man salad a defender.

Kipling set the tone, kicking off and dribbling the ball not at the Police goal, but at the sole Police player, Afficer Hibbet, known in the station and on the pitch as Killa Hibbert. The other Beach players shouted 'down de left, man, pass it!' and 'gi' it a mi, man!', but Kipling took it forward on his own, and then tried to chip it neatly over Hibbert's head to collect it on the other side. But the chip was too low and Killa took it on his chest, controlled it, and left Kipling sprawling on the turf behind him. Nobody ran in to tackle Hibbert. They had the more important task of abusing Kipling to attend to.

'Come on! Constentrate,' urged Busta, in the Beach goal.

'Dat nat mi fault,' Kipling shouted back.

'Ya man dat ya fault. Ya lose de ball,' shouted Vinton. 'Who fault ya believe it is?'

'Stop ya noise,' yelled Cedric, as Hibbert steamed into the Beach half with the ball at his feet, and Biggar, his bosoms bouncing up and down, trundling along behind him. Hibbert's shot went wide, and Busta took the goal kick, which was picked up by Kipling in the centre. This time he had only the Police keeper to beat. On his left were four players and on his right, three, all bearing down on the goal alongside him. Ten yards out he dummied a pass to Maxwell, sent the keeper to the right, and drove the ball into the net.

'Ya salad him!' Flossie shouted triumphantly from the touchline.

4–1, with eleven minutes plus injury time left. A second goal somehow kept evading the boys; two easy shots at an open goal went wide, on both occasions because the striker (first Vinton and then Maxwell) chose to hammer the ball as hard as possible rather than just slide it into the goal safely. As time ticked away, Beach's old friend defeat came clearly into view, and mesmerised Cedric and the boys with its hateful familiarity. Beaten by a team of only two players. It was something that could only happen to a Beach outfit, and everybody seemed to know it. They began to laugh at their own mistakes, and make light of their bungled attempts to stop the ball, or kick it straight, as if preparing themselves for defeat. The Beach supporters fell silent, and the Police supporters became voluble. Word of the state of play, whisked along by a speeding minibus, reached Sandy Island and Firefly Bay, bringing out astounded onlookers who would normally have no interest in the match, to see for themselves the spectacle of a whole football team being beaten by two men.

Kipling finally scored a second goal, and then with his third goal began at last to make it look easy. But that goal gave him his hat-trick – an achievement only equalled once before in Beach footballing history by Wordswort, and therefore merited a sluggish run all round the pitch, followed by a general mobbing of Kipling by players and spectators alike, all of which took valuable minutes – though everybody felt it was still an absolute necessity.

4–4, with two minutes of time to play.

'Dis easy.' laughed Vices, taking the ball upfield.

'Ya man,' agreed the other eight strikers, tagging along beside him. They were euphoric. Even if they didn't score, the draw was their best result in ages. Unless of course Killa Hibbert scored a fifth for the Police, which for one heart-stopping moment, when the whole Beach team, including the keeper were caught up in the Police half, it looked like he might do. Fortunately enough Beach players got back to cover the goal.

It was during injury time, in the last seconds of the game, that Barrington 'Vices' Cooke dummied at Hibbert to salad him, and found himself running at the goal with only the keeper to beat. Kipling, seeing that Vices was about to remove from him the chances of scoring four goals in one match, and going down in the annals of Beach sporting history as a record-breaking striker, tore into Vices from behind and with a sweeping tackle dispossessed him of the ball. Vices got off the ground and started to cuss and use bad word, but Kipling now had the ball, so Vices grabbed his shirt and pulled him over. The ball went loose, six yards in front of the goal, right in the path of Biggar, who was thundering towards it at maximum speed, thighs flapping, untied bootlaces flicking from side to side. As the ref checked his watch and put the whistle in his mouth to blow full time Biggar booted the ball harder than it had ever been hit, straight at the goal. He kicked it so hard, in fact, that he split the ball in two, one half of which audibly whizzed past Holt's outstretched fingers into the roof of the net.

Biggar, his arms outstretched like an aeroplane, ran towards the Beach supporters crying 'GOAAAAAAAAAALLLLL!'

The fate of the other half of the ball was somewhat different. It also took the full force of Biggar's size fourteen right boot, but skewed off to the right, skidding along the ground wide of the goal, spreading a large group of Police supporters who were jumping up and down shouting 'Ya miss! Ya miss! Draw! Draw!'

A second later, all the players and all the supporters converged on the match officials, arguing furiously about the rules that covered this eventuality. The referee, jostled by the crowd, part-terrified, part-dumbstruck and completely unsure of what to do made it through to Liar Brown and Shepherd Bush George.

'That was no goal, ya haffi disallow it, ref,' Liar Brown averred. The ref assumed that was what he was going to say, knowing his close relationship with the Police.

'Linesman,' the ref addressed Shepherd Bush George, 'what you think?'

Shepherd Bush George was pretty certain that a new ball should be found, and play started again from before the goal, which should be disallowed, but something made him hesitate. It was perhaps the sight of his large and comfortable concrete house on the far side of the ballground, surrounded by the many lesser board houses of his neighbours' yards. 'Under rule number twenty-two of the English Football Association,' he stated evenly, 'of Lancaster Gate, London S.W.7, it states quite clearly that where a ball splits into two, the piece that remains on the field of play shall be deemed in play.'

People were not immediately certain what this meant, but the words were so fine and sounded so authentic that the ref grabbed at them, blew his whistle and pointed to the centre spot, a moment later blowing again for full-time.

There was tumult. The Beach team ran in a pack around the pitch, shouting and whooping in celebration of the first victory in living memory. The Police supporters moved in on Shepherd Bush George, and began to push and punch him. It was only the appearance of two off-duty Police from Mo-Bay who escorted Shepherd Bush George off the pitch, which prevented violence. Though as soon as they were out of sight behind a house they pulled their service revolvers on him and threatened to kill him if he ever 'tief de Police a nex time.'

Up until that afternoon, Shepherd Bush George had growing doubts about whether he was right to have left Shepherds Bush for Jamaica for his retirement. But from then on, although he had the same old suspicion that he was being avoided, he felt that when he did talk to his neighbours they had more respect for him – and he liked it. Sometimes,

Vices, or one of the other yout dem of the village would say, 'Shepherd Bush George. Ri-spec! What dat English Football Sociation clob rule dat ya mek up for de Police match?' and laugh.

Shepherd Bush George replied the same each time: 'I did not make that rule up. That rule is in the book. I would never cheat. Never,' adding, to himself, 'unless it was for Angel Beach.' And thus he settled into a long and happy retirement.

A week after the game, Vinton said, 'Give tanks to you, Shepherd Bush George, for nex year we are in de Westmorland and St John Football League, and wid de Lard's help and Shepherd Bush George rule nomber twenty-two, can be we will lick down de appasition an' win de league nex year.'

'Angel Beach, win the league?' laughed Shepherd Bush George, 'That is about as likely as the Jamaican National Team qualifying for the World Cup Finals.'

THE PEOPLE'S GANGSTA

When Tyrone 'Natty' Morgan held up the drinks truck on a stretch of the Main beyond Lemon Grove, the job went better than he could have hoped: not only did he get away with 41,000 J, but the robbery was reported by Radio Waves, the new Mo-Bay station, and made Crime of the Month on RJR, which meant that his name, with the prefix 'notorious gang leader' was broadcast twice a day, every day. It was the kind of publicity that gangsters dreamt of. He became such a celebrity a minibus owner in Sandy Bay renamed his unit 'Natty Morgan'.

Before this break, Natty was an unknown member of a Kingston gang run by Heart Disease, so called because according to a government broadcast on JBC radio, that was 'the nation's number one killer'. Natty decided to get famous by killing his old friend Heart Disease, but the job went wrong, he only wounded him, and had to leave the metropolitan area in a hurry, so headed for West Jamaica, where twenty years before he was born an' raise.

Sergeant Delroy Pinnock of Sandy Island, St John's hardest cop, was put on the drinks chock robbery. Everyone knew and feared Pinnock, who had shot dead six people including his wife.

Natty hid up inna de hills while tings cool dung, but 41,000J in cash began to mad him in a backwater where the people still bartered for goods, and money was virtually useless, unless you wanted kerosene – not the commodity the gangster had planned to celebrate his heist with. His single thrill was hearing his name on the radio, and so, long before it was safe, he took the minibus down the pot-holed road to Montego Bay to drink rum and sport wid de gal dem.

The moment he alighted on Sam Sharpe Square he could tell people recognised him from wanted posters Pinnock had distributed. It was his first direct brush with fame and he loved it so much he swaggered brazenly down Barrett Street trailing a gaggle of awe-struck picknee chanting, 'Natty, Natty, Natty …' only shooing them away half-heartedly before climbing the stairs to an iniquitous go-go bar where he was confident of being recognised by the criminal clientele.

Natty had a couple ounce of rum in him belly and his arm around a bit of browning in a bra and G-string when feet pounded up the narrow staircase and two uniformed cops burst into the bar. Even though they had guns in their hands, and Natty had something altogether different in his, he managed to shoot first, killing one and leaving the other writhing on the floor. With the sound of reinforcements charging up the stairs Natty gave his go-go dancer an un-hurried kiss, vaulted the bar, ran through to the back and smashed a window with a chair. Shoving his Beretta into his belt he climbed onto the sill, leapt across the alley and grabbed a loose drainpipe on the other side. He would have got away if he hadn't stopped to hail up som yout dem who'd heard the shots and shattered glass and run into the alley to see what was going on. He was still striking poses and spinning his pistol on his trigger finger when Sergeant Pinnock, six foot four with a wide jaw and thick moustache, rounded the corner with his .44 in his hand and squeezed off a shot. Natty still didn't run; he waved his fist and shouted, 'Ya miss, raas claat!' making the yout dem roar with laughter.

Pinnock didn't miss the second time, and Natty half fell, half slid, down the pipe and collapsed bleeding on the filthy alley floor. Pinnock picked up Natty's Beretta and spilled three live rounds into the palm of his hand.

Cocking his own pistol with a click at Natty's brown temple he said, 'Nyam dem.' It was classic Pinnock: make suspects eat live bullets to soften them up for interrogation. Holding Natty by his short dreadlocks he stuffed the ammunition into his slack mouth. Natty's eyes opened and he spat them out along with a stream of abuse, so Pinnock forced him face-down in the gutter, and with a boot between his shoulder blades slapped handcuffs on his wrists. He then dragged Natty past the yout dem to the Police car. Seeing the boys made Natty defiant. Not wanting to disappoint his public he began to cuss and use bad word.

'Nuh touch mi, pussy claat,' he shouted, but Pinnock just lick im across the head and tipped his body into the boot of the car which he slammed and locked.

On the way to Sandy Island Pinnock deliberately drove slowly, and stopped for an hour fi check one gal in Sandy Bay, carefully parking so the bonnet and cab were in the thick shade of an almond tree and the boot in the searing sunlight.

Word that the gangster was in Sandy Island lock-up flashed up and down the Main. People held up their heads with pride that such an important individual as a gang member and Police killer was for once on the north coast and not in Kingston. The story of his capture quickly penetrated deep into the hills and valleys, and well-wishers gathered at the gate of the Police station so that when Natty awoke from unconsciousness on the floor of his cell, the first thing he heard was his name being called from beyond the bars.

After Natty nyam a dinner of chicken-foot and rice, spurred by a hatred of Pinnock and a desire to do something for the crowd at the gate, he formed a plan of escape, and in the darkness before dawn, he struggled through a hole in his ceiling, crept across the roof of the lock-up, leapt off into a thicket and ran away into the bush.

Mr Crooks of Angel Beach was responsible for Natty's escape, though he didn't know it, for he was the contractor who had supplied the load of contaminated sea sand that had produced the substandard concrete roof which Natty had burrowed a hole through with nothing more than a spoon.

Natty spent the day sleeping in the upper branches of a guango tree with Police and Army vehicles speeding along the road beneath him. When night fell he slipped through the bush to a silent coastal village where a long time before he did friend with a shy, pretty girl whom he knew he could count on. He hadn't seen her for four years but figured she'd be where he left her, as she was tied to her yard by a huge dragon of a mother to do the chores.

It was late, and the people who had grouped up to discuss Natty's escape and speculate on his next move had dispersed to their yards, little thinking that he was passing silently through their midst. He crept to the girl's house and whispered her name through the rotting siding boards, trying not to wake her mother, who had, he remembered, often predicted he'd end up in trouble with the Police.

'Who dat?' came a voice.

'Nerine?' whispered Natty again.

'Who dat?'

'Nerine, it Natty Morgan. Mi beg ya som help.'

Nerine got up quickly and quietly and tiptoed to the door.
'Natty?' she asked anxiously.

He took her hand and squeezed it.

'Ya in trouble.'

'Dem nuh gonna capture mi. But mi beg ya someting fi
eat and som place fi hide till tings cool dung.'

'Mi can tek ya to de cave dem. Wait while mi get fi mi
dress.' She pushed the door to, and turned to see Miss Dahlia
in the moonlight sitting up in bed on one massive elbow,
tree likker picknee nuzzled up to her bulk.

'Who dat?' she shrieked.

Outside, Natty winced.

'Nobady Mumma.'

'Dat Natty Morgan.'

'Ssh Mumma.' There were seven children and two other
adults in the three-roomed house and Nerine wanted none
of them to wake up.

'What he want?'

'Someting fi eat.'

'Give him dat fry fish inna de pot.'

'Ya Mumma.'

'And mek him pay.'

'Mumma!' said Nerine.

'Mi don't have no money,' Natty growled through the
boards.

'Him never change,' sighed Miss Dahlia, then she asked
'What bout de farty-one tousand dallar from de drink chock
robbery?'

'Mi nuh have dat now.'

'Ya nuh spend down all dat money, ya liard,' Miss Dahlia
said.

'Mi hide dat far away. Now let de gal com,' he whispered impatiently.

'Who dat?' a small voice asked. Everyone fell silent. A five year old boy sat up in Nerine's bed rubbing his big eyes.

'Go back a sleep, Kermit,' Nerine whispered.

'Dat Natty Morgan?' he asked excitedly.

'Hush up, picknee,' Miss Dahlia growled.

'But Mumma, mi hear one man say him Natty Morgan,' Kermit said. 'Mi did.'

'Top ya noise picknee or mi lick ya,' shouted Miss Dahlia, and he lay down, but was too excited to sleep.

Nerine grabbed half a bread, tree fry fish an one jack dompling, shoved the plate out of the door and hurried to the mirror to work on her hair. Dawn broke as they left the yard and headed across the pasture to the dark hills. Nerine planned to hide Natty in Hopton's Rocktop Cave which, although Beach's premier tourist attraction, was reliably deserted at all times. Occasionally Hopton, who had painstakingly erected a sign on the Main, and built a bar and turnstile at the cave entrance, wandered up there to moon about on his own, to daydream about tourists and money, but he rarely went into the limestone caves, which Nerine, like everyone else raise in Beach, knew so well. Well, perhaps not so well; Vinton once went in with Mooney for a quick game of hide and seek and emerged shaken ten hours later.

Nerine and Natty walked fast through the salady grass with their heads down, and only looked behind them once they reached the mouth of the cave. They then saw hurrying along in their footsteps a barefoot boy in a torn shorts and ganzi. It was her nephew, Kermit.

'Go in,' Nerine whispered to Natty, who darted into the cave. 'Kermit!' she shouted. 'What ya do here, picknee?'

A large, round face with big blinking eyes and long lashes

looked up innocently. 'Mi want fi hail up Natty Morgan,' he said, 'so mi can tell mi bredren.'

'Ya nuh tell nobady nuttin, annerstan?' Nerine said.

'Bot mi moss tell Leroy mi see Natty.' Leroy was two years Kermit's senior and an object of adulation.

'Natty Morgan nat here, annerstan? Ya never hear him, ya never saw him. Now gwaan back a yard.'

'Ya, man, but first mi hail up im.'

'Hail up who?'

'Natty.' Kermit stood square to his aunt with his hands plunged into his pockets.

'Mi tell ya. Natty nuh here. Now gwaan.' She raised her hand to lick him.

'Him is here. Him in de cave mout,' Kermit stated implacably. 'Mi see him go in.'

She tried to strike him but years of practice enabled him to evade the blow.

'Him in der,' he shouted, 'mi will show ya.'

'Bredren,' Natty uttered quietly, emerging into the light with his hand held out to Kermit, 'hush now. Com ya,' he beckoned to Kermit, whose eyes tripled in size and whose chin dropped onto his chest. He shot a satisfied smirk at Nerine and approached the gangster. 'Let we go inna de cave mout,' Natty said, taking Kermit's hand. But Kermit shook his hand out, puffed out his chest, and walked beside Natty like a man. Nerine followed them in, and in the cool of the cave dabbed aloe on a wound on Natty's foot bottom while Kermit stared at his swollen and cut face.

'Pinnock beat ya?' Kermit asked.

'´Top your noise, Kermit,' snapped Nerine.

'It nottin,' replied Natty. 'Bot mi gonna kill him for it.'

'Look at dis.' Kermit pulled down his shorts to reveal a welt across the top of his buttock.

'Ya Momma lick ya?' Natty asked.

'It nottin,' Kermit said, pulling up his shorts, 'but mi maybe gonna kill her for it.'

Nerine slapped him across the back of his head.

'Ya one bad boy, picknee!' laughed Natty.

'Ya man,' exclaimed Kermit proudly. 'Mi bad like you.'

'Ya one bad raas claat, mi can see,' said Natty, before turning serious. He took hold of Kermit's hand, and this time wouldn't be shaken off. 'Will ya do someting for mi?'

'Ya man.'

'Listen careful. When ya go back a yard ya nah tell nobady ya see and talk wid Natty Morgan. Nobady, annerstan?'

Kermit looked into Natty's bloodshot eyes and felt scared. 'Ya sah.'

'Nobady. Not one friend or nobady. Cas Natty ron from de Police and nobady moss know where him de hide. Annerstan?'

'Ya man,' he gulped.

'If ya tell somebady, picknee, ya know what a-happen? Natty com an find ya in de night. Ya man. And ya know what him do den?'

Kermit felt his hand being squeezed hard – harder than he liked. But he did not complain. He just stared into Natty's dark and dangerous eyes.

'Mi will slit ya wid one ratchet knife from ya belly to ya troat. Annerstan?'

The boy's face crumpled and tears poured down his cheeks. 'Ya sah,' he sobbed.

'But dat nuh gonna happen,' said Natty, releasing his hand and patting him on the back.

'Nuh bawl,' snapped Nerine.

'Gwaan now,' Natty waved them away. 'Tek a long way back a yard. And wuman, com tomorrow. Bring mi food, ya?'

Nerine cuss and use bad word to Kermit all the way home. 'Ya nuh tell nobady. Nobady, or Natty will kill ya. For sure. Him will.'

'Uh-hu,' murmured Kermit miserably, by now resigned to a horrible death in the middle of the night at Natty's hands because, sneaking out of Miss Dahlia's yard at dawn after Nerine and Natty, he buck up on Sandra, a neighbour, who was returning from a night's work in Negril, and had boasted to her that he was off to see Natty Morgan. When she called him a liard he pointed out Nerine and Natty hurrying across the pasture.

Sandra Swing was a newcomer to the village, who worked in the tourist industry as a prostitute on the beach in Negril, and therefore for professional reasons did friend wid whole 'eap o' police. She was very pretty, nice and fat, with brazen, seductive eyes. She considered herself Beach's leading authority on Natty, because her boyfriend of the moment, Afficer Donovan, was stationed at Sandy Island, and leaked the latest Police intelligence on the case to her.

There was a battery-operated portable TV in Larmonds novelty store, in Content, which Sandra had coveted for months. Its moulded pink plastic attracted pilgrims from miles away, but Sandra was determined to make it hers. She was too superior to use the benches Shepherd Bush George had kindly arranged in his yard for people to sit on to peer through his windows at his 36″ Grundig. It vex Sandra to watch Shepherd Bush George on his settee eating fried chicken by electric light while she sat salivating out in his yard. Others felt differently: for them, the luxurious composition framed by the open window, of the settee, the picture of the square rigger, the floral carpet, the lava lamp and Shepherd Bush George eating chicken, were as much of a draw as the rather incomprehensible foreign television programmes.

After watching Kermit run after Nerine and Natty, Sandra went into her house and shook Afficer Donovan out of his sleep.

'What ya want?' he groaned. 'Gwaan an' mek mi breakfast.'

'Mi know where Natty Morgan de,' she blurted.

His eyes opened. 'What, wuman?'

'Mi know where Natty Morgan de,' she repeated urgently.

He sat up in bed. 'Where?'

'What ya give mi fi know?' Sandra said, her rich red lips widening into a corrupt smile.

Donovan lay back down and closed his eyes. 'Ya know nottin, ya liard.'

'Mi nah liard. Mi see him dis marning.'

'Wishart ya see him?'

'What will ya give mi fi tell ya?'

'Pussy claat, Sandra ...' he sighed. 'Mi give you one shoes last week wuman. Ya never have enough new ting?'

'Him wear one green ganzi,' she said, 'and him foot limp.'

Donovan leapt from the bed and pinned Sandra to the wall by the throat. 'Where ya see him? Tell mi.'

'What ya give mi?' she croaked.

Donovan squeezed her larynx. Her bright red fingernails clawed impotently at him. 'Talk, blood claat ...'

'Alright. Alright,' she gurgled. 'Mi tell ya.' He loosened his grip. 'Mi tell ya if you buy mi dat pink teevee in Larmonds.' He tightened his grip and began to beat her head against the partition wall. Next door, Kadim, her three year old daughter, woke up and began crying. 'Mi nuh tell ya,' Sandra screeched. 'Mi never tell ya.' He threw her back on the grey sheet, grabbed his Police issue pistol from under the pillow, and pointed it at her head.

'In the name of the law, pussy claat, tell mi or mi kill ya.'

Killing Sandra often crossed Donovan's mind. An afficer called Buckingham shot his girlfriend and Pinnock promoted him a week later.

'Ya kill mi Donovan, ya never find Natty, ya idiot.'

Paying for the TV meant hanging around for hours at illegal roadblocks near the big hotels to get bribes from terrified tourists with ganja. But leading Sergeant Pinnock to Natty Morgan would please Pinnock even more than shooting a girl.

'Ow much dallar is dis teevee?'

It was 2820 J, but Sandra also desired a pair of spangled plastic high heels for her daughter, Kadim, so added the cost of them to the figure. 'Tree tousan J.'

Donovan thought for a moment. 'Alright. Wishart Natty?'

'Ya swear ya gonna give mi tree tousan J?'

'Dat what mi say wuman.'

'Ya swear?'

'Mi swear.'

''Pon de Bible?'

'Ya man, now where Natty Morgan de?'

'Hol' an.' Sandra picked up her Bible – the only book in the house. Raising her voice over the sound of Kadim's bawling she said, 'Put ya hand 'pon it and swear ya will pay mi.'

Donovan, his gun in his left hand, did so, and with his right hand still on the Bible said, 'Tell mi where de blaad claat is, now.'

'Mi nah know.'

'Bumber claat!' he shouted and grabbed her again in fury.

'... Bot mi know who know ...' she screamed. 'Mi know who hide him and who tek him food.'

'Who?'

✳   ✳   ✳

Nerine did not panic when she saw the Police car in the road by Miss Dahlia's yard. It had been up and down so much she thought it must have burn out of gas, but when Sergeant Delroy Pinnock hail up her from the driving seat she felt her heart miss whole heap o beat.

'You Christella Knibb?'

'Ya,' said Nerine, letting her bag with the length of aloe and blood-soaked cloth drop softly by her feet.

'Gimme dat lada bag, gal.'

Pinnock glanced in the bag. 'Get in de car, gal.'

Miss Dahlia, who'd watched from the house, staving off a heart attack with Old Testament prayers, pushed herself up onto her feet and hobbled down from the house and across the yard. To Nerine she whispered, 'If ya haffi tell him, mek him pay.'

Like all Jamaican cars, the door hangle brok, so Pinnock leant across to let Nerine in, lingering in the position to pat her on her knee. 'Ya gonna tell mi where he is now, or we gonna ride back a Police Station an' talk der?'

'Mi nuh understan ya question sah.'

'Good, cas mi like fi interrogate a pretty gal.'

He started the engine, and without looking behind, executed a swift U-turn, forcing Wilbert, who was trotting by on his donkey, off the road and into a tree.

Kermit crept into the house and hid under Miss Dahlia's bed, remaining there all day, watching her swollen ankles and waiting for Natty Morgan to kill him. At dusk, when he heard the picknee in the yard play a game called Natty a com fi we, he could bear it no longer and decided to commit suicide. Once, when hungry, he'd eaten fistfuls of foam rubber torn from Nerine's mattress, and Miss Dahlia, while beating his botty, screeched, 'Nah nyam sponge, ya craven picknee. Ya eat sponge ya will dead.' So he solemnly consumed two square feet of six-inch foam rubber and waited to die.

All night he felt as though he were about to expire, but in the morning found he was still alive. He decided that God must have saved him, and in return for this made a promise never to speak again, which was a big undertaking for the most talkative boy in a talkative village.

Pinnock posted nine men in Angel Beach to search for Natty, and set to work on Nerine. Police Commissioner Cuthbert Macmillan telephoned from Mo-Bay and told Pinnock to go easy on the girl. Three politicians had made specific complaints about the treatment of suspects at Sandy Island, and the Commissioner asked Pinnock what plans he had to prevent similar complaints arising in the future.

'Mi gonna kill dem tree raas claat PNP politician,' he laughed. 'No Commissioner, seriously, the witness will not be harmed.'

The truth was that Pinnock never planned to use violence during interrogation. He invariably ended up using it, but that was out of irritation rather than by design, because suspects never talked. The brutality of slavery days, and the difficult years that followed, hardened the likkle people far beyond the point at which a beating could break them. Nothing could break a people who'd survived slavery. The Police knew it, and they knew it, which was why Bob Marley's taunt at the Police: 'Cas dem saft! Yeh dem saft! We know dem saft!' was so loved by Jamaicans. The silent strength of the slim, barefoot and badly clothed suspects did mad the well fed, well clothed and well shod Police. And out of sheer frustration, Pinnock, like the other cops, always gave them a kicking before letting them go. But after speaking to the Commissioner, Pinnock was determined in the case of Nerine not to lay so much as a finger on her.

Sandy Island Police station was a new, and run down, flat roofed concrete bungalow protected from the people by a tall fence and heavy gates. On one side a cell block housed suspects whose hands could be seen clasping the bars of the high windows, and whose shouts could be heard by their friends and enemies who waited for them, sometimes for days, at the gate. Inside the station it looked as though the place had been ransacked, as though a civil war had swept through the place: the large rooms were empty but for broken furniture, bloodstains and papers strewn across the cement floor. The Police lounged apathetically on the front step or in the charge room, concerned only with the visitors who brought vegetables, meat and sometimes even cash as gifts. Anyone who came with a grievance was carefully parried by an interminable wait before being half listened to, and run back to their yard in a Police car. No constable had any interest in the crimes of the likker people dem, so the likker people dem devised their own system of justice, handed out by the village mob.

For two days Nerine was walked back and forth from the cell block to a room with two chairs for interrogation.

'Wishart Natty hide?' Pinnock asked.

'Mi nuh say nuttin.'

'Christella,' Pinnock said gently, 'I am trying to help you. Keep you from big trouble. I'm your friend. Tell me, if dat towel in de lada bag not for Natty, who it for?'

'Mi nuh say nuttin.'

'Ya nuh say nuttin.' Pinnock sighed. 'If ya nuh say nuttin, I will charge you wid obstruction of de law.'

'Mi nuh say nuttin.'

'And aiding and abetting a convicted criminal, and being an accessory to murder.'

'Nuttin …'

'Gal, ya can get ten year inna Spanish Town Jail for dat.'

'Mi nuh say nuttin.'

But Pinnock didn't want to charge Nerine. It was the last thing he wanted. Pushing a case through the Content Court was an exceedingly painful business, and he didn't want to waste days of hard work on this girl. He wanted Natty Morgan.

'Mi know ya know wishart Natty. Ya nuh leave dis room till ya tell we.'

'Mi nuh say nuttin to you, Pinnock. Mi nuh say nuttin to no Police.'

Back in Beach Natty tried to slip out of the cave, but was thwarted by one of Pinnock's constables who concentrated his search on Rocky's yard, near to Hopton's Rocktop Cave, because he fancied Rocky's sister Marcia, a fawn-like fifteen year old who caused a lot of men to waste a good many hours hanging around her yard in a backwater of Beach called Egypt. Natty was also nearly discovered where he lurked inside the cave by Hopton, the proprietor of the dud tourist attraction, who, searching for a spot to make some ancient Arawak paintings, walked within feet of the fugitive who withdrew into the deep shadows clutching Nerine's kitchen knife.

Pinnock couldn't make Nerine talk. For the first time in her life she had something a big person wanted, and she wasn't giving it away. She even made Pinnock doubt his instinct: when Donovan woke him for the midnight session on Nerine, Pinnock waved him away. 'Leave de gal. She nah know nuttin. Ya gal friend one liard, Donovan. She waste we time bad. Now go way fra here.'

When Donovan got back to Sandra's yard he beat her bad. 'Ya jinall mi fi get one blaad claat teevee!' he shouted as he smacked her with the flat side of a machete.

'Mi nuh one liard Donovan,' Sandra shouted back. 'Believe mi, believe mi. Mek dat gal talk and she will tell ya. She know where Natty de. Mi swear. Mi see dem pon de pasture. Mi can mek dat bitch talk. Give her to mi.'

Then something occurred to Sandra. 'It nat only Nerine dat know where Natty de,' she said.

'Who else know?'

'De licker picknee Kermit. Him know. Him follow dem dat morning. Mi see him too. Tell Pinnock fi talk wid de picknee.'

Miss Dahlia lay on her bed feverishly studying the Bible when Pinnock drew up with Nerine. Her reading wasn't so good, but she could feel the benefit of simply staring at God's words. Nerine got out of the car slowly. Her hair was matted with blood, her face twice the right size, and her limp tortuous to watch. Miss Dahlia heaved herself onto her feet and hobbled across her yard.

'Sergeant Pinnock, 'ow can ya abuse de young gal like dat? She never done nottin wrong and ya beat her bad, man. Serious ...'

'De Police cannat be eld responsible for haccident dat occur to suspect durin custody. De gal buck up on one table and juke her foot. She clumsy, aunty. Dat nat Police fault. Annerstan? Now. True ya have one picknee in de yard name Kermit Barrett?'

'Ya man.'

'Mi want fi talk wid him.'

'Wid de picknee?'

'Ya man. Call him.'

Up went the shout so familiar to all those who lived within a mile of Miss Dahlia's yard: 'KIEEEEEEEEERMIT!'

A few minutes later, Kermit ran smiling round the sound of the house, making the guttural growl of the ice chock toiling up the slope from the seaside, and mimed changing down from second to first with his hand. He halted with a hiss of air brakes at the Police car.

'Get inna de car boy.'

'Ya man!' Kermit exclaimed excitedly. He loved riding in cars. He could hail up all his friends on the Beach Primary playground, the school he was kept from so he could ketch water for him Momma.

'Mi want fi talk wid you.'

'Mi?' he said, pointing at his chest. He was pleased to be thought important enough for anyone, not least a Police, to have a conversation with. 'No problem,' he smiled. 'Let we go.'

'... Tell I 'bout Natty Morgan,' said Pinnock starting the engine.

Kermit stopped smiling. Nerine shouted, 'Nuh say nuttin, Kermit. Nuttin!' at the departing car, adding, 'Oh lard, oh lard,' to herself.

Tyres screamed as Pinnock pulled out into the path of a tourist bus full of whities, whose brakes were so badly adjusted it swerved sickeningly and looked for a moment as if it were going to roll. Vinton, watching, said to Mooney: 'Tour bos nearly stop in Angel Beach at last.'

Kermit made a second promise to himself (for the first he'd broken thirty minutes after making it), to say nothing at all. Mi get Natty inna dis trouble, he told himself, and it mi moss get him out.

Within two hours of Pinnock sweeping Kermit through the gate of Sandy Island Police Station, news that Natty's fate was in the hands of a five year old boy reached as far as Ocho Rios, a hundred miles to the east. Another five hours later it got to the ghettos of West Kingston. Despite not being mentioned on the radio or TV, it was the lead news item for the whole of Jamaica.

Wherever people group up, harrowing and pitiful accounts of Kermit's screams and whimpers were passed from one indignant person to another, in a long chain of tiny links that stretched across Jamaica. Kermit's mother in Savannah La Mar, forty miles south of Sandy Island told everyone she met she was going to Pinnock to complain, but she had too much washing, and never made it.

As the hours passed, the crowd at the gate swelled and grew silent with outrage. By nightfall on the second day, when he had been held for thirty-seven hours, Police constables coming and going told Pinnock that the people dem wouldn't stand for it if Kermit was held much longer. By the following afternoon a riot was said to be imminent. Inside the lock-up, Kermit sat on a chair, both hands gripping the seat, his exhausted face stained with tears, his mouth firmly shut, and for the thousandth time Pinnock said, 'Tell we, Kermit. Where Natty?' And the tousand and oneth time Kermit shook his head from side to side as his eyes filled with tears.

Nearly all of the twenty-three members of Angel Beach's population walked the five miles to Sandy Island to join the crowd at the gates of the Police Station. Only Nerine, who was too weak, Mr Crooks, who, when he heard how Natty escaped from jail, decided to give Sandy Island Police Station a wide berth for a few months, and Shepherd Bush George, who secretly sympathised with the Police, were not present. When Afficer Buckingham emerged from the back door for a quick pee, he was jeered, and someone (six people claimed it was they) fling one rock stone at him that missed and shattered the window of the office where Pinnock was taking a nap.

Pinnock awoke so shaken that half an hour later Miss Dahlia proudly led Kermit by the hand out of the station. The moment he was through the gates, the crowd closed around them to slap the boy on the back and hail up a hero.

Everyone in the minibus back to Beach felt honoured to travel with Kermit – Miss Dahlia made sure of that – and the conductor waived both their fares – at Miss Dahlia's suggestion. At Angel Beach, Kermit staggered out of the minibus, crossed the yard and climbed up into the house where Nerine was lying on the bed next to the cooker, looking distraught.

He looked at his aunt with a serious expression. 'Mi nuh say nuttin, Nerine,' he said, and collapsed beside her.

He lay on that bed for two days, and every one of Beach's twenty-three residents came fi check him, though Shepherd Bush George pretended he had only called round to borrow a machete. It was a glorious time for Kermit and for Angel Beach. Complete strangers, some of them big people dem, speeding importantly between Montego Bay and Negril in criss car, drew up in the village and asked after the picknee who hadn't grassed on Natty.

Pinnock finally withdrew his men, and Natty took the opportunity to excape inna de hills, coolly strolling into a barber in Grange Hill for a shave and trim in full view of the general public. The barber told the story of Kermit, and Natty said, 'Mi remember dat picknee. Im cool. Mi respect im,' words which were in due course relayed to Kermit, and made the whole of Angel Beach walk with their heads held up proudly, even in Content.

As the barber dusted Natty's neck with powder, to help remove the cut hair, he listened to Natty outline his plans. By this time the shop was full, and at every window faces looked in and listened to Natty: 'Mi gonna get one gun, bredren, and mi gonna find Sergeant Pinnock wherever he de, and mi gonna kill him for what him don.'

The news, carried on packed minibuses and crammed old taxis, spread from Grange Hill deep into the most silent, overgrown hills and valleys, and down onto the noisy Main, where it sped by word of mouth east and west so that within days everyone in North Jamaica knew that Natty was going to kill Pinnock. With one notable exception: Pinnock himself, whom no-one dared tell.

It was only when a four year old boy in Salt Spring asked, 'When Natty gonna kill ya dead, sah?' that Pinnock began to suspect why everyone was acting so nervously around him. It also explained why his two best girlfriends said he couldn't stay in their yards till Natty was inna de lock-up or dead. In a quiet corner of the Police Station he asked Buckingham if it were true. Buckingham said it was.

Pinnock grew windy, and was unable to sleep soundly at home, so decided to move into the Police station until Natty was back in custody. When he passed through the crowd at the gate with a sponge mattress on the roof of his car, they laughed and jeered at him. 'Ya can hide, bot Natty a com an' find ya Pinnock,' they taunted.

Even in the station with his bed right under a cast-iron desk his dreams were bad and sleep patchy, and once, when Commissioner Macmillan burst in without knocking, he jumped so badly he nearly fractured his skull on the bottom of the desk. There was a heatwave and sweat dripped off him even as he sat motionless in the station's three-legged armchair, daydreaming of Natty coming steathily down the corridor with a knife in his hand, but he couldn't go out to clear his head with a breath of fresh air because of the people at the gate whom he knew were only there because they wanted to be around when Natty killed him. Worse still, he could not prevent Hyacinth, the wife, visiting whenever she felt like it. He couldn't shoot her, because two dead wives was hard to explain, so he had to tolerate the visits. It was an attack on the very being of a Sandy Island Police to be accessible at all times to the wife. At the end of the day when the men went off in happy groups to find women to have fun with, they laughed to think that all Pinnock could look forward to was Hyacinth and a big plate of jack domplin.

Pinnock's public humiliation ended a week later, when Natty was caught in a shoot-out in Negril and died in a hail of Police bullets. He was interred at the Dovecote Memorial Park, which was besieged by people wanting to file past his corpse in its silk-lined coffin. The funeral was reported on JBC TV, and Sandra promised Kermit he could watch it on her new pink portable, if he cut her yard, but he ended up standing on the roof of her house holding the aerial while she lounged on the bed to watch TV and nyam fried chicken.

THE SPOILS OF THE WAR
AGAINST DRUGS

In the 1980s the Reagan administration declared war on drugs and made Jamaica a front line. Two United States Air Force helicopters were dispatched to recce for ganja plantations. They did not represent a threat to the Jamaican industry which was formed by numerous small growers with crops too insignificant to be spotted from the air. Ten dozen goats would have harmed the trade more, and saved the Pentagon a few bucks to boot.

In Angel Beach the arrival, each week, of the helicopter, was a keenly anticipated event. It made them feel important to be the object of American interest. On top of this, items sometimes dropped from the pockets of the airmen as they leant out to survey the bush. Maxwell sported a pair of Ray-Ban shades that fell from the aircraft, and for a week, Busta built spliffs with a packet of American cigarette papers that wafted down beside his bar after the chopper had clattered away over the hills.

The Americans rewarded those parishes where the Police made drug seizures: the Ambassador came to the north coast in a criss Cadillac to give the hospitals of St James 25,000 US of, confusingly, drugs, and present Content, St John's principal town, with a big red American fire engine.

The fire engine was designed for a crew of four, 'though it never left Content with less than eleven men on board, and often with many more. Eight fire-proof uniforms, including coats, pants, boots, gloves and helmets were also supplied. These were shared by the twenty-three men of the Content Fire Brigade, who were all prepared to enter burning buildings only partially clad in protective gear. It soon became clear, however, that they weren't likely to come to any harm. In a place where no-one had a telephone, and the wooden houses took ten minutes to bung down, it was a safe bet the firemen were never going to confront anything more dangerous than a heap of smouldering ashes.

The Brigade's telephone rang incessantly, but always for one of the Swing girls, whose yard lay in the shadow of the fire station. Jackie gave out the number as her own, and both her husbands, European men who'd fallen for her startling good looks and sexy body while on holiday, kept in touch with her regularly. This stopped only when the phone was disconnected for non-payment of the bill, which grew huge because the crew used it to chat to dem relative inna foreign. Appeals were made to the Jamaica Telephone Company to write off the debt in an act of civic responsibility, but the executives, who lived far from Content and would never need the fire brigade, refused to. The local member of parliament, Andy Chin, who'd recently been promoted to Foreign Minister, intervened, but was told to 'mind him own PNP business' by the JLP phone executives. He did as he was told for fear that the phones in his ministry, like those in the Ministry of Agriculture the month before, would be disconnected in an act of malice. It took the intervention of the only man more powerful than a telephone executive on the island, the US Ambassador, to get the fire station reconnected, and that was only to take incoming calls.

When Gaddaffi burned down G. Silk's shed in Beach because tourists kept passing Gaddaffi's bamboo bar, and stopping at G. Silk's – not, as Gaddaffi thought, because of an Obeah curse, but because G. Silk alone amongst Beach bar owners had cleared a spot beside the road for tourists to pull over and park on – people group up to watch the shed blaze away. It was customary to ask the first vehicle that passed on the road in the direction of Content to alert the fire brigade. The sound of a gear box changing down to negotiate the Beach bridge heralded a Lada station wagon driven by Hopton, the fastest man in St John and St James, towing his minibus, the nose of which was buckled by yet another accident. It was a bad time for Hopton; first, he'd bounce and killed a crazy man in Little London, which was easy enough to laugh about and forget, but then a week later he bounce one picknee in Sandy Bay, who was struggling for his life in Mo-Bay hospital. Leroy Mckenzie, Hopton's boss, had vex bad at the cost of the bodywork to the minibus, and that was before Hopton tore a hole in the front of the unit when he scraped a tourist car which wasn't driving close enough to the kerb.

Hopton could not work out why he was having such bad luck. But he was determined to regain his reputation as the Main's fastest tourist bus driver, and had found something which steadied his nerves, helped his concentration, and made him drive harder and faster, though not necessarily more accurately, than ever before. It was called cocaine.

When G. Silk frantically waved down the two vehicles, Hopton pulled over to check out what was going on.

'Mi shed bung down, man,' wailed G. Silk.

'Nuh worry, G. Silk, mi go a Content fi fetch de fire chock – fast. Mi will getti here before ya shed destroy. Tross mi.' With that, Hopton nipped around the back of the two massive almond trees on the beach, had a swift pipe of cocaine, then ran back to the Lada. 'Nobody can drive fasterer dan I,' he announced before piling into the car through the passenger door.

'Ya man!' shouted a supporter in the crowd. 'Nabady can beat Hopton.'

'Unhitch de minibus, man,' Busta helpfully suggested.

'Ya man,' shouted the driver of the minibus, a friend of Hopton's.

'Nuh man,' said Hopton, fired up by the drug coursing through his body.

'Ya kiant drive fass and tow one minibus, man,' pointed out Busta.

'We nuh have time fi unhitch de minibus, man,' replied Hopton, who needed the minibus in Content for repairs. 'Like mi say: us in one horry.'

The Lada shot off with wheels spinning, the tow rope cracked taut, and the minibus lurched forward, its driver thrown back against his seat.

Getting to the fire station fast was a way to salvage his reputation, and Hopton screeched and howled his way through the twists and turns of the coast road at a suicidal speed, his minibus barrelling crazily along behind him. At Sandy Island he overtook a nervous tourist in a rental car which was clinging to the tight bend, nearly driving him off the edge into the sea.

It was not the habit of minibus drivers to use their rear view mirrors when in motion, their main purpose being to enable drivers to admire their hairstyles during stops, so it was only when Hopton drew to a halt at the fire station that he looked in his mirror for the first time.

'Where is mi minibus!' he cried, when he saw that there was nothing behind the Lada but a length of frayed rope.

His minibus was in fact at that moment sinking gently into the swamp by the new pork sausage factory outside Content, which it had glided into when the tow rope finally snapped as Hopton gassed the Lada as he came off the corner and onto the straight.

Everyone at the fire station knew it was too late to save a bamboo shed as far away as Angel Beach, but the crew still sped into action, threw on their odd bits of uniform, climbed aboard and switched on the bell and siren. Jackie Swing, the most beautiful of the sexy Swing sisters, on the phone to her Austrian husband, shouted out, 'Wishart de fire?'

'Angel Beach,' someone answered.

'Hol' on, mi go dat way too,' she shouted back.

It was hard to believe that nothing rested on the speed of the brigade's response, when you saw how fast and dangerously the fire engine was piloted through Content and down the Main. A tourist, recently recovered from a near heart-attack when a car chased by a truly insane minibus driver practically drove him off a cliff into the sea, received a second life-endangering shock when a fire engine loaded down with men and women in fancy dress appeared suddenly around a tight bend and missed him by a gap no wider than the air ticket he had just decided to buy to get off the island as fast as he could.

Things were made worse by the siren, which in the US may have scattered people in front of the vehicle, but which in St John attracted them to its path. The vehicle was gunned at sickening speed down a twisting, narrow path, in places no more than ten feet wide, lined with adults, children and unleashed animals. As usual, the act of summoning the Content fire brigade put more lives at risk than any fire.

The truck drew up at the cooling pile of ashes which had

been G. Silk's shed, but few considered its journey wasted, for the sight of the gleaming American machine and the wail of the siren thrilled the assembled crowd. It seemed to them to more than make up for the disaster to G. Silk's shed. G. Silk didn't share this view and did not join the chorus of thanks and congratulations. While a fireman wearing shorts, T-shirt, and one fire-proof gauntlet hoisted a picknee onto the engine, and Beach men took turns sitting behind the steering wheel, G. Silk picked among the burnt-out ruins for any possessions that might have survived.

People felt sorry for G. Silk, a young, charming man who'd worked hard to clear a bit of bush, erect a shed and get a little business going, but no-one condemned Gaddaffi for the arson attack, although all knew he was responsible. It was G. Silk's own fault, they argued, for trying to capture land so near to the seaside where Busta, Blender and Gaddaffi all had bars. G. Silk was cool, but G. Silk was an outsider. You could tell he wasn't from Beach – he ran a successful business. He came from the hills, not the Level. No amount of good vibes could efface that. But when he rebuilt on a piece of land nearer the edge of the village, everyone was pleased, and Gaddaffi knew that this time G. Silk did it with the blessing of the village, and even though, once again, because G. Silk bothered to clear a spot for cars to park on, tourists started to pull over and patronise his bar, Gaddaffi could not bung down fi G. Silk shed a second time without public condemnation. But that didn't stop him thinking about doing it night and day, night and day.

TREE BAD GAL

CARLENE

Carlene was the village bad gal, until Jackie Swing turned up on the fire-chock the day G. Silk's shed bung down. Carlene was bad. But Jackie was badder, and a year or two after Jackie, came her sister Sandra, who was the badderest.

Carlene worked as a prostitute in Negril, or indeed anywhere, and spend down all him money on coke. She had a yard on the hill above Beach where her five picknee fended for themselves during her frequent stays in Pegasus – the new Police station in Negril that was named by the little people dem after the international hotel in Kingston that they thought looked just like it. In Beach, Carlene was called Gregory, after Gregory Isaacs the reggae singer who was always being busted for cocaine. He, like Carlene, was in such a bad way he disgraced himself on stage during a show at Zion House. The audience bokkle him and once again looted the bar and box office which Lord Locks had only just refitted after the last riot.

Carlene was strikingly tall, with a slender, aristocratic neck, Egyptian eyes, flattened nose and wide mouth out of which obscenities emerged thick and fast as she strode through the hail of friendly abuse the villagers shouted whenever she got out of the minibus and walked the curving path across the pasture and up through the thickening bush to her yard.

People knew that when Carlene's kids were hungry she'd still spend her last cent on cocaine, so they turned a blind eye when they saw them tief fruit from another man's tree. Carlene did friend wid anybady when she needed money, but only one man meant anything to her: Humble Dread, a silent, dreadlocked Rastafarian from deep back a bush, with a deeply lined face, matted grey locks and a mouth empty of teeth. Omble Dread was a Bongo Dread – that is, a real Rastaman who kept strictly to the salt free, pork free, ital diet, sang incantations to Jah, smoked ganja religiously, and led a peaceful, harmless, meditative life. There were two other kinds of Dread. The Commercial Dread, like Busta or Blender in Beach, who had the dreadlocks and knew all the Rasta rules but liked Dragon Stout and jerk pork too much to observe them all the time. The other kind of Rasta was the Rental Dread, to whom the whole thing was little more than a hairstyle which white wuman dem found sexy. They ate anything, smoked coke and tief money without hesitation. The centre of the Rental Dread community was the Cotton Tree Cafe in Negril, where scores of them grouped up every afternoon before setting out into the hot sweet night to seduce overweight whitey spinsters and divorcees. All they wanted to do was have sex and sport on the women's money, and, marvellously, that was all the women wanted as well.

When Omble Dread came down from the hills fi turn wid Gregory for a couple night she didn't take the minibus to the beach at Negril, but rake de yard, sweep de house, shine de floor, got a fire going, put a pot on it and cooked up some dumpling and yam for Omble Dread and the picknee. She put on weight and smiled when Omble Dread was staying, but when he picked up his rod and his bag and left wordlessly at dawn for the blue hills she went straight to Negril, took coke, and draw weight till she look so grey and maigre not even Rayon Fairfax, who was not that choosy when it came to women, would pay 15 J to friend with her.

Jackie

Jackie was badder than Carlene, but in a different way. Like Carlene, Jackie wanted many things she did not possess; she wanted clothes and shoes, she wanted meals in restaurants and rides in fast cars – but most of all she wanted to get off the island of Jamaica. She wanted to board an orange and green Air Jamaica 727, leave far below her the squalor of her crowded, dirty yard behind the fire station in Content, disembark inna foreign and walk through immigration to a job, a decent home, and the easy life.

At fifteen, Jackie was told by the careers master at Rusea Comprehensive in Content that with her brain she could win a scholarship to Arthur Mannings Technological College to train to be a teacher or accountant. But neither of these professions would get her off the island. Even if she earned money at them, she could never change it for US dollars, and even if she found an illegal way of getting hold of US dollars, most countries, particularly the ones Jackie wanted to go to, banned Jamaican visitors. An American, or European, went to the airport and boarded any flight they could afford to. To the Jamaicans, no matter how rich they were, half the destinations on the departure board were barred. It was impossible to get a visa for America, Canada, Britain, Germany or Austria unless you had family there, which Jackie didn't. If a Jamaican wanted to see the world it was Central and South America, or a geography text book. But Jackie didn't want to live in Belize or the Caymans. She wanted to go up in the world, not sideways.

Instead of going to Arthur Mannings Technological

College in Montego Bay, Jackie went to the beach in Negril, a place far more likely to yield a US or German visa to someone with Jackie's fresh, sexy looks and gravity-defying body, than any Embassy in Kingston. And on the beach she joined a much more highly regarded profession than accountancy or teaching, on the beach she became a prostitute.

Negril beach attracted a different kind of tourist to the ones who congregated in the cement bars and restaurants on Gloucester Avenue in Mo-Bay to eat American food and watch American satellite television, or sat in linen suits, red-faced and thinking vaguely racialist thoughts, being served rum punches by gloved waiters at the Jamaica Inn or Tryall Villas Hotel. The tourist who went to Negril was more of a traveller than holiday-maker, and tended to be interested in discovering something about Jamaica and Jamaicans, and this set him apart from the rest of the island's guests.

The people of Negril welcomed these travellers with open arms, literally. They were rich, and generous and friendly, and never got into conflict with the locals over lovers because the white men liked thin Jamaican girls, whereas Jamaican men liked only good size wuman, and the whitey wuman dem loved Dreadlocks men, who were held in contempt by most self-respecting Jamaican girls, so everyone got along fine.

On the beach at Negril, the traveller found things arranged particularly congenially. For a start, the place was fabulously beautiful. Fabulous, because it seemed as though, when you first kicked off your shoes and felt the talcum-fine sand press your instep, under the grove of coconuts that fringed the beach, that you were walking into some kind of perfect, fictional location. The seven-mile white sand beach had not a single stone to step uncomfortably upon. It shelved at the gentlest of inclines into turquoise, transparent, bath-warm water under a deep blue sky. Immersion in this sea, which lapped onto the beach in soothing, stroking curls, no more than a few inches high, was akin to drifting off into a dreamy sleep, and certainly no more strenuous.

Against this background, fine-looking barefooted Jamaicans ambled up and down wearing only the flimsiest of garments, many of which were easily slipped out of, like the sexual inhibitions and moral constraints the tourists left strewn behind them as they began to enjoy themselves. They learnt from their new Jamaican friends not to judge strangers, nor feel guilty about something done in the name of sport. Negril beach was magical: it made the fat feel slender, the pale feel cool, the self-conscious feel sexy, the provincial feel pioneering, the mean feel rich, the poor feel generous, and the timid feel brave. Everyone fell in love on the beach, and made quixotic declarations of lifelong devotion, which were cooled only by the drive back along the Main, the air-conditioned airport, and the gathering thoughts of forgotten responsibilities and commitments back home. In the early days, before the big hoteliers and coke dealers moved in, the tourists and the Negrilites were the same kind of people: easy-going, fun-seeking and peace-loving. Most of the tourists wanted to stay forever with the Jamaicans, but couldn't, and most of the Jamaicans wanted to leave with them, but couldn't. This made the last goodbye, on the porch of the cottage in the coconut grove, or by the mouth of the tent at the hippy campsite, all the more sweetly poignant.

Jackie was so alluring in her silver bikini it did not take long before she was betrothed. Her fiancé was a large fifty-five year old Belgian called Hubert. In the company of Jackie, who was then sixteen and a half, he smiled a lot and sweated gently. They married and honeymooned in Zoo, which was what the staff called Hedonism Hotel, because of its high chain-link boundary fence and the unrestrained behaviour of the guests kept behind it. Hubert returned to Brussels with the marriage certificate, and promised to get Jackie's emigration papers organised so she could follow him to Europe. But nothing ever happened. He telephoned Jackie at the fire station when he was drunk or lonely, but when Hubert twice put down the phone when a woman called his name, Jackie could tell that he wasn't going to get her off the island. So without bothering with divorce, she married Rudy, from Vienna, the nineteen year old son of a prosperous industrialist. He also returned to Vienna to fix her papers and passport, but when he telephoned he had bad news: he had showed his parents a picture of Jackie and they had demanded he divorce her. Of course he said he wouldn't, and that he loved Jackie and had made a solemn promise to stand by her, but they threatened to take away his flat, car and all his money. 'Jackie,' Rudy said to her on the fire station phone, 'please don't vurry, I haff a plan. I vill come back to Jamaica and find verk as a vaiter, und ve can live together in a liddle hut in the hills.'

'No, Rudy, nuh com dung a Jamaica wid nuh money. Tell ya farda, him kiant mek judgment pon mi, till dem meet mi. Dem moss fly mi inna foreign and moss meet mi, annerstan?'

'But Jackie, ve love each uzzer, ve don't need my farder's money ...'

'No, Rudy, nuh com dung a Jamaica widout monny.'

Rudy rang the fire station three or four times a week, and Jackie found it increasingly difficult to keep him in Austria. Meanwhile, her attention was caught by someone else. Passing through Angel Beach on her way to and from work, she noticed a white man constructing a board house on a piece of land that sloped down from the Main to a little lagoon that opened onto the creek. Every time she flashed through Beach on the minibus, she caught glimpses of him first clearing a space in the jungle and then erecting a three-room clapboard house with a pitched zinc roof, in the old style.

She only found out who this was when one day she found herself in Beach on a search for sick picknee. Jackie liked the high status prostitution gave her, with its enviable contacts amongst the tourists and Police, fine new clothes and easy cash but, for some reason no-one knew, the Police started coming down hard on prostitutes, so she developed lucrative sidelines, like drug dealing, massage, hair braiding, and her sick children scam. She hit on the sick picknee idea when Yatta, her eleven year old brother who lurked under the coconut trees on the beach learning the art of the hossler, was suffering from an oozing eye infection. An American who wrangled for half an hour over paying 15 US for sex with Jackie, when he saw Yatta's eye, took a 10 US bill from the wallet in his swimming trunks and gave it to the boy.

'You seen the doc about that, son?'

'Ya man. Him give me one pill paper,' Yatta said, showing the whitey the prescription, 'but mi kiant afford fi buy i'.'

'Go and get that prescription right away,' he told Yatta. 'I'm serious, or you could lose that eye.'

Yatta ran off across the sand with the 10 US in his fist, and Jackie only caught up with him after a very hurried sex session, at a tourist stall buying himself a T-shirt. She ripped the note out of his hand.

'Tief,' she shouted, cuffing him over the head.

'Mi nuh tief, de white man give I dat.'

'Raas claat,' Jackie shouted.

'Dat fi mi money,' Yatta said impotently. 'Dat fi mi

money,' and stamped off across the sand, rubbing his inflamed eye.

'Com, ya, picknee,' Jackie called, and pulling out a filthy, soft Jamaican bank note from her bikini briefs, said, 'Tek dis. Nex time mi give ya more.'

'Nex time?' Yatta asked.

'Ya man.'

Thus was their business partnership born, which led to the sick picknee scheme. With the prescription, the steadily worsening eye infection, and Yatta's pathetic assertion that he had no money, Jackie took hundreds of dollars off men and women on the beach. It only came to a stop when one day Yatta took some money and bought the antibiotic cream at the pharmacy because his eye was hurting so much. Jackie tried to get the tube of ointment off him, but he hid it in a hiding place in the coconut grove, and try as she might, she couldn't prevent him applying it. She was philosophical about the set-back; one thing the back streets of Negril were not short of was sick and suffering children, and she went out to get hold of a new one. For a week she had a boy with a foot wound that, as it turned green and began to smell rank, raised money faster than the beach's best hookers, and for a few days she worked with the victim of a minibus crash with a terrible head wound. He was going very well but died suddenly one night after work. After this, Negril baby mudder dem grew wary of leasing their sick children to Jackie, so her search took her beyond the town boundaries, which were themselves moving outwards by the day, to places further down the line like Angel Beach, where one afternoon, on her way to work, she stopped the minibus because she saw a promisingly malnourished little girl hurrying down the road.

The girl was Joy, Carlene's eldest, and she was on a mission to Miss Netta's shop to beg for half a bread on credit for her mother and for her siblings, Sanjay, 10, Simone, 9, Marshalyn, 8, Kaysia, 8 (but not a twin), Andy, 6, and Tulia, 5. Carlene had spend down all her money on coke and the youngest picknee had moaned through the night with hunger. Actually, Carlene had done more than spend down the money, she'd stripped siding boards off the house and sold them to Mr Crooks for money for coke, so the breeze now blew straight through the house across the bed the children all slept on. But at six o'clock that morning, when Carlene cuss and use bad word at Mr Crooks because he refused to give her any more money unless she stripped the corrugated zinc off the roof, because he didn't want any more siding boards, Joy set off down the hill to beg one bread, so as to save the zinc and keep the family dry when rain farl.

'Picknee,' Jackie called to Joy, 'com ya.'

Joy approached Jackie shyly. Jackie looked appreciatively at her open sores, and the bones that prodded at her skin. She would raise a couple dollar pon de beach.

'Ya want fi earn a few dollar, gal?'

Joy could tell Jackie was a prostitute from her expensive denim clothes, pink lipstick and yellow hair extensions.

'Mi go a shop fi mi mudda,' she told Jackie, and tried to get away.

'Tek me to ya yard. Mek we talk wid ya mama.'

Joy beg Miss Netta for a bread, and took Jackie back up the hill. As they climbed the steep and muddy path through jungle dripping with dew, Joy heard Carlene screaming at Mr Crooks, who stood impassively in the yard, a box-like figure wearing heavy government boot, watching her struggle to peel back a section of roofing, a faint smile on his blunt features.

'Ya want fi tek de raas claat roof from mi picknee head,

man. Ya have no heart?' Carlene shouted. 'Gimme a couple blaad claat dollar. Gwaan. Raas claat. An' mi will pay ya back anudder day.'

'I will give you fifty dallar for one zinc,' said Mister Crooks in his gruff voice. 'Horry up and lift it now.'

'Carlene, w'appen?' Jackie greeted her, for they knew each other from the beach. 'Gal, if ya need fifty dallar, mi can giv' i' ya.'

Carlene stopped levering at the roof, and stood up, swinging the hammer at her side. 'What ya want fi de money?'

'Jus' let ya darter here com an' work wid mi on a likker tourist bizness.'

Joy looked at her mother imploringly; she didn't want to work on the beach as a prostitute.

'Fifty dallar ya give mi far her?' Carlene asked.

Joy looked down, miserably.

'Ya man. Fifty now, and mebbe de gal bring a likker more home later.'

'Raas claat Jackie,' she shouted. 'Ya com fram de devil, wuman. Ya tink mi tek one cent fi turn mi own darter prostitute?'

'Mi nuh say she turn prostitute. When mi say dat?'

'If she go a beach wid you, she nuh gonna turn blaad claat Christian. Ya is one beach prostitute, Jackie, and so also is mi one beach prostitute, but mi nuh gonna mek mi darter one, not for ten tousan dallar mi will nat do dat.'

The sound of an altercation always drew people towards it in Angel Beach, where two people losing their tempers, and maybe even coming to blows, was considered top entertainment. Maxwell, searching for goats that had slipped their tether, rushed to the yard gleefully, and from other directions came ten or fifteen adults and picknee dem to watch the action, and stir it up a bit if it looked like fizzling out.

'Nuh call mi one prostitute, Carlene,' Jackie shouted. 'Mi work pon de beach in tourist bizness now. You is one prostitute. Ya would tek five dallar to fuck one donkey excep the donkey never wan to.'

'Blaad claat!' Carlene screamed, and hurled the hammer, which sped, spinning slowly, through the air. It missed Carlene and struck Mr Crooks on the shin.

'Ya blaad claat wuman,' he shouted and stomped off into the bush.

'Ya let one wuman lick ya?' shouted someone after him, but he didn't rise to the provocation, and muttered to himself all the way back to his yard.

Jackie left the yard and descended the path to the Main, putting the incident behind her. Being a prostitute had taught her the gift of stopping herself remembering selected events from even the most recent past. Without this gift the job would mad her, the way it did so many other girls.

She waited on the Main for the minibus back to Content in the shade of a tree shared by two boys, Vinton and Mooney, who were idling pon de roadside, watching the white man in his yard on the other side of the road planing timber for furniture. She noticed how he didn't fling his tools into the dirt the moment he'd finished with them, the way Jamaican men did.

'Who dat white man?' she asked the boys.

'Him one teacher de England government send down since tree mont fi teach de ignorant picknee fi read and write and learn carpenter bizness.'

'He cool?'

Mooney laughed. 'Him kinda cool, but him nuh drink liquor or go wid prostitute, so forget 'im.'

'Cho!' chided Jackie. 'Ya chat nuff likker boy. Him marry?'
'Nuh man, 'im live pon him own.'

The thud of a bass line, first detectable in her feet, and then ears, followed by the whine of a VW Combi engine gunned at full throttle, heralded a minibus, which Jackie stopped and boarded, climbing in beside the driver in the comfy front seat – the prerogative of respected citizens like Policemen, footballers and prostitutes.

Back at the Swing yard in the shadow of the fire station, where seven adults lived in three rooms, there was a flood. She picked her way around and over deep muddy puddles and jumped onto the porch, which shuddered when she landed. The house had smelled of mildew ever since her brother O'ell, and her father Red Rat, tief the gutter from the fire station to sell, so that when rain farl, water swept off the eaves like Dunn's River Falls onto the Swings' previous roof.

The thought of Wilfred's soundly built house with its brand new roof was one thing Jackie could not erase from her memory, and when a week later she was on the phone to Rudy, and heard the fire chock was going to Angel Beach, she shouted, 'Hol' on!' to the boys. 'Mi soon com back,' and dashed to her yard to dress up for the whitey with the new house. It took a few minutes, naturally, but the guys on the fire truck were happy to wait for Jackie. When she arrived she had stripped off her jewellery and wore her mother's print cotton church dress, which buttoned chastely to her throat, had long sleeves, and a full skirt that came down unflatteringly over her knees.

'Mi kiant believe it,' the driver of the fire truck shouted. 'Jackie give up whore bizness and turn Christian.' Then without any urgency, he activated the siren and bell, and floored the gas pedal.

At Beach she alighted from the truck and walked to the white man's yard, through all the rushing villagers, drawn in the opposite direction by the siren, bell and smoke from G. Silk's shed. She found the white man working on his furniture beside his lagoon. Crouched next to him, a youth, Nickretta Crooks, older brother of Vash and Mooney, carefully watched his every move.

Short, with narrow shoulders, a wide bottom and splayed feet, Wilfred Poole had a long nose on a sad face, and looked as if a great deal of effort had been repaid with only the most limited success, yet undaunted, he persevered. He originated in Bolton, a small northern English city, where he'd lived uneventfully for twenty-seven years before accepting a Voluntary Service Overseas posting to Jamaica.

'Ya mind if mi sit in the shade of ya tree, sah?' Jackie asked.

'No, lass. Sit right down. Make yourself comfortable. Hang about, that needs a wipe. You be happier if I fetched you a chair?'

'Tank you.'

When Wilfred dashed off, Jackie said, 'What ya do here?' to the boy.

'Mi learn carpenter trade,' Nickretta answered her. 'Mister Poole one good teacher.'

'Mi nuh want ya here. Go way. Go way. Gwaan, run on ...'

The boy, drilled into obedience by his bullying father, Mr Crooks, obeyed without a word.

'Where's Nicky gone?' Wilfred asked sunnily when he got back with the chair.

'Soon as teacher back turn, student run off. It alway de same.'

'He's a good lad, got a good eye and a strong arm.'

Jackie said, 'Mi try an' stop him. Ya nah mind if I watch you?'

'Goodness me no,' said Wilfred.

'Only I never talk to no white man before,' she continued.

Later, she asked if she could swim, which seemed to necessitate unbuttoning every single one of the fifteen buttons down the front of her mother's dress, even though she could have slipped out of it easily after opening only four. She turned modestly away from Wilfred, but felt his eyes boring into her back, and heard the saw he held stuttering for the first time in its groove.

'Mi can bathe in mi brassiere and panties?' she asked, turning to him in her white lingerie. Wilfred could not take his eyes off her gorgeous body. 'Only I don't got no swimsuit.'

The closest Wilfred had got to sex in Jamaica was a few tentative conversations with a certain Miss Markham. Miss Markham stood six feet two inches tall, had greying hair and a matronly, no-nonsense attitude, with which she ran the Post Office counter in Content. When she saw Wilfred through the plate-glass Post Office window, she took his mail out of the pigeon hole to be ready to call, 'Mister Poole! Mister Poole! Your mail,' when he came in. Wilfred was embarrassed at jumping the three-quarter hour queue, but that never occurred to Miss Markham, who flashed him her toothy smile, because she was a bit buck-toothed, and chatted a while about this and that. Everybody knew the white man liked Miss Markham, but it seemed like both of them were too scared to make the first move.

Making the first move was not something Jackie had a problem with. She swam for about thirty seconds, keeping her feet on the ground, emerged wet, and stood before a deeply blushing Wilfred asking if he had a towel. Flossie, passing down the road, glimpsed the two of them out of the corner of her eye, and thought, This mash op Miss Blanche Markham's chance with Wilfred.

Jackie noticed Wilfred's outdoor shower, housed in a shoulder-high corrugated zinc booth in the shade of banana trees that nodded in the breeze wafting off the sea. When Wilfred came out of the house flapping a towel, and checking it over for dirty marks, Jackie shouted, 'Over here, Wilfred, ya didn't mind me taking a fresh?'

'A shower? Of course not.'

When she took the towel, she allowed the door of the shower to swing open a little more than necessary, and her nude wet body was branded onto his memory. From that moment, Wilfred Poole was smitten.

Ten days later, Jackie moved into Wilfred's yard. Miss Dahlia saw her taking her bags of clothes out of the back of a minibus, and that eveling the whole village was sombre.

'It look like Jackie control Wilfred now,' Flossie said to Miss Myrtle, with a laugh.

'Ya man,' agreed Miss Myrtle. 'She run out fram Wilfred yard all de picknee dat Wilfred teach carpenter trade. It terrible, man, terrible. Mi kiant believe he kiant see Jackie is one whore.'

Love blinded Wilfred. And Jackie never put a foot wrong while she courted the poor man, though when he left the house, she went to a little carved cupboard he had made and mounted on the wall, and took out and handled Wilfred's dark blue passport, her head a blizzard of stratagems. Pretending to be a virgin, she allowed him to deflower her. Wilfred had no idea sex could be that good; he emerged shaky and stunned from his bedroom every morning, and taught his lessons at Beach Primary with his head full of what he and Jackie had done the night before in the candle-light of their room.

The village lived in mourning for the old Wilfred, whose yard was open to children, and whose tools were always available to be borrowed – for Jackie told him to say no when people came and beg him for one pick, or buster, or hax, or ammer. She turned him against the village, and filled his head with lies about Miss Dahlia, Miss Myrtle, Nerine, and everyone else, so he walked past them without stopping to talk. No-one dared tell him the truth about Jackie; you could easily get killed for doing something like that, and anyway Jackie would somehow lie her way out of it.

It was only when Vinton hurried off the minibus from Content one afternoon, saying he'd seen Rudy, Jackie's second husband, looking for Jackie in town, that the village saw some good in the whole episode, for this surely meant they were going to be entertained. People grouped up casually at Wilfred's end of the village waiting for the bearded German youth to turn up, which he did, with a rucksack, on a minibus.

'Excuse me, but I am looking for Jackie Swing,' Rudy asked Miss Myrtle, who had escaped from Mr Crooks with some excuse, and come down from her yard as soon as she'd heard the news.

'Ya can find ya wife in dat yard,' Miss Myrtle said. And Rudy set off, followed by Wilbert, Miss Dahlia, Nerine, Miss Myrtle, Flossie, Vinton, Mooney, his brother Squeecher, little Maxwell and a half dozen picknee.

Jackie was in Wilfred's house looking at photographs of life in Bradford in the photograph album. Wilfred was at Beach Primary, putting in overtime, due home at any time.

'Jackie!' Rudy called.

The Beach crowd smiled.

'Oo dat?' came from inside, in a sharp, angry voice.

'Jackie. It iz Rudy.'

Jackie came to the porch, scowling. Rudy walked across the yard in filthy jeans, T-shirt and worn trainers, his shoulders sloped depressingly downwards by a week of arguments with his parents, a long, long flight, a difficult search for Jackie, and a rucksack with twenty kilos of his most loved possessions. He was not a happy boy; he had just experienced the first three days of his life without a car, a house or his generous allowance, and it had not been enjoyable.

'Rudy, ya carry dung mi air-ticket an' passport?' she snapped.

'Jackie. I carry down nussink but my love,' Rudy replied, hitching off his rucksack, and looking around with delight at the pretty yard and inviting creek. 'But remember ze song, All you need is love, Jackie.'

'If ya nah have no air ticket, den go way, den, ya rass claat German fool. Gwaan! Hitch up ya bag and leave.'

Rudy flinched at the severity of his wife's words. 'But Jackie, vot is vrong? Haff I done somesing I am not knowing?'

Jackie looked up the Main in the direction of the primary school. Little Kermit ran down the middle of the road, his eyes sparkling and his front teeth clearly visible.

'Wilfred de com!' he called excitedly. 'Wilfred de com!'

A few hundred yards behind him, Wilfred hurried to his yard, the prospect of another early night with his fiancée quickening his paces.

'I haf come to live wiz you, as man unt wife, Jackie,' Rudy said.

Jackie dashed back into the house and came out with the kitchen knife. This wooden-handled stainless steel knife looked like an innocent cooking implement, but it had form: it had been a murder weapon once, in the hands of Red Rat, the father and moral guide of all the Swing siblings; he had inflicted many gashes, and countless times it had been pressed threateningly against the flesh of both enemies and friends.

The look in Jackie's eyes as she advanced holding the knife in the air so terrified Rudy that he was rooted to the spot. His mind raced: it wasn't too late to ring his father and beg forgiveness. His BMW would still be in the garage, his flat still unsold.

'But Jackie vot is vrong? We can liff here most happily togezzer – and I will try to get my farter to send some money, I promise.'

'Dis marriage finish,' she said, somewhat unnecessarily, and brought down the knife, gashing his arm.

'Lick her, lick her!' Maxwell shouted from the road.

But Rudy knew Jackie better than that.

'Mein Gott, Jackie, you could haf kilt me. Haf you gone mad?' he stuttered, backing away from her.

'Ya man, and mi will kill ya if ya nah get out av mi yard. Gwaan, ron now ...'

Rudy grabbed his rucksack, and ran, clutching his forearm, out of the yard and down the Main, disappearing from view just as Wilfred, whistling merrily, came into view. Rudy ended up in Blender's bar down by the seashore, clutching a T-shirt to the wound, which looked rather worryingly superficial, considering how fast he had run. The heavily dreadlocked Blender brought him a Red Stripe that he'd opened on a pair of rusty nails, which Rudy swigged on, tasting the slightly fishy smell that lingered around the cap of every bottle served in Beach.

'Spliff?' Blender asked.

'Ya, danke, tank ya.'

'No problem.'

Blender reached for his stash under the cane thatch roof and bil one spliff, which he lit, the white smoke obscuring his head and locks, before passing it to Rudy. Rudy pulled deeply on it. This was his first spliff since landing in Jamaica. It tasted lemony, and full of blossom.

After a long, easeful silence, Blender, who of course knew what had happened to Rudy, because everyone in Beach knew everything, said, 'Life go on, eh?'

And Rudy smiled. 'Ya man,' he said, 'life go on.'

When Wilfred got back to his yard he saw the knife in Jackie's hand.

'What are you up to with that knife, Jackie?' he asked cheerily.

'Cutting flower dem far de table,' answered Jackie sweetly, slicing through the stem of an hibiscus.

He put his arm around her waist and smiled into her eyes. 'Flowers for the table,' he said. 'You know I think I'm the luckiest man in Jamaica, to have someone as wonderful as you.'

Three weeks later they were wed. The day after the wedding, Jackie dragged Wilfred to the Post Office to make sure he posted their passports, marriage certificate and application for her British citizenship to the consulate in Kingston. As usual, Miss Markham served Wilfred. Naturally, she knew exactly who Jackie was and what was in the envelope. Miss Myrtle had told her. She had heard it from Miss Dahlia, who had heard it from Nerine, who had seen it while she palish an' shine de flaar in Jackie's house. Miss Markham took the envelope from his hand and hid it at the back of a drawer under some old papers in her desk in her office, where it remained for seven months, until questions from Head Office forced her to put it into the postal system.

There is not a single nation which welcomes applications for citizenship from Jamaicans, with perhaps the exception of Colombia, and it therefore took a long time for the passport to come, the British Immigration Service erecting every legal obstacle they could to Jackie's quest, but she was patient, determined, and prepared to wait. And while she waited, she played the part of Wilfred's wife as well as she could.

Wilfred taught at Beach Primary and worked without rest on improving the house, the yard, which was almost now a garden, and building more beautiful furniture. After eight months, Jackie gave birth to a boy, called Chris. He was laid in a carved cedarwood crib Wilfred had constructed in the shade of the sea-grape tree on weekends. The boy reached his first birthday, but still the Immigration Department at the Consulate wanted more questions answered and more documents produced.

After a couple of years, Jackie's hopes of getting out of Jamaica began to fade. She grew bored with Wilfred, and became careless. When he went off to the primary school to teach, she wandered over to Gucci's to drink Appleton and idle with him under the almond tree outside his bar, and listen to his stories of life in big cities and travels abroad with people like Bob Marley. She friend with Gucci, causing Wilfred incalculable anxiety and suffering. When Jackie gave birth to a second child, a girl, Wilfred knew the infant was too dark-skinned to be his, but loved the baby all the same. Everyone laughed at a man who had a jacket, as another man's child was called, but Wilfred didn't seem to care; he pull it round him till it fit.

Twice a week for three years, Jackie went fruitlessly to the Post Office at Content, to see if her passport had arrived. As a white man's wife she could go straight to the front of the line, where Miss Markham told her with an ambiguous smile that she had no mail, except from time to time a Jamaica Public Service bill, as electricity had finally been brought to Angel Beach. Then one hot and rainy morning in June, she was given a package which contained her new deep blue British passport.

By that time her marriage had lasted over three years, and people in Beach wondered if Jackie had changed, or if she was still one bad gal. Their doubts were cleared up the day she received her deep blue British passport, because she stepped out of the minibus in Beach clutching her package, went into her yard and threw all Wilfred's clothes out of the house. When he came back from work, whistling a tune as he walked down the road, she met him at the little gate he'd erected to stop Chris wandering onto the Main, and run him off, exactly the same way she run Rudy off. Everyone in Beach either watched, or knew about the incident.

'Leopard kiant change him spot dem,' opined Miss Dahlia.

'Ya man,' said Flossie. 'Jackie alway one bad gal.'

Wilfred came back every day for a month to remonstrate with her, his tearful and increasingly desperate appeals entertaining the crowd drawn from the Back Street, but she cuss and use bad word and run him out of the yard time after time, much to everyone's amusement, until he went back no more, and people said he'd gone to live inna foreign.

Jackie set about selling Wilfred's house and furniture. She found three interested parties: a Swiss dentist, a blue-blooded Boston ganja smuggler, and an American tourist. She then sold the house, and took the money, from each of them. No-one knew quite how it happened, but most agreed Liar Brown, Jackie's lawyer, had a lot to do with the plan. It was certainly by no means the last time a house or piece of land in Beach was sold to more than one whitey at a time.

Jackie took the money and emigrated with Chris and May to London, where she soon realised that she didn't have to lie or use people to get what she had always wanted, which was a job, a decent home and the easy life. She was soon settled in a council flat, went back to college, and within four years she was deputy manager of a small building society branch in Balham. She's still working on the easy life, but she's happy with things as they are.

Back in Beach, while the three purchasers argued over whose house it was, Sandra, Jackie's younger sister, moved into Wilfred Poole's yard and held the place by force with her elder bothers Dagga and Shox, shortly before they were both jailed for murder, when the whities dropped their claims.

Sandra

Sandra was as pretty as Jackie, but because she was shorter, plumper and had an enormous posterior, a bumpa botty, covered in cellulite, she was considered much sexier than Jackie by those who declared themselves experts on the matter, i.e. every man in Angel Beach. She had none of Jackie's elegance, and in the place of her sister's intelligence was a short-sighted, even stupid, cunning, but she had courage, and few people or things scared her. She was a shining example of someone with no conscience, and keenly followed her siblings into the family trades: petty crime and prostitution, but didn't have their determination or brains to be a success. It wasn't easy to follow the high achievements of Jackie – at one point Negril's highest paid whore – and two elder brothers, both of whom were serving impressively long stretches in Spanish Town Jail for robbery and murder. Sandra managed little more than stealing towels on the beach, and diluting the pure orange juice she sold in Negril with squash and water.

Although essentially a failure in the world of crime, Sandra felt big and bad in Angel Beach, which was a peculiarly forgiving and encouraging community for low achievers. You could be the best, or at the very least brilliant, in your chosen field, without achieving a thing. It was enough simply to talk about it. Dreams were as highly regarded as actions; words were as valued as deeds. Everyone had a money-making scheme in the planning stage, and no-one felt any pressure to get it off the ground.

Those who did actually do something, as opposed to talk about it, were assured of success – though it must be pointed out that the threshold for success in Angel Beach was low and wide. The cricket team, which won only one game the season after the famous match against the Police, was still 'de best inna de island. Serious'. The top athlete, a star of track and field, was Vinton, with his knock knees and immense flat feet which looked like batter poured into a deep frying pan, who each successive year left Beach for the inter-parish trials in Content, full of hope, with many slaps on the back, firm shakes of the hand, and injunctions to 'lick dem down', and 'mash dem op', and was knocked out in the first, or very occasionally, second, heat of every event he entered. He was knocked out, in fact, as often as Beach's other great sporting champion, Boydie the boxer, who at twenty-five had trouble finding his words after so many blows to his head.

Beach's top tourist operator was Busta, whose newly built bar stood on rocks beside the seashore, not far from the shed he built with Blender, whom he had parted from acrimoniously after an argument about Blender's tendency to long change customers. Busta's new shed was about twelve foot square, with bamboo walls, a pitched zinc roof, and a concrete floor on which was built a mahoe wood bar. Behind the bar was one crate of dusty soft drinks, one of Red Stripe and one of Dragon Stout, a framed black and white photograph of Haile Selassie, the Ethiopian Emperor, and another, unframed, of Bob Marley. In front of the bar were three stools whose height placed your chin at the level of the bar if you sat down. On the bar, in common with every other rum shop in Jamaica, was a ghetto blaster half tuned to a radio station at full volume, and a glass cabinet whose feet stood in bottle tops of water to prevent ants climbing up them and swarming over the buller, bon, rack cake, or fry fish which sat in the warm gloom of the showcase for whole weeks before being consumed. The bamboo walls were painted blue, yellow, white and dark green, as each half pot of paint he beg from friends ran out.

After everyone in Beach had visited it, looked around, and said 'criss bar, man' to Busta, it fell silent and empty – except for Busta, on a stool behind the bar, his dreadlocked head resting on his folded arms, week after week, listening to the air-conditioned coaches half full of tourists hissing at the bridge, changing down, and then roaring up the hill past his bar, changing back up as they hit the straight out of Angel Beach. Locals patronised the bar, but they had little money, and had to make one Red Stripe or saff drink last three or four hours; yet somehow, like most businesses in Beach, the bar just managed to keep its head above water, being saved from total immersion by the arrival, every six weeks or so, of a car-load of tourists, bored by their hotel and resort town, doing a little exploring. They would fill the bar with their big American bodies and voices, and within an hour triple the monthly takings. Tourists were everything people said they were. If you happened to be passing Busta's at the time, you could easily be asked in, and bought one, or even, in one extraordinary reported incident, three, Red

Stripe (and it would have been four, but all Busta's beer done), and get to chat with the whitey dem, all of whom were incredibly rich, madly generous and extremely friendly.

It was Sandra who managed to get tourists to stop in Beach for more than an hour or so, and everybady respect her for that. She found out that Wilfred Poole's yard had some magical qualities for the white man. She brought parties out from Negril, and sometimes white men would stay the night, but she was useless at whore bizness because she always bugged them for too much money too soon, and they scurried back to Negril. There was one couple Sandra met on the beach, called Don and Marlene, who came to Jamaica every year around November-time when it was just getting seriously cold in Chicago where they lived, who always stopped by Sandra's yard on their way to their hotel from the airport.

Don and Marlene had visited two years running when, around November 1990, Sandra began to think they might reappear. And indeed one dry autumn day, Sandra, hearing a car pull off the road into the yard, rolled over on her bed, peered through a crack in the woodwork, and shouted, 'It Dun an' Marlene,' to Vinton excitedly.

She had recently taken Vinton off the side of the road where he scratched a living, just, selling stolen or scavenged fruit in tiny quantities to passing motorists. Since escaping Miss Liza's yard, he had no yard to call home, and slept at night wherever he could. Up 'n' down, it was called. He was always careful to leave before his welcome wore thin or, before it wore too thin, anyway, and never returned to the same yard too soon. In sixteen years alive in Beach he had managed to accumulate only four, treasured, possessions: one brief, and tree shirt, two of which he had to lend to his cousin Barrington, to borrow back one trousers, so he could walk up and down 'pon de street widout shame. He wanted most of all a gold chain, so girls would talk to him, no, notice him, and one shoes. His attendance at Sandy Island Secondary School trailed off two summers ago, well before he learnt to read or write – but in a world with no books, paper or pens, it was not a problem. He knew that others were doing better than he, and had more to show for sixteen years than one pair of underpants and three T-shirts, but Vinton felt that his life was by no means irretrievable, and with the right breaks he could come good – find a girl who would talk to him – and even make some bills.

When Sandra installed him in her yard to babysit, guard against tief, wash up, cut and rake the yard, in return for a roof over his head (unless Sandra had friends staying, when Vinton had to sleep under the house in the housebottom), and the occasional look at her snowy portable TV, his real education was about to begin.

After they all said hello, and Don and Marlene said how warm it was and how beautiful the sea looked, Sandra said, 'Ya need a drink after ya journey. What ya want?'

'Well, what are you offering?' Don asked.

'Anyting. Beer or saff drink.'

'I'll have a Red Stripe.'

'Don! It's only four o'clock!' said Marlene.

'Relax. We're on vacation, and this is Jamaica, honey.'

'Ya man. In Jamaica it no problem.'

'Well I'll take an orange juice,' said Marlene. 'Do you have fresh orange juice?'

'Ya man,' said Sandra, going into the gloom of the house. Vinton had come round to the back door.

'Get mi one Red Stripe and one saff drink, orange. Horry. Hol' on.'

'Dun,' she called. 'Ya need one spliff to chill out?'

'Oh wow,' said Don. 'Well, I guess so ...' he replied.

'It is a little early, honey,' said Marlene, 'and we still have a way to go on that terrible road.'

'No problem,' said Sandra. 'Spliff can clear the brain for drive. Den ya can constentrate. Alright, just a small one.' She thrust a few notes at Vinton, and whispered, 'Get mi one spliff. Run. Horry now.'

Down at Busta's he found the bar shut. Quite often Busta was so high when he arrived at work, he went round the back under a fig tree, climbed into his hammock and waited for a customer without noticing the front door was closed until he came to shut up at the end of the day.

Vinton called his uncle's name. 'Dread!' he shouted, but nothing came in reply, so he went on down to Blender's shed on the seashore.

'Dread,' he called to Blender, who was crouching by a pot on a charcoal fire in the little kitchen behind his bar. 'Ya have one Red Stripe and one saff drink?'

Blender moved slowly to the cold store, a hole in the sandy ground behind the bar where half a dozen bottles – his entire stock – sat in warm water that three days before had been chunks of ice, bought off the dripping ice chock that supplied all the bars along the Main from Mo-Bay to Negril. He found a bottle of beer and a fizzy orange.

'An' mi need one spliff,' Vinton added when Blender wiped the bottles on a rag that smelled of fish. Blender returned from his stashing place under the cane thatch, and Vinton said, 'Ow much for dat?'

Blender looked long and hard at the two bottles. Then he said, 'Red Stripe six dallar, saff drink tree. Dat ... dat ...' his voice trailed off, and he was left gazing intently at the bottles in silence.

Vinton wished his youngest sister Amoy was there. She

was nine years old and the village's champion mathematician, reader, writer and speller.

'Dat nine dallar,' said Vinton quite confidently.

'Ya man,' smiled the dread.

'Ow much far de spliff and wizla?'

'Say ... say ... say ... five dallar. Dat mek ... dat mek ...' he started laughing softly to himself.

'Nine dallar an' five dallar. Dat fourteen.'

'Ya man.'

Vinton gave him an orange twenty-dollar bill with the picture of a bauxite mine on it. Blender drifted off into the dark recesses of the shed and returned with a handful of notes, which he then looked at in a surprised way, as if they had landed in his hands by magic. He shook his head and laughed. 'It com to ... It com to ...'

'Fourteen dallar.'

'Ya man.' He stopped and stared at the money again. 'Ow much ya give mi?'

'Mi give ya one twenty bill.'

'Ya man.' Long pause.

'Ya owe mi six dallar.'

Blender looked at the money in his hand. 'Mi nah have six, man. Me only have four dallar bills an' one ten dallar bill.'

Vinton was aware that there was a solution to the problem, but felt that Don and Marlene were going to be gone before Blender and he got it. White people did everything so fast.

'Tek de twenty. Give me de change later.'

'Ya man. Respec.'

Vinton left the shed and ambled back to Sandra's yard, running the last few yards.

'Ow much?' Sandra shot at him as he handed the drinks and ganja in the back door.

'Twenty. Drinks nine. Ganje eleven,' he answered, giving Sandra back her change. He knew she knew the price of drinks, but had gambled on the ganja, whose price fluctuated with supply and demand.

'Dun!' she called, and gave him the ganja where he sat on the porch.

'Oh wow. How much do I owe for the draw?'

'Fifty J. Call it four US. An maybe a likker tip far de boy who ron and carry it.'

'Sure,' said Don, digging in his pocket again.

Vinton, standing shyly at the corner of the house thought to himself how Sandra was a hard task mistress, but had a soft side to her.

'Here.' Don gave a single US bill to Vinton. A US dollar! His first! Wickid.

'Tank ya, sah,' he said, fingering the bill lovingly.

'What ya carry dung fram a foreign far mi?' Sandra impatiently asked Don. 'Ya know ya got to give mi someting,' she piped gaily. He made the mistake of not bringing Sandra a present last year – she was so demanding he had been lucky to get away without her peeling Marlene's watch and jewellery off her body – so he didn't make the mistake twice.

Sandra unwrapped her gift hungrily until she saw what it was – a kitchen apron with Don's company logo on it – and lost interest so quickly she didn't even say thank you. Vinton looked at it and thought he could wear it on the street and the girls might love it. It was worth a try, anyway.

After a spliff and a drink – Marlene taking only one sip of the bright orange confection in her bottle, but upon seeing Don with his spliff she said, 'All right, maybe I'll have a quick pull on that' – the procedure was as follows: Don went to the car, took out masks, snorkels, fins and swim suits, and they swam for twenty minutes before taking a shower and driving on to Negril. Vinton led them to the water's edge, carrying their state of the art diving equipment just to get a feel of the newness of it, even if only fleetingly, saw them safely in, and said, 'Ya wan ya car clean, sah, while ya swim?'

'Oh right, great. And keep an eye on it, thanks,' Don called, and pulled down his mask.

The reef, through a snorkelling mask, was a teeming, bright and beautiful world. The coral, predominantly red, grew in extraordinary shapes – in huge pillars that seemed about to teeter to the sandy sea floor; great mansions, hollowed out like catacombs with giant bulging brain corals protruding from their sides; and near the surface, in pale fingers of delicate traceries, reaching through the water to the sunlight. Amongst this ruined underwater world darted thousands of bright fish; from tiny electric blue minnows in shoals half a million strong, through striped, spotted, brindled even, fish, to giant rays that swept out from the shadows with the sinister, deliberate slowness of a dangerous and fearless animal. While Don and Marlene were immersed in this world, only stopping to stand on the coral every now and again to clear their masks and exclaim, 'Wow, isn't it just unbelievable. I mean really?' before dipping down back into it, Vinton made his way back to clean the car.

'Gi' mi dat one US dallar,' Sandra snapped at him, as he gazed with stunned admiration at the Civic.

'Nuh sah! Dun give i' a mi, Sandra ...' But it was useless, so he pulled it out of his pocket and handed it over. At the pipe under the avocado pear tree, he filled a pan with water, found an old discarded sock of Sandra's and went back to the car, moving fast so as to have plenty of time touching the beautiful automobile. It was a five year old Honda Civic, and you couldn't get much grander or newer than that in Angel Beach.

He had never, in his whole life, handled, let alone owned, any new manufactured object, until he worked for Sandra. Everything that he got hold of was second-hand, no, fifteenth-hand, at least, and had long before lost the lustre, feel and smell of newness. He longed for something with a price label on it, something straight from a shop, with plastic and cardboard packaging to strip off, but only ever got his hands on things picked from the dust of a yard where they had been thrown down by the last owner.

While wiping the back window, Vinton saw, on the back seat of the car, a photographic bag with something metallic, and new-looking, sticking out of it. It was a camera, a criss camera, with one wickid big lens, and the name PENTAX written across its top. He tried the door; it opened. He sat in the back seat with his legs out the door, and picked up the camera. It was heavy, and felt good. He lifted it to his eye, and after a few difficulties was looking at the steering-wheel and speedometer through the viewfinder. Ya man. That would make one nice phota. He made the click and whirring wind-on noise with his mouth. He knew the sound from the tourists who always took photographs of the old fishing canoes from Busta's Bar. He couldn't work out why anyone would want a picture of Jagwar and Oncle Dicky's dug-out canoes. If he were them, he would have taken a picture of the Rental car, or Busta's flush toilet, or the street light – something new and criss like that.

He saw a pair of sunglasses under the bag, and pulled them out. They had a weight, too, like all the expensive things tourists brought with them. He tried them on and looked in the wing mirror. He brought the camera near his face so he could see it in the reflection, too. Ya man, dat look kinda cool. When he slipped the glasses back, the big bag moved and revealed Marlene's handbag beneath. Vinton saw the pale green edge of some bank notes, and after investigating a little, had Marlene's wallet open and was fingering four or five hundred US dollars in cash.

'Put i' back, ya idiot, Vinton,' Sandra snapped, slapping the top of his head. 'Dat nat de way fi get de money. Ya want fi we to go a jail? Den nuh touch i'. Gwaan, move out a here. Go dung a sea an' keep watch far Dun an' Marlene.'

'What is you gonna do?'

'I,' said Sandra, slipping into the driver's seat and touching the key in the ignition, 'am gonna tek de rental far one likker spin.'

'But ya kiant drive, Sandra,' Vinton blurted out. He knew she had only got a licence because Afficer Donovan of Sandy Island Police Force (Traffic Division) had given it to her for sex.

'It easy fi drive. If Shepherd Bush George can do i', any fool can do i'. Go an watch far Dun.'

Vinton stood back and watched Sandra pilot the Honda unsteadily onto the road. When its front wheels were half way across the tarmac she pulled on the handbrake, got out of the car, leaving it in the middle of the road, and dashed back across the yard and into the house. A minibus and car came abreast round the blind corner and swerved with a cry of tyres, narrowly avoiding the Honda, then Sandra appeared carrying a pair of sunglasses, and climbed back in the car.

She had no destination in mind, nor errand to run, but there was nevertheless a definite purpose to her journey. Her object was to cruise up and down the Main and possibly onto the Back Street, so that as many people as possible could see her driving the criss rental car and be reminded of how big her status was, before getting the car back to the yard and parking it.

Sandra was the most glamorous person in Angel Beach. The people knew she was bad, but loved her for the new and exciting things she brought into their lives: the long bamboo pole that waved in the breeze above her roof, with the rusting antennae tied by string to its top, was the source of immense civic pride, even though the pink portable TV at its other end barely produced an intelligible picture. It meant, though, to people passing through, that Angel Beach had a TV. Sandra loved the glamour of being the most modern girl in the village, and felt a certain responsibility to live up to expectations. Whenever she got her hands on a new appliance she proudly brandish it to the likker people dem of Beach. It was she who gave people their first feel of a Walkman. The headphones were passed from head to head producing startled and awed expressions as Kenny Rogers, slurring on underpowered batteries, growled out his lyrics. So powerful was the little machine that even Wilbert, deaf to everything else, caught a snatch of music and laughed joyfully at his first aural contact with the outside world for decades. Sandra also introduced the camera to Beach, taking a lot of pictures of people which were never developed because they didn't have the money to clean de film. No-one minded though – posing for the pictures was enough of a thrill. She also bought the pressure cooker to Beach. She had gone into Larmonds Record and Novelty store in One Way Street, Content, to buy a Hi-Fi, but discovering that she didn't have enough money, went for a pressure cooker instead. With the remains of her funds she bought some diced beef, and hurried home to impress everyone in Beach. On the long journey from the factory in Taiwan, where the pressure cooker was manufactured, to Content in St John, where it had sat in the shop for three and a half years, it had become parted from the instruction manual, so Sandra relied on instinct to discover how it worked. One thing she knew about beef: it took a lot of cooking. She dropped it into the pot, added some water, seasoning, scallions and carrot, screwed the lid down hard, put it on the paraffin flame, and stood back. Within quarter of an hour a wonderful scent of beef stew filled the room. It was time to call in the small crowd gathered in the yard. In trooped Miss Dahlia, Nerine, Kermit, Nakissia, Mooney, Wilbert (who since the Walkman, believed Sandra had access to miraculous inventions) and Miss Myrtle, all of whom admired the clean lines of the pressure cooker and commented favourably on the smells emanating in hisses from it.

'Mi go a Negril now, and nyam de beef when me com back tonight when it cook proper,' Sandra announced, as everyone left the house. 'Vinton,' she commanded. 'Sit here and watch de pressure pot till me com back.' Negril being six miles to the west, and Sandra's mode of transport being a minibus, Vinton settled in for a minimum two and a half hour wait in front of the sizzling pot. After an hour, though, when he had invited Mooney into the house for company, the smell of well seasoned beef stew became too much for the two hungry boys to resist.

'Let we tek off de top an' eat a couple spoonful of meat before put it back to cook. Sandra never gonna know,' Vinton suggested.

'Ya man,' agreed Mooney, 'she never gonna give we no beef herself.' Too often Mooney had sat with Vinton in Sandra's yard, and out of the corner of their eyes watched Sandra single-handedly consume a meal for three, before shouting at Vinton to wash up the plate and pot.

Vinton had trouble unscrewing the lid, but Mooney, who

was good with his hands, saw that a hammer and piece of wood would do the trick. He put the wood in place against the boiling pot, and gave it a sharp crack with the hammer.

There was a mighty explosion. The lid flew off the pot, and a fine layer of beef stew was spread evenly over the walls, ceiling, faces and clothes of Vinton and Mooney.

'Jeeezus, Chris'!' laughed Mooney.

'De pressure pot vex!' said Vinton.

'Mi kiant believe i'. But i' taste good,' Mooney said, picking a strip of meat off a T-shirt that said MY DAD WENT TO JAMAICA AND ALL I GOT WAS THIS LOUSY T-SHIRT, and putting it in his mouth.

'Mmm. It can go on,' agreed Vinton.

'But what Sandra gonna say?'

'Sandra never gonna know. Sandra kiant know or else she gonna kill we.' So the two of them, armed with a wide-headed screw-driver and a general purpose kitchen cloth scraped up the mess, put what they could of it back into the pot and screwed the lid back on. When Sandra returned she ate her stew and pronounced it an unqualified success.

That had been months before Don and Marlene called by, and she felt it was time to reassert her position as Beach's most exciting resident. She turned the car right, and took it slowly up the Main towards Shepherd Bush George's house, where she knew it would out-trump his immense Grundig TV. Vinton watched her leave on her Royal Tour of Angel Beach, and made his way back to the sea.

It wasn't long before Don and Marlene's snorkel pipes began to move back across the reef towards Vinton, where he sat anxiously on the rocks. Behind him, there was no sign of Sandra or the car. Soon they were drawing themselves out of the water, ripping off their masks and saying, 'Oh wow, that really is incredible, I mean that's awesome, it really is. Jesus, there are people who'd pay hundreds of bucks to do that ...'

'It sure beats the D train down town on a cold Monday morning,' laughed Marlene.

When Don noticed Vinton sitting on the rock, he said, 'Hi, there. Everything okay?'

'Ya man,' said Vinton, and had recourse to the phrase Sandra always used in a crisis with tourists: 'This is Jamaica, man. No problem!'

'Sure!' laughed Don.

Vinton looked up through the seagrape trees for signs of Sandra. All he could see was Kermit, hanging around hoping for a tip from the white man. He thought he could probably get Don dem to the shower and then to Sandra's bedroom, where they had left their clothes, without seeing the rental wasn't there, because Wilfred Poole's hibiscus hedge hid it, but after that Sandra had better get back, or there was gonna be one 'ole 'eap o' trouble. He wondered where she was, imagining her taking the rental gently down the Back Street on the way back to her yard. In fact, she had her foot hard down on the gas pedal and was five miles out of Beach on the road up to Blenheim. Having cruised past Shepherd Bush George and ensured he saw her in the car with Marlene's Pentax round her neck, she decided to go up into the hills to check a Police who had been giving her the eye on the beach for a couple of weeks. Maybe he'd want to take a ride with her. She thought about Don and Marlene. Yes, she'd have to hurry a little.

On the way to the shower Marlene said, 'Did you lock the car?' and in a lower tone added, 'Only my bag and money are in it.'

'Will you relax, Marlene,' Don replied. 'I've known Sandra years. We're amongst friends.'

'So you didn't.'

'I'm not sure. Hey! you ...'

'Ya man,' replied Vinton.

'No-one's been inside the car, have they?'

'No man,' replied Vinton.

'See?' said Don. 'Now just relax. Please.'

They loved the open-air shower, and ran laughing to the house and Sandra's bedroom while Vinton sat unhappily on the porch looking out onto the empty road. Suddenly Don came to Sandra's bedroom door with a towel round his waist.

'Anyone been in here while we were swimming?'

'Nah sah,' answered Vinton.

'There must have been,' Marlene screeched from inside, 'my watch has been stolen.'

'Darling, we don't know for sure yet ...'

'Yes I do. I put it here with my clothes. I told you this place was fucking unsafe. I knew we should have gone to Tahiti. The South Sea islanders just aren't into this stealing shit.' She, too, appeared at the door. 'You see anyone sneak in here?'

'No. Nobady com in here.'

'Well where the hell is my watch then? It was a fucking Rolex. I paid over a thousand bucks for that watch. Just what is it with Jamaicans? Did you come in here while we were swimming?'

'No. Mi swear mi didn't. Mi sit pon de rock dem while ya bade.'

'Oh, right, sure, you just acted as lookout for your pals.'

'Let me have one look,' Vinton said, approaching them. He'd seen this before. White people get high, lose tings and say dem tief. He entered Sandra's room, and began a search. In the little cupboard on the wall that Wilfred Poole had made and Jackie had been unable to prise off and sell, Vinton found Sandra's Bible, with a woman's wristwatch pushed under it. He took it out.

'That's where I put it. I forgot I hid it.'

'No prablem,' said Vinton.

'VINTAN!' he heard shouted.

'Please excuse me,' he said to the whities, 'that is Sandra.'

She was back. But the car wasn't in the yard. 'VINTAN!' he heard Sandra scream again.

He followed the shout out onto the road, where Sandra stood twitching by the car thirty yards from the yard, the Pentax resting on her full bosom.

'It burn outa gas,' she said to him. 'Wishart Dun dem?'

'Dem change in fi you room.'

'Quick. Ron now to Ranald and beg some gas fram him.'

Vinton sprinted off up to Ranald's yard and managed to get some gas, though the only receptacle available for its transportation was a washbowl, round which the pint of petrol swilled as Vinton trotted back to Sandra.

'Give me dat,' she snapped, pushing him out of the way, but when she brought it to the gas tank the fluid dribbled off the bottom of the bowl in an arc onto the tarmac. 'It want one fonnel. Ron and fetch one fonnel.'

But Vinton knew there wasn't a serviceable funnel in St John, let alone Angel Beach. He dashed into the hedge and plucked a wide and waxy leaf from an almond tree.

'What ya doin' wid dat? Mi need one fonnel ya idiot.'

'Dis can work, Sandra. Pour it now.'

With remarkable smoothness, the gas ran down the groove of the folded leaf and disappeared into the gas tank. 'Now get ou' de way,' Sandra said, and started the car.

Marlene and Don sat on Sandra's bed, too consumed by embarrassment at falsely accusing Vinton of theft to notice the sound of their car returning. They emerged sheepishly a few minutes later, when Kadim, Sandra's high-heeled, six year old daughter, was coming home from school.

'Vinton,' Sandra whispered out of the back door.

'Yes?' answered the boy.

'Lock off de current.'

He went to the main fuse box and threw the switch to off.

'Go inside an do ya homework,' Sandra ordered Kadim, 'it late.'

The sun was indeed setting. Kadim went in, and then came back to the door and addressed her mother.

'Momma, mi kiant see to read book cas it too dark.'

'Switch on light, ya idiot.'

'Mi kiant switch on light, cas corrent gone.'

'It bad for child to read in dark?' Sandra asked Marlene.

'Sure, it can ruin a child's eyes. What's wrong with your lights?'

'Mi kiant pay de bill and dem disconnect we. Only ten US, but mi poor and kiant afford it.'

'Oh Don, did you hear that?' Marlene said. 'The little girl has to do her homework in the dark because Sandra can't pay the ten dollar electricity bill. Can't we do something?'

Marlene was thankful for this opportunity to efface her earlier meanness – and for such a tiny sum.

'Sure, hon,' Don reached into his pocket. 'But I've only got eight bucks on me.'

'Don't worry,' said Marlene, moving off the porch and going to the car. 'I have some.'

She came back with her handbag. Vinton looked at Sandra, upon whose deadpan features he searched in vain for a hint of a smile. Marlene took out her wallet and withdrew a ten dollar note.

'Here,' she said, quietly and enjoyably, as she gave it to Sandra.

'Ten dollar for bill, but twenty-five bucks for reconnection fee,' Sandra said.

'They do that here, too? That's what they do in the States. They're terrible these big corporations. Here.'

The sun was submerged in the sea, and the short sweet cool Jamaican dusk was upon them. Don said they had to get on. As they kissed Sandra goodbye, and promised to see her again the following year, she said, 'Nuh forget mi present.'

They drew out of the yard and headed west to Negril.

'That was a great stop,' Marlene said. 'The swim was out of this world, and that boy was sweet, you know? And it was real nice to be able to help out, wasn't it?'

'Sure was,' said Don, smiling as he thought about the week of sun and fun and harmony that lay ahead of them. The visit had completely changed his wife's mood. 'It's right what they say, isn't it? Jamaica – no problem.'

Back at Sandra's yard, as Sandra put the 35 dollars into her pocket, she caught Vinton looking at her.

'Mi one teevee?'

'No,' replied Vinton.

'Well why ya look pon mi den?'

'Mi nah look pon ya,' he answered.

'Good,' she said. 'Now switch on de current an' cook up some rice and peas far mi. Mi ongry. Horry.'

And Vinton proudly tied Don's apron with the company logo on it around his waist, and set about his duties.

DROGS BIZNIS

When Gaddaffi get back from a turn inna Kingston at him mumma's yard, he came down from his yard inna de ills to show off the sunglasses he stole from his brother, and inquire amongst friends who was the best fisherman in Beach. His elder brother Buru had some gangsta buddies in Allmans Town, Kingston 4, who do some drogs biznis with Colombians, and needed a reliable sailor to pick up a consignment of cocaine dropped into the sea at a prearranged spot off the north-west coast of Jamaica. Living inna de ghetto they knew no fishermen, but Buru told them that his brother Gaddaffi lived near the coast in St John, and he could ask him to find someone to do the pick-up.

Gaddaffi first buck up pon Rayon U-Roy Fairfax, who idle in the deep shade of the big almond tree by the fishermen's canoes.

'Whuppen'?' Rayon greeted Gaddaffi.

'Yes, Rayon,' said Gaddaffi, settling on a fat root that threaded in and out of the sand. 'Tell me one ting, which de wickedest fisherman in all of Beach?' he asked.

'De best fisherman? Con, Wadder, and de udder shooter-man dem catch nuff pound of fish. Dem clean lick down all de fish dem in de Beach wid speargon.'

'Mi nuh mean shooter men, mi mean boat fishermen.'

'Boat fishermen? Dat easy. Jagwar de best. Him fish far

tirty odd year and know all de sea up an' down. Dat man can see straight trough water. And de fish love him, dem haffi love him, cas dem alway catch by him. Or Oncle Tom. Even when nobady op and down de coast fram Negril to Ochi kiant catch nuttin, Oncle Tom come back wid a boat full of snapper.'

'Which fisherman de best boatman?'

'De best boatman?'

'Ya man. Which fisherman know de sea and boat and ting better dan de udders?'

'Gaddaffi, why ya want fi know dis?'

'Cas Buru need one man wid a boat fi do a likker drogs biznis wid.'

'What kinda biznis?'

'Dat mi nuh know, cas him nuh tell me no detail plan dem. All mi know is dem need de bess boatman in de village.'

'For de purpose ya state, de answer easy: ya look pon de man right now.'

'Uuuh?'

'Mi can elp ya brudder no problem. Ya com to the right guy.'

'Bot Rayon, ya stop fish since four year, and ya nuh ave no boat, and ya lost easy out at sea when ya have ya boat. Remember dat time one starm come up fast and the sea rough up, and nobady kiant find ya till de coast guard ketch ya baffling for life off Negril Point?'

'Dat cas fi Wordswort canoe weak.'

'Ya man. Now mi remember, ya tief Wordswort canoe dat day.'

'Shot op, man. Dis biznis serious. Mi know what ya brudder want – one boat fi pick op drog fram sea. Dat easy, and mi can beg one fibreglass craft fram som fool in Firefly Bay wid big engine, so nuttin kiant wrong.'

'No sah,' laughed Gaddaffi, 'ya nat gonna do no biznis wid Buru ...'

'Mi know what biznis dis is. Dis cocaine biznis, tross me. And dat coke wort 'ole eap o' money ...'

'Ya man, mi know,' said Gaddaffi, 'and the dealer dem know too, and ya kiant mess wid dem or dem kill ya. Serious.'

'Dem kill ya, sure.' Rayon paused, then grinned, adding, 'If dem catch ya.'

'If ya mess wid dem, dem ketch ya. Tross mi. Dem rut'less. Dem love fi kill, dem love i'.'

'Listen,' said Rayon, drawing Gaddaffi closer, 'ya tell ya brudder dat mi de wickedest fisherman ...'

'Nor!'

'... and you and mi got out fi check de drogs ...'

'Nor, Rayon ...'

'Out at sea we tief maybe half pound or tree pound ...'

'... No!'

'... and leave it tie up by fish pot, com back fram a sea and tell dem dat when we find de coke one bag brok and coke lost.'

'Rayon, ya kiant do dat wid dis posse. Dem roff, trost me. Dem kill ya quick as dem smile at ya.'

'Ya know how much dallar half pound coke wort'?'

'No, an' mi nah want fi know.'

'Five tousan' US. Half pound ... Tree pound wort near twenty tousand US.'

'Twenty tousan' US?'

'Ya man.' Rayon's obeah mathematics worked its magic on Gaddaffi's resistance. 'Dat twelve tousand five ondred US for each o' we.'

Rayon borrowed a boat, which six weeks later, shortly after dark, they pushed off the sand, clambered into, and pointed out to the black sea, scraping the hull horribly, because Rayon'd forgotten the lanes in the coral reef. They had no charts, no watch and no compass with which to find the rendezvous.

Far out at sea Rayon shouted, ''Top de engine ...'top de engine.' When Gaddaffi killed the outboard, Rayon said, 'Ssh. Mi tought mi 'ear one airplane.' Gaddaffi looked terrified. They sat and listened to the lapping of the warm black sea on the hull. The moonlight illuminated the buoy, plastic bag, tape and scissor in the bottom of the boat. 'Nottin,' announced Rayon. The next thing he said, half an hour later, was, 'It soon com. Tross mi.'

When, nine hours later, dawn broke greyly over the slither of land on the horizon, Rayon got Gaddaffi to start the engine, and pointed the prow back to Angel Beach. As they bounced along, Gaddaffi scrabbled around the bottom of the boat for the tape, scissors and other equipment related to their planned deception, and threw it overboard.

'What ya do, ya idiot?' shouted Rayon.

'Mi dash i' all away.'

'Mi need dat tape! Nat de bouy, no! ... Jeeezuss.'

'It all got a go, Rayon. Dis a problem situation we is in. Mi nuh gonna take no chances.'

'Us don't do nottin wrong. We do everyting right. Relax, tek it easy. Dem nuh gonna vex wid we.'

They roared past the fleet of fishing canoes paddling out to sea at dawn, pulled the boat carelessly onto the sand and were just about to disappear for a few days inna de bush when they noticed a group of men sitting under a tree watching them. It was Buru, looking excited, his Kingston friend from Telaviv posse, an out of uniform policeman called Nini Hibbert, and two strangers. One had a bald head and a pair of silver revolvers wagging under his earlobes, the other was a short, fat, moustached Latin man.

'Whuppen'?' Buru asked.

'Alright,' said Rayon.

'Everyting cool den?' Buru asked, unable to contain his happy excitement.

'Ya get trough?' asked the Kingston yout, who was called Fumes.

Rayon looked about him at the mangrove bushes, and lowered his voice. 'The plane don't come,' he said.

'What do you mean?' asked the man with the moustache.

'We sit an' wait all night, but we nah hear or see nottin. De airplane never com. Mebbe it have problems and kiant leave to com up.'

'Were you on the right grid reference?'

'Ya man, for sure. We was der. We was der, waitin, and nottin don't com.'

'So where is your map and compass?' asked the man.

'We trow it inna de sea when we come in. Don't we destroy all incriminating evidence, Gaddaffi?'

'Ya man,' said Gaddaffi miserably.

The guy with gun earrings told the others to search the boat. Rayon said to him: 'No plane com, man, believe mi.'

'Ya man, plane come. Now it sit at Montego Bay airport,' said Fumes.

'And it don't got no coke on it?' Rayon gulped.

'No. It hasn't. Because the consignment was tipped overboard,' said the boss, the short man with the moustache.

'Where?' asked Rayon.

'At the correct position at the correct time.'

Rayon leant towards the little Colombian. 'Dat what de pilot say?'

'Yes. Yes.'

'Him musta drop it someplace else where him bredren wait, so him can tief it fram you.'

'That's not possible.'

'Why nat? Is you one o' de pasingers on de plane?'

'No.'

'Ow many people on board wid de pilot?'

'He was alone.'

'Well den, bas.' Rayon lowered his voice to a whisper. 'Ya kiant trust nobady. Dat pilot one tief. Believe Rayon Fairfax. De pilot one traitor.'

'No he's not.'

'Bot 'ow can ya know, bas?' Rayon whined, in his most paranoia-inducing manner.

'Because I am the pilot,' the man answered, 'and I threw it out.'

Without pausing, Rayon said, 'Good. Dat rule out dat den. So. Us know the coke drop. Some fisherman most see it come, dem most. Let mi go and talk to mi bredren and aks a couple question up and down. Mi will have ya coke back by tonight. Tross mi. Nuh problem.'

Everybody watched Rayon closely. Gaddaffi cleared his throat. Rayon smiled weakly.

'Ready?' he asked brightly. 'De quicker mi go, de quicker ya get ya coke.' He made as if to go, but Afficer Nini Hibbert stood in his way.

'Ya nuh go nowhere till de bas tell you, annerstan?'

'For sure, no problem afficer.'

The man with the revolver earrings talked in a foreign language to the boss. Then he nodded at the cop. The cop leant towards Rayon. 'Ya have till tonight to find the consignment.'

'We meet back here at sunset. Understand?' the boss said.

'Mi annerstan,' said Rayon.

Gaddaffi nodded sickly.

'Dem annerstan,' said Buru. 'Dem annerstan that if dem nuh find we coke, dem gonna dead.'

'Get de message?' the cop asked.

'And no funny stuff, all right?' said earrings.

'Dem kiant try no funny stoff, cas dem know mi will find dem, wid ease,' said the cop.

'Sure,' said Rayon, sunnily. 'Tross we, tross we.'

When the men had left, all crammed in Nini Hibbert's police car, driver turned on Rayon. 'Ya idiot!' He ran his hands through his locks and stamped his foot. 'Mi told ya not to mess wid Buru. Why mi listen to you? Why?'

'Cas mi clever, and mi alway have a nex idea.'

'Ya alway have a nex bad idea.'

'Not dis time. Not dis time, Gaddaffi. Listen. What we want fi happen?'

'Fi find de lass coke.'

'Right. Or fi lose de Colombia man and him friend dem.'

'Dem nuh gonna go nowhere widout dem coke, Rayon.'

'Bot maybe someting can happen to dem. Someting bad, eh?' A smile curled his sly features.

'Cho,' spat Gaddaffi. 'Ya kiant kill dem, Rayon. Dat kiant work.'

'Nat kill dem, Gaddaffi. Get dem remove.'

'Who remove dem?'

'Police.'

'Police?' repeated Gaddaffi, trying to work out another of Rayon's stratagems.

'Mi talk 'bout Crimestop.'

'Crimestop,' said Gaddaffi, and then recited the radio advert: 'Don't hide it, tell it. Crimestop.' Crimestop was a confidential Police phone line for informers.

'Com ya,' said Rayon, 'us gonna mek one phone call.'

The two of them spent most of the afternoon looking for a serviceable telephone box, ending up outside Sandy Island Police Station, both crammed into the public phone box at its gate. Rayon punched the number into the phone.

'Dis gonna deal wid de prablem,' he said, sweating profusely. 'Yes sah!' he suddenly said into the receiver.

It had been a quiet morning on the Crimestop desk in Montego Bay, so when the line rang, Afficer Nini Hibbert, who had just come on shift, answered it within two rings.

'Crimestap,' he said, without enthusiasm. Since his suspension pending the inquiry into his robbery of the Sav La Mar Post Office, and his subsequent acquittal, the Superintendent put him on the Crimestop desk because his presence on the street in uniform was found to be too inflammatory.

'Ya sah. Dis one citizen callin bout drog dealer dem in de parish av St John.'

'What ya information?' Afficer Hibbert asked, disinterestedly, bored of the succession of interfering nobodies and malicious liards who were the only people to call Crimestop.

'Mi know where ya can arrest two Colombia cork dealer, two Kinston dealer and one corrupt Police,' Rayon said.

'Dat so. Where?' Hibbert said, not bothering to stifle a yawn.

'Ya know Beach?'

Hibbert sat up abruptly. 'Angel Beach?'

'Ya man. Go dung a Beach 'bout sunset, ya can pick dem up near the seaside. Ya kiant miss dem. Dem have one airplane at de airport dem use for smuggle cork.'

'Interesting information. How you learn bout dis?'

'Inside information. But it true.'

'May I ask your name?'

'Jost call mi a concern citizen.'

'Yes sah. Tell me, sah. You want a reward for this information receive?'

In the phone booth Rayon smiled at Gaddaffi, put his hand over the receiver, and said, 'Dem even gonna give mi money for dis!' Into the receiver he said, 'Afficer, mi do dis far mi country, ya know? Dis country is full of drog dealer and criminal and it drag we down in de eye of de world, ya know? People inna foreign say al dem Jamaicans jost drogs dealers and bad boys and prostitute. It de job of de honest citizen, fi clean out de contagion of dishonesty and criminality, bot, bot if you want fi give mi a couple dollar for outa pocket expense and ting, dem can be mi will give it to mi ole momma, cas mi nah want nottin fi miself, bot fo him mi will trouble ya.'

'Alright. Where ya want to meet mi?'

The good thing about working in Negril was you saw plenty of new things. Cedric had one of the best jobs in tourism, standing all morning waist deep in the water off Zoo, raking out the weeds so the whiteys didn't have to step on any plants when they went for a swim. He saw ole heap o gal dem widout bra. Bla had a good job too: wiping bar seats at Rick's Cafe in Negril when customers in damp swimming costumes got up to leave. Nerine have a job lowering the chain at the gatehouse of the Negril Tree House to let cars in and out. She saw some wickid cars in that job. The bad thing about working in Negril was you lost touch with the latest events in Beach. But when the tourism workers got back after their shift that evening, they were all brought up to date with the latest developments as soon as they stepped off the minibus, because the whole village chat nuff bout Rayon and Gaddaffi an de drogs biznis. Sitting on the rail of porches at dusk, standing semi-naked around standpipes, and in the middle of the backstreet, people group up fi talk pon de subject.

Flossie's shed was a bar Vinton and Mooney built out of ironwood posts and bamboo on captured land beside Sandra's yard. It listed heavily to the left when you stood in its doorway looking into the gloomy interior, where Flossie usually stood behind the bar in front of her stock of six Red Stripe, four Dragon Stout and half a dozen saff drink. She once tried to extend her lines to tin milk, mackrel, and peanut, but Vinton and his younger sister Amoy nyam down all de stock whenever her back was turned so she gave up. The bar had a bench, on which, that evening, she lay peacefully sleeping, her big shiny body rising and falling, and a stool, on which Wilbert, Miss Dahlia's brother, sat. Wilbert was a white-haired, sleepy-faced man, whose amiable features formed easily into a one-toothed smile. Vinton, seeing the old farmer inside, pulled Mooney into the shed to tell Wilbert the news. Vinton knew that Wilbert was the only person who hadn't heard the story five times, on account of his acute deafness, and wanted to tell it again.

'RAYON IN SOME DROGS BIZNIS DAT GO WRONG!' Vinton shouted.

A smile spread across Wilbert's face. 'HIM DOUBLE CROSS DEM?'

'MI NUH KNOW. CAN BE. SOMETING GO BAD. MAXWELL SEE SOME HEAVY YOUT FROM KINGSTON SHOUT AT RAYON DIS MARNING AFTER HIM COME BACK FROM INNA DE DEEP.'

'And he didn't take no bait when him and Gaddaffi go a sea, but leave it on the seashore, and never com back for it, so dem nuh fish,' interjected Mooney, though Wilbert got none of it.

'DEM KILL RAYON?' Wilbert shouted happily.

'NO MAN, DEM LET HIM GO. BUT DEM WANT HIM NOW, CAS RAYON GO A SANDY ISLAND AND RING CRIMESTOP FI TELL DEM ABOUT DE DRUGS DEALERS AND EVERYTING EXCEPT HIMSELF AND TOLD DEM FI ARREST TWO COLOMBIAN AND SEND HIM BACK DOWN. AND HIM ASK FI ONE TOUSAND DALLAR FOR HIM INFORMATION. ONE AFFICER KNOW RAYON VOICE AND DE POLICE COM A BEACH FI BEAT RAYON. WHEN RAYON HEAR HE RUN OFF INNA BUSH.'

Wilbert was laughing at the thought of Rayon spending a few days on the run.

'Mi kiant believe 't. Him call Crimestop and dem com after him,' said Mooney.

'Dem say now dem try fi find de cocaine inna de sea,' said Vinton wistfully, 'so mebbe somewhere out dere,' Vinton looked out to sea through the unglazed window in his mother's shed, 'there's a ole eap o' cocaine float around.'

'De yout from Kingston and de Colombia man rent all motorboat fram Kim's Bay to Sandy Island fi go out and look for dat coke. Can be dem will find i',' Mooney said.

'Remember dat time Maas Percival find ten fifty gallon drums of gas floating out a sea inna de deep, and bring dem all in tie wid cord behind him canoe?' asked Mooney.

'Dem find all kinda ting out a sea; one time dem find airplane,' said Vinton excitedly. It was a Cessna ditched by a drunken American smuggler on a Christmas morning ganja run that went horribly wrong.

'WHADDAT?' shouted Wilbert.

'MI SAY YA CAN FIND ALL SORT O TING AT SEA.'

'YA MAN. YA NEVER KNOW WHAT YA CAN FIND PON DE BEACH,' Wilbert shouted back. 'DIS MARNING MI DE DOWN DE SEASIDE EARLY AND MI FIND FOUR

BAG O' BREEZE WASHING POWDER WASH UP PON
DE SAND. MI KIANT BELIEVE I'. IT MOSS BE A GIFF
FRAM GOD.' Washing powder was sold cheaply at the
market in transparent plastic bags.

'WHAT YA DO WID DEM?' Vinton asked.

'WHAT? WHA' YA SAY DER?'

'SO WHA' YA DO WID DEM?'

'MI TEK DEM BACK A YARD AND MI WASH FI MI
CLOTHE DEM. WHAT ELSE MI GONNA DO WID DEM?'

'YA TEK UP ALL FOUR BAG?'

'Nuh shout, ya fool,' Mooney advised Vinton. 'Ya wake
Flossie,' he added in a whisper.

'Ow mi gonna find out bout it if mi nuh shout, idiot?'

'AV COURSE! YA TINK MI WASTE WASH POWDER?'

'DO IT CLEAN CLOTHES?' asked Vinton, laughing.

'YA MAN, BUT DER SOMETING WRONG WID DAT
POWDER. IT CLEAN GOOD, BUT IT NAH SUD, AND I'
NUMB UP FI MI ARM DEM WHEN ME WASH DE
CLOTHES DEM. DAT WHY SOMEBADY TROW IT INNA
DE SEA.'

'YA ARM GO NUMB? OW MUCH YA USE?'

'MAYBE NEAR QUARTER POUND.'

'Jeezus,' said Mooney quietly. 'Mi kiant believe dis.'

'SO DE REST LEAVE?'

'TREE OR FOUR POUND LEAVE. BUT MI NUH WANT
IT, SO MI GET RID A I'.'

'WHAT YOU DO WID I'?' Vinton and Mooney held their
breaths. Vinton checked to see Flossie was still sound asleep.
This wasn't the kind of thing you wanted your mother in
on.

'MI DASH IT AWAY.'

'YA DASH I' AWAY? WHERE?'

'WHERE? IN DE TOILET PIT INNA MI YARD.'

Leroy Mckenzie was the biggest drugs dealer Vinton knew. There was Rankin, Beach Boy, and recently Jingles in the village, but they weren't really drugs dealers, they just hustle a couple spliff when tourist stop and the opportunity arose. Leroy Mckenzie was a real drugs dealer. He had a Benz, and a big wall house on the hill far above Sandy Island Secondary. He smuggled enormous volumes of ganje, by boat and plane, and built a legitimate business on some of the proceeds, buying an 800 acre estate near Lemon Grove, with its own private harbour, well out of sight of curious eyes. He planted and soon harvested rows and rows of mango, banana and coconut trees, and built two long sheds to breed chickens. He was a clever man; everyone said it. Before dealing drugs he was head of English at Sandy Island Secondary School, where he'd married one of his star pupils, beautiful sixteen year old Sunita, Hopton of Rack Top fame's sister. He sometimes threw a couple dallar to the picknee dem playing at the pipe in Egypt when he drove up to see his in-laws behind Beach.

But Leroy Mckenzie was a ganja dealer; coke dealers were different. There was one in Negril with a sports Benz with a gold grill and mascot, and a blue neon frame around his number plate. Vinton had seen him. Jeezus. Ya kiant believe i'. Trailer load of gold chain roun him neck, wickid watch, and choperators roun him hand and ole heap o ring, size ya kiant believe, tross mi, roun him finger and thomb dem. With just a single piece of his jewellery, Vinton could pull every girl in Beach, except Bubbles, who at sixteen had grown so plump and beautiful it'd take two or maybe three.

'Mi gonna do a likker business, den,' Vinton said to Mooney.

Outside, in the snowy moonlight, Mooney said, 'Ya nah gonna go dung a Wilbert yard?'

'Ya man. Fi sure,' Vinton said across Mooney's laughter.

'Ya gonna, ya gonna, ya gonna put fi ya hand inna Wilbert do-do?'

Vinton looked at Mooney seriously.

'Not Wilbert do-do?' Mooney shouted again, laughing as he staggered backwards.

'Ya know how much coke wort'?' Vinton asked.

'It nat wort dat, man. Nuttin wort dat.'

' 'Top ya noise, ya eediot. One bag o' coke, say two pound, wort ...' Vinton, having no idea, thought of the largest sum of money he hoped it was worth, and said it: '... it wort sixty US.'

'Sixty US dallar?'

'Ya man.'

Mooney laughed. 'It wort more dan dat. Come on,' he said, and headed off across the pasture towards Wilbert's yard.

Vinton stopped him. 'We want one flashlight,' he said. 'Vices have one but it want one bulp.'

'Con have bulp. Vices have battery dem?'

'No. Sandra have battery in fi her tee vee. She in Negril tonight. Mi will get de battery and de flashlight. Ya get de bulp.'

They met up on the road outside Flossie's shop, and assembled the torch, which produced a faint yellow pool of light on the tarmac.

'Give it mi,' said Vinton.

'No man,' said Mooney, laughing and running off towards Wilbert's yard and tilet pit.

There were three sanitary sytems in Beach. Most of the little people dem feed de crab, that is, crouched in a thicket, or edging, or bit of bush, and afterwards covered it in leaves or the sandy soil. However, privacy was becoming harder to come by; more and more people were clearing bush and building houses. The second way was the tilet pit, one of which Wilbert had, amongst maybe ten others; this was a two-metre deep hole covered by concrete with a small opening, on which, when no expense was spared, a wooden thunder box was poised.

The third kind was the flush tilet. There were only two of those in Beach: one in Shepherd Bush George's yard, which had a padlock on the outside of the door to deter toilet tourists, i.e. those many people who wanted to come and stare and wonder at a flush toilet. The other one was in Panda's new wall house, which stood in his yard not far up the Main from Miss Dahlia's. Panda grew rich quickly, driving tourists around in his criss minibus. For a short while he employed Mooney to clean the minibus and his house while he was working. While Panda was out, Mooney invited in his friends to look at Panda's possessions, and Vinton accidentally took a photograph with Panda's camera of Mooney with his feet on Panda's sofa – yes, sofa, even Shepherd Bush George didn't have a sofa – watching Panda's pornography on the video. Four weeks later Panda clean de film and saw the picture. He ran Mooney out of the yard and never paid the last six weeks' money, but there was nothing Mooney could do about that. Naturally, Vinton and Mooney had closely inspected Panda's flush tilet ... The flush itself, triggered by the neat little chrome hangle, was impressive, and they tested it so often it broke, and Mooney had to take the top off the cistern and fiddle about with it until he got it going, though it was never the same again. Both sat on it for hours but were unable to give it a full test because they couldn't relax enough on the seat to do do-do.

Wilbert's tilet pit smell rank. It caught the boys' nostrils before they pulled back the rusty zinc door of the hut and stepped inside. The torch panned across the box sending a dozen teenagers, two-inch cockroaches with glistening brown backs, slyly to cover.

'Point him down der,' Mooney said, removing the thunder box.

They moved towards the hole, which Vinton grimly estimated to be about the size of his waist. The light went down the hole. Neither said anything, then Mooney hissed, 'Jeeez. Us. Chrise.'

Vinton giggled.

They saw a one and a half metre pyramid of faeces, the whole surface of which was crawling with cockroaches and maggots.

'Over dere. Dere.'

'Ya man.'

Wilbert had thrown the bags in at an angle, so they were embedded about halfway down one side of the pyramid. Mooney counted them. 'One, two, tree ...'

'No,' said Vinton. 'I'll count dem. You get dem.'

Mooney laughed, 'Tree.'

'Dere is de brok one.' The torch caught the white powder spilling from a split packet. Three cockroaches investigated it with long twitching antennae.

'Cockroach coke yard,' said Mooney.

'Dem want fi party.'

'De coke can reach?'

'Dat mi nah know,' said Mooney.

'Try,' urged Vinton.

'Bwoy, ya kiant talk to ya bredren like dat!' exploded Mooney, standing back and crossing his arms. 'So why you nuh try fi reach i'?'

'Cas ya hand longerer dan fi mi hand.'

It was true; once he was the tallest gangliest yout in Beach, but recently it had become St John, and possibly western Jamaica. That's why one of his names was Longboy. Mooney sighed, and lay down on the floor with his head over the hole. A cockroach sped out onto his shoulder, and then his face, jinking to avoid Mooney's slaps and running down his neck into his T-shirt, where it was finally flattened with a mighty blow against his chest.

''Top ya noise,' Mooney shouted at Vinton, who started giggling again.

He put his hand into the hole; more roaches jumped onto it, but he ignored them as they scurried over his head and across his mouth. 'Hold de flashlight steady, ya'eediot and 'top laughing. Here. One ... two ... tree ...'

Thus he recovered each bag, including the broken one. Vinton took two of them down to the standpipe on the road at Egypt, a minute or two away, rinsed them down and hid them in the grass before going back for the other two. As they gasped for breath in the fetid heat of the hut, both tried to think only of what they would do with the money. Vinton first imagined huge quantities of food – dumpling, roast breadfruit, yam, and rice, all cooked by Mama who, though hard on him, and had many times beaten him with machete and stick, and thrown rock stones at him, could cook up a plate of fry fish and rice and peas like nobody else. But he was going to be rich. Rice? Rice was for de likker people dem, de sufferers, de poor people. Rich people ate chips. He conjured up vast tables covered in Whoppers, cheeseburgers, chicken nuggets and chips – all from Burger King Gloucester Avenue, Mo-Bay. But then he thought of clothes: jean trousers and shirt, matching, with pearly buttons, and Bally shoes, or Nike, or, the very thought sent a thrill through him as he washed a bag clean with his hand, both! He could be the only yout in Beach with two pairs of shoes. And flies with a functioning zip. Nobody in Beach had one of those. And he could get a socks. But then came thoughts of girls. If you were rich you could have a trailer load of girls. Go-go girls, who knew how to dance; he'd keep one all for himself, or two; he could afford it.

Mooney's fantasies ran on different lines: first he would buy Miss Myrtle, his mother, a TV and video, and a fridge freezer if he could afford it, and afterwards some clothes for his sisters Marvia and Marcia, and a shoes and a visit to Dr Bury for granny. For himself, he bought a saw, plane, tape, plumb line, hammer and set of three chisels, so he could follow his brother Nickretta into the carpentry trade. If you could work wood well, and quickly, you could really make money, he thought to himself as he brought up the last pound bag of cocaine. He then dashed to the pipe, stripped to his underpants, and gave himself a thorough bade with little bits of soap you can always find in the long lush grass around a pipe. Vinton rolled Mooney's trousers and shirt around the bags of cocaine, and walked, with Mooney striding alongside in his underpants, back towards Flossie's shed.

They decided to secrete the drugs in a hollow guango tree by the pasture, and sleep close by to keep a watch out. They were soon on the Main, feeling the warm tarmac under their feet, when they heard an argument in progress down by the fishing boats, deep in the mangrove trees, out of sight. But it wasn't like a normal fight, when two people cuss and use bad word with each other at the top of their voices and everyone in earshot grouped up to listen and laugh.

It was the Colombian with the silver gun earrings. He was shouting, but no-one was shouting back at him. The boys crept closer through the bush to see: four uniformed Police, the moustached Colombian and another Jamaican yout were ducking three gasping, choking men in the shallows. Two Police cars were pulled off the road and hidden in the bush behind them.

They heard a voice splutter, 'Please God believe we. Mi nuh touch ya cork. Mi swear i'. Mi swear i'.' There was another splash, and silence.

'Look like dem ketch Rayon,' Mooney whispered.

'An' Gaddaffi and Gaddaffi brudder Buru,' Vinton whispered back.

The four pounds of cocaine he was carrying seemed suddenly a very dangerous load for someone with his keen sense of self-preservation. Mooney crouched down, the moon glinting on his long thigh. Vinton crouched too, and suddenly heard a loud retort, like a length of calico being ripped at speed, explode from his bottom, the inevitable consequence of a double portion of Flossie's jack domplin, mackrel an' dasheen hastily consumed for lunch on top of two saff drink and eleven ripe mangoes.

'Oo dat?' shouted one of the Police. There was silence but for Buru, Gaddaffi and Rayon's gasping. The Police walked towards the boys, a flashlight glinting in his hand. 'What ya do der?' He shouted when he saw them.

'Mi a go a do-do, sah,' Vinton replied.

'Wha dat ya hold?'

'Washing far mama fi do.' Vinton held up the bundle to show the Police; a trickle of cocaine spilled from the open bag onto the ground.

'Ya Persil bag brok,' said the Police. 'Ron on now, find someplace else fi do-do.'

'Can be too late fi dat,' Vinton said under his breath.

'Ya sah,' said Mooney.

✳   ✳   ✳

The idea that night-time was for sleeping and day-time for waking never caught on in Angel Beach. In other villages, when night fell, they climbed exhaustedly into bed and woke only at dawn. But to many men and women in Angel Beach, dusk was the signal to get up and sample the unmissable tropical night. When the moon was bright and high in the starry sky, the opportunity for meeting members of the opposite sex to chat with and make friends with in the moonlight was too good to stay at home. People had to get out the yard and walk up an down. As the moon waned over the following days, and the nights perceptibly darkened, the friendships formed under the full moon were consolidated in the moonshadows, and finally consummated when the new moon set early near the end of the month, and darkness offered sweet secrecy.

During the days, Vinton and Mooney hovered always within sight of the guango tree, and at night they chill out under it – sleeping fitfully, waking with a start, and talking in lowered voices to friends and girls who passed by in the dark.

About every four hours for ten days, Vinton said to Mooney, 'Nah tell nobady, bout dis, annerstan? Nobady. Too much people looking for it fi take no risk.'

Mooney looked at him skeptically, knowing that it was he, Vinton, who was the big mouth.

The next day, at dusk, as the setting sun reddened the cliffs at the mouth of the cove, Trouble crossed the pasture and approached Vinton and Mooney.

'Mi can tek a look at de drog dem?' he asked Vinton.

Mooney looked at Vinton. Vinton said, 'Mi only tell him cas him can help we sell it. Ya have connection, true, Trouble?'

Fifteen year old Trouble said, 'Ya man. Fi sure. Mi have associates, ya know? Seen?'

They led Trouble to the tree. Vinton said, 'It five days since nobady see de Colombian or no Police. Even Rayon and Gaddaffi walk up and down pon de Main now.'

Both had emerged three or four days after the beating, Gaddaffi with a limp and Rayon with a black eye and a new name, Drogs, which everyone called out when they saw him.

'Dem nah a com back,' said Trouble, staring at the bags of coke. 'It time to market de merchandise.' He used terms he'd picked up from videos Miss Dahlia watched.

'Where we gonna sell i'? Tek it a Negril?'

'No man,' counselled Trouble. 'Dem will rob you of i' and den kill ya. Sell i' here in Beach.'

'Mi kiant sell i' from Sandra yard. She have two whities stay.'

'An' Mister Crooks gonna kill we if mi sell drog from him yard.'

'Ya man,' Trouble and Vinton agreed. 'All o' dat.'

'Let we sell i' from fi mi yard,' said Trouble.

'What 'bout Miss Dahlia?' asked Vinton.

'Tip her couple dallar, she cool.'

The following day they took a pound-bag of cocaine to the back room at Miss Dahlia's, and with Kermit looking on closely, and the toddlers Nakissia and Najia crawling amongst them, the three boys filled a hundred plastic bags each with about two grams of cocaine, and knotted the tops.

'How much we charge for each one?' asked Vinton.

Trouble picked a figure out of the air. 'Six US, or ninety J,' he said.

Vinton smiled and shook his head slowly from side to side as he filled another bag. 'Mi kiant believe dis. Mi gonna rich.'

For a day or two, business was slow. Hopton and Carlene came round, but had no money, so just stood for hours looking at the bags of coke. A couple of yout tried to hustle it to tourists who stopped at Busta's Coffee Shop, but they were the wrong type, and Busta told them to quit it. Then a whitey called Barney, the son of a prosperous New York businessman and poet, who had dropped out in Jamaica on a generous allowance, and who lived in a little house on some land his father had bought, was brought to Miss Dahlia's house by Kermit. He put a ten-inch line the thickness of a pencil out on the top of the broken television, and made all the children laugh when him sniff it. After that he bought three bags for cash, and left with Carlene and Hopton following him to his house. From then on, business picked up. Rankin's elder brother stopped by in his minibus and bought a few bags to take to Negril, and he too was soon back, along with a couple of heavy yout, who took ten bags, and paid in US dollars. The next evening, Mooney had to run back to the tree for another pound. By the end of that week, people were calling at Miss Dahlia's yard all hours of the day and night. She didn't mind. She loved it, and would prod Trouble or Vinton or Mooney if they were sleeping and scream at them to serve the customer.

Vinton was meanwhile also in demand at Sandra's yard, where he was cooking, cleaning and helping out a couple of whitey tourists called Jane and Chris from London, England who rented the place from Sandra for a couple of weeks. They looked respectable, like Christian, so he tried to give an impression of being reliable and incorruptible to them, and kept quiet about the coke yard he ran on the other side of the road, that by now was never empty, because not only were people always pulling up to buy coke and drive off, but quite a few customers were living in the yard, smoking on the front porch or lying twitchily asleep by the back step till dem spend down all dem money. Things were so hectic that Miss Dahlia only managed to keep going by stirring a tablespoon of coke into a big jug of beveridge – sugar and water – which she, and the picknee, sipped all day.

Vinton's and Mooney's coke yard was a big secret that nobody knew about except the whole of Beach and a few score others, but they were protected from betrayal because the village was proud of the huge find, and overjoyed at last to witness a commercial success within the village limits. Everybody except the Christians wanted to see it flourish, but the Christians knew better than to report them to the Police.

Chris and Jane left Sandra's yard for the airport at the end of their holiday. They thanked Vinton for looking after them, gave him their address in London and told him to look them up if he was ever over. Having a foreign address on a bit of paper was almost as glamorous as foreign travel in Angel Beach, so Vinton treasured the scrap, and kept it in a lada bag inna de bush with his few other personal possessions.

Sandra came back wearing new clothes of stone-wash denim she'd bought with the rent money.

'Vintan,' she snapped. 'Clear up de back room and shine de flaar dem. Some guest from Kingston come fi turn in mi yard for a couple day fram tomorrow. An' rake de yard, an' ron an' buy mi one tin mackerel fram Maas Greville, an',' she added, perhaps sensing it was getting a bit harder to push Vinton around, 'tek tree dallar fram de change fi yasel.'

Later, when he was on all fours rubbing at the dyed pine floor with the coconut brush, sweat dripping off his nose, Sandra stood watching him, greedily eating a bun and cheese. Only the thought that he had sixty US dollars hidden away, and a half share in the remaining few pounds of coke, sustained him.

'Dem say sambady buck up pon de coke dat lost,' Sandra said as she bit off another knob of bun and cheese.

'Dat so?'

'Dat whad mi hear,' Sandra said, her pretty mouth chewing cake. 'Ya ever hear of Telaviv posse?'

'Ya man. Everybady hear o' dat.'

'De men dat com fi stay tomorrer fram Tel Aviv. Dem want fi find who have dem coke. Dem bredren o' mine from old days. Dem heavy, man, heavy,' she added with a dreamy smile.

'Dat so?'

'Ya man, so look after dem good while dem stay in mi yard. What dem want ya give dem it. Annerstan?'

'Sure, Sandra, no problem.'

They arrived late at night, when the village, except for Miss Dahlia's yard, was silent, emerging from a blacked-out BMW wearing sunglasses, one of the bredren carrying a sports holdall. Vinton was immediately dispatched by Sandra to wake Flossie and open up the shed for a dozen hot Dragon Stout.

'Shed close,' she shouted through her wooden wall.

'No Mumma, ya got to open up. Sandra friend dem want couple drink.'

'Tell dem fi drink water from de pipe.'

'Mumma, dem from Telaviv posse inna Kinstan.'

There was rustling inside, and the wooden louvred shutters opened. Flossie's podgy hand held out the key to the padlock on the shed. 'Nuh touch nuttin yaself, boy.'

'Yes Mumma.'

Vinton entered Sandra's house to see the holdall lying open on the floor, with the men sitting round oiling two handguns and one Uzi. He steadied himself on the lintel, and then handed out the bottles, getting no thanks, or even acknowledgement of his presence. Only Sandra addressed him.

'Wait outside in the yard,' she snapped. 'And nuh com near de house.'

Vinton crouched beside the road thinking about the guns when a car drew up from the direction of Negril, and a guy shouted, 'Wishart de coke yard, boy?' out of the window.

'Der not no coke yard ere,' he replied, choking on the fry fish an' buller he tief from Flossie shed. A motorbike then drew up from the other direction with four youth on it, two white and two Jamaicans. They all got off and the bike fell over, but they just laughed before stumbling across the verge to Miss Dahlia's yard.

'Dat where i' is,' said the man in the car.

Vinton called out to Kermit, who was patrolling the Main, despite it being four in the morning, for customers.

'Ron fetch me Mooney,' Vinton whispered to him over Mister Poole's old hibiscus hedge.

When Mooney came, Vinton told him all he had seen and heard.

'Us moss stop Dahlia sell more coke straight way,' Vinton said with terror in his voice.

'Let I ron over and tell Dahlia fi stop sell coke, close down de yard and cool out for a couple day till de posse ride outta town.'

'Ya tink dat kian work?'

'No, but mi kiant tink o' nottin else dat might.'

With those hopeful words Mooney slipped away into the darkness, passing the four men on the motorbike who were arguing at the tops of their voices about who could drive the fastest with them all on board.

Mooney came back with Trouble flashing his ratchet knife at his side.

'Wishart de gun men?' he shouted. 'Nobady gonna tief ya coke fram ya, Vinton! Dem try, mi cut dem troat.'

Trouble had clearly been at Miss Dahlia's beverage.

'Nuh joke man,' said Vinton desperately, while Mooney tried to hold him back.

Then someone came onto Sandra's porch.

'Ssh,' said Vinton to his friends.

'Vintan,' Sandra whispered, sharply.

'Mi de com,' he replied, pushing Trouble behind the hedge.

'Tek dis man inna de bush and show him where fi hide him bag, and den stay wid i' until mi call ya.'

'Ya man.'

Thus Vinton led the gunman, who he heard being addressed as Fumes, into the thicket of sea grape and wist that grew up around Sandra's yard. In a darkened clearing he said, 'Dis place good fi hide.'

Fumes passed him the bag effortlessly, said, 'Nuh bodder de bag, and no let nobady elkse touch i', annerstan?' and then moved off silently the way he came. The bag was heavy. Vinton put it down with a muffled clinking noise on the sandy ground and crouched beside it. He could smell the gun oil. A moment later there was a rustling of the bushes and Mooney appeared.

'What Miss Dahlia say?' Vinton asked.

'He gonna try fi ease back de cork deal dem.'

Vinton looked down and shook his head. 'Dis ting gonna bad,' he said.

Mooney said, 'What inna de bag?'

'Gon dem,' said Vinton.

'Gon?'

'Ya man. One tirty-eight Taurus revolver, an' a tirty-two

semi-automatic, and even one Uzi.' The youth of Jamaica knew the names of all the guns.

'Why dem want one Uzi in Angel Beach?' Mooney asked.

'Fi kill we,' answered Vinton miserably.

'Jeezus,' said Mooney slowly, as he absorbed the truth. 'So what we gonna do?'

'Dis,' said Vinton seriously. 'Load up de magazines. Mi tek de Uzi, you hangle de two pistol dem. Mi kick down de front door and squeeze off couple hundred round inna de house, and you hide roun' the back and kill anybady who run out the back door.' He looked at his wrist. He had no watch, but said, 'Alright. Synchronise watches.'

Mooney said, 'Ya idiot. How can ya joke at time like dis?'

'Mi nuh joke,' said Vinton. 'Now is time for de Angel Beach posse fi strike back at Telaviv. Ya man. It gonna easy now us ave de weaponry.'

'Vinton mi know yah too coward fi even open up dat bag.'

'Cho! Nuh talk to de don like dat.'

'So what we gonna do?' Mooney asked again.

After a long pause Vinton said, 'Mi tink mi better try fi talk wid Sandra. Maybe she can elp we.'

When later he tapped on Sandra's bedroom wall, there was the sound of rustling and a man's low voice. He should have known Sandra would link op wid one o' de bredren.

'Sandra, it Vinton. Mi need fi talk wid ya.'

'Wishart de bag?' the man's voice snapped.

'Mooney watch de bag.'

There was some murmuring in the room, then the door opened and Sandra slipped out.

When they were away from the house, standing by the lapping sea at the edge of the yard, Vinton said, 'Sandra, ya know ya say dat somebady buck up pon de coke?'

'Ya man. Ya hear who?' she asked excitedly.

'Ya, mi know.'

'Good boy. Tell mi. 'Oo?'

'Mi an' Mooney.'

'You an' Mooney? You an' Garnett?'

'Yes.'

Sandra paused while her mind raced over the possibilities for personal gain that this intelligence presented her. Her first thought was not, it must be admitted, for the welfare of her employee and his friend.

'You an' Mooney?' she repeated.

'Ya,' said Vinton miserably, hanging his head.

'Wishart de coke?'

'Mi hide it inna one tree.'

'Good boy. Ow much ya ave?'

'Two bag and one half.'

'Ow big de bag dem?'

'Like bag o' sugar. One pound. Ya tink mi gonna dead?'

'Mebbe nat if ya do as mi say. Anybady elkse know bout de coke?'

'Ya.'

'Mooney.'

'Anybady elkse?'

'Ya man. Ole heap o' people know.'

'Bumber claat. Ya eediot, why ya tell dem?'

'Cas mi sell some o' de coke fram Miss Dahlia yard.'

'Ow much ya sell?'

'Mebbe two or tree hondred US.'

'Jos a couple of gram. Dat no problem.'

'Good,' said Vinton, smiling for the first time in three hours. Then he asked, 'Ow big is one gram? Like half a bag o' sugar? Gram like pound?' But Sandra wasn't listening.

'If ya nuh wanna dead, den bring mi all de coke and all

de money. All av it, an me try fi cool out de Telaviv bredren. Gwaan now, and com back soon.'

Back in the seagrape thicket, Vinton said to Mooney, 'Ow much dallar we gonna give back?'

'Mi ave two ondred and ninety US, an six ondred J.'

'Ow much ya gonna give back?'

'What ya mean, boy? Cho! Jus do what de woman say or de don kill ya.'

'Dem nuh scare mi,' laughed Vinton. 'Mi ave two ondred and mi gonna give one ondred and ten US and couple ondred J.'

Early the next morning Vinton and Mooney were lined up in Sandra's house in front of Fumes and his two bredren from the Telaviv posse. On the table that Mr Poole had made so lovingly for Jackie and the kids, stood two pound bags of white cocaine. Vinton had given Sandra two and a half, but the half bag had mysteriously disappeared. Next to the cocaine were two hundred and ten US dollars in crumpled notes. Beside that was a 9mm pistol, and beside that was Fumes' hand, ready to pick it up and use it.

'Ya want we fi believe dat ya find four bag o' coke pon de beach, and sell tree pound, dat twelve ondred gram, an get tree ondred US far it?'

'De yout one liard,' said one of the gunmen, darkly. He stood up, took the gun off the table and put it against Vinton's temple. Vinton thought to himself that he had two options: one, to bluff it out, and the other to tell the truth and beg for mercy.

'Tell de man de trut' Vinton,' Sandra said.

Vinton thought: Come on. Be like a bad boy. Big up your status. Bluff it. But he said, 'Mi sorry sah, mi just remember mi have anudder couple dallar dat mi forget complete about. Mebbe mi kian ron an' fetch i'.'

He ran to and from his hiding place in the bush and was soon back with the money, which he laid on the table.

The sinister small gunman laughed. 'Ya want we fi believe dat all de money ya have?'

'Ya sah. Dat all de money we take.'

'Far twelve ondred gram?' The man brought the gun up to Vinton's head again.

'Mi swear.'

'Ease up, Badeye, de yout tell de trut',' said Sandra, with a little look at Vinton which said you are going to shine a lot of floors and run a lot of errands for this.

With the exception of Badeye, the gunmen inexplicably started to laugh. Vinton was hurt. 'Why ya laugh?' he asked.

'Why we laugh? Cas ya sell out cocaine wort forty tousand dallar.'

'Ya nah have no more coke leave noplace? Nobady have no more?' asked Badeye.

Out of the corner of his eye, Vinton saw Sandra look at him. He felt the gun jab into his side.

'None leave but dis, sah,' he said, and gave Sandra a look which said I don't think I'll be shining quite as many floors or running so many errands as you thought.

'And ya no give no money to nobady elkse?' asked Badeye.

'We give a couple dollar to Miss Dahlia,' Mooney said.

'Oo dat?' they asked Sandra.

'De lady who yard dem use over de road,' Sandra explained.

'Ow much ya give her?'

'Mi nah remember.' Out came the gun again, this time to be pressed into Vinton's kidneys from behind. 'Two ondred and tharty US, bout.'

There was a small crowd already assembled at Miss

Dahlia's yard all looking for coke before Badeye strode out of Sandra's yard and, pausing for a huge coach of tourists to roar by, trotted across the road. Kermit saw the dark, oiled metal of the gun he held nonchalantly at his side, yelped 'Wickid!' and skipped along behind him.

'Wishart Miss Dahlia?' Badeye shouted at the house. 'Com ya.'

'Oo want her?' Miss Dahlia called from inside.

'One man 'bout a likker business.'

'Mi nah have no coke leave. Go way fram ere. Dat finish.'

'Mi know dat finish. It mi who tek i'. Now come out, mi want fi talk wid ya.'

Miss Dahlia came to the door. She sweated and had to support her enormous bulk on the frame.

'Granny,' said the man, 'mi hear ya ave someting dat belong fi mi.'

'Nuh sah. Everyting mi ave, belong fi mi. Now go out mi yard yout, before mi mek ya.'

The assembled and fast-growing crowd of spectators drew in their breath with admiration. There was Kermit and his sisters Nakissia and Najia, the girls with buckets of water from the pipe on their heads, there was Linda from the Back Street, wearing one high heel shoe and one trainer, there was Trouble, looking bleary, and Trevor looking excited, and there was Miss Liza, who stopped on the way to catch a minibus to Content, in addition to a few assorted coke heads. All of them saw Miss Dahlia insult the gun-man, and turn casually into her house, and all of them saw the gunman's face twist in fury at being dis by an old woman.

'Yo, Granny. Mi talk wid ya. When mi talk wid ya, nuh move off till mi tell ya. Somebady tell mi ya sell drog here.'

'Dat no concern of you,' Miss Dahlia shouted from inside.

'Ya man. It is so. Cas the cork ya sell is fi mi and mi bredren cork.'

'It nuh go so, boy,' Miss Dahlia answered, coming to the door again. 'Dat coke lost at sea, and somebady find i'. Mi no tief. You is de tief, come fi get mi money. But you nah gonna ave i', so ron on, ya likker man now.'

'Dat coke belong to me, so give mi mi money.' He lifted his gun for the first time.

'Ya want fi kill mi? Go on, shoot, ya blaad claat fool. Kill mi. Bot ya nah gonna get no money, cas dat belong to mi.'

Badeye started to talk, but Miss Dahlia turned into her house, saying, 'Bumber claat,' and pushed the door closed behind her. Badeye lost his temper at this. He ran at the house, leapt onto the porch and burst inside after her, slipping his gun into the back of his belt as he moved. He was inside for only a moment before the crowd heard the horrible crack of fist on flesh and bone, followed by the thud of a foot well practised at brutal violence stabbing into an abdomen again and again, with sickening force. There followed the terrible sound of a body crashing heavily onto splintering furniture, and the moan that came from a spasm of tortuous pain.

Half a minute later the door opened slowly, and the hunched, groaning figure of Badeye half-crawled, and half-stumbled out onto the porch. Miss Dahlia appeared in the door frame, holding the gun.

'Gwaan back a Kinstan!' she shouted. 'An' nuh com back ya if ya nuh want mi fi beat ya again.'

In Sandra's house, Fumes and his brudder were loading the coke and the guns into the holdall. When they heard Badeye call them, all three got into the BMW and sped out of the yard and out of Beach on the road to Mo-Bay, Ocho Rios, Fern Gully and Kingston.

Miss Dahlia sold the gun to some bad boys in Negril for thirty US dollars, Sandra sold her half pound of cocaine to the Police in Negril for one thousand US, and Vinton and Mooney spent the next few weeks in each other's company, tending to avoid their friends, with their tedious jokes about selling forty thousand US dollars of coke for three hundred dollars. One of their favourite occupations was sitting on the rocks behind Flossie's shed, staring out to sea, looking for anything small and white floating free on the water.

YAMI AVE A VISION

Giarbage was no problem in Beach. If you have giarbage, you dash i' away inna de bush or inna de sea. Den it no problem. 'Cept the whitey always complain 'bout litter an' giarbage, and that make the government do someting 'bout i'. A tourist in a criss Rental would pull up by Busta's bar, or Blender's shed, step out on the soft pale sand, gaze at the sparkling sea in the pretty bay with miles of wet green jungle all around him, and then notice a candy wrapper maybe the size of a postage stamp that was hidden in the grass and say to his wife, 'Can you believe this, honey? Look. Litter. How can they ruin it like this?'

But in Negril the problem got serious. The hotels were flinging their garbage into the sea, and sometimes it drifted back onto the beach right in front of the sunbathing tourists. The coloured plastic packaging looked good floating on the water, but it vex the tourists, and they just called it dirty. Nobody had the courage to tell them that the plastic garbage wasn't nearly as dirty as the raw hotel sewage being flushed into the sea by underwater pipe just beyond the rubbish.

The big people dem dat own Zoo, Sclandals, Negril Tree 'Ouse and the other big hotels found a piece of government land by the Main in Lemon Grove and mek it turn domp. There were a few yards on it, but most of the likker people dem who lived in them were happy about the bounty that suddenly came their way, for the dump was a big success: chocks loaded with giarbage com dung from every hotel, restaurant and bar in Negril in the west and as far as Content in the east. Soon the domp was six chains wide and nearly a mile long, an immense, stinking, smouldering treasure trove, for the white man binned all kinds of things which were by local standards not rubbish at all. A cursory search yielded pornographic magazines, batteries that weren't flat, lada bags, books, children's toys, and razors. An hour spent in the company of the limping dogs, busy children and slow-moving adults of the tip, could be rewarded by a camera or watch, which although non-functioning, was nevertheless a prize.

The smell was not good, everybody admitted that, and it grew thicker and more noxious when the new slaughter house near Grange Hill began dumping scraps of cattle hide and rendered carcasses which festered spectacularly in the hot sun. In the heavy humidity and soaring forty-degree afternoons of the summer, the stench grew so bad people said you could see it. When the wind blew from the east, you could smell the Lemon Grove dump so unmistakably nine miles down the coast in Beach that it became one of the seven wonders of the village.

High on the hill above Lemon Grove there was a criss new housing estate for the rich people. The homes were all wall houses, with fancy concrete walls around the gardens, car-ports with a door that went straight into the house, and ornate wrought-iron security bars on the porch, where the big people sat to enjoy the breeze wafting off the Caribbean. Everyone said that if the smell got as far up the hill as the Lemon Grove Estate the dump would be closed. It did, and no lesser man than Judge Horace Walpole led the campaign to close it. He wrote a long letter to the Gleaner, he made representations to Andy Chin, the local Member of Parliament, and attended a special meeting of the Negril Town Council. He even rang Barbara Gludon on RJR radio to complain about 'the deplorable pollution caused as a result of the instigation of an unauthorised rubbish facility at Aringe Bay', but none of this worked. The Negril Chamber of Commerce said that the dump had to stay if the government wanted tourism to increase in western Jamaica. As the tourist industry was the only thing keeping Jamaica from absolute bankruptcy, nothing was done. The domp grew and grew, and smelled worse than ever, so bad, in fact, people were forced to invent a new word to describe it. They stopped saying, 'Dat domp smell bud,' and said instead, 'Dat domp green, man. It green bud. Serious. It greeeen.'

Right on the top of the hill, some quarter of a mile above the big people's housing estate at Lemon Grove, lived Leroy Mckenzie, the biggest ganje dealer in western Jamaica. He built an ornate white concrete house with four balconies and dozens of yards of concrete balusters. There was a swimming pool full of his fat children and extensive grounds patrolled, they said, by armed bredren of the Don. When the stench reached Mckenzie he spoke to the Negril Chamber of Commerce. They explained once again the impossibility of moving the dump or closing it down. He spoke to them again. The next week news came through to the people that the domp was moving.

The question was where would the domp go? There were certain limitations: it had to be on the Main, or near it, and could be no further than twenty miles from Negril. The Negril Chamber of Commerce identified various pieces of land: and each time a place was mentioned, the people dem rise op gainst i'. Little London was suggested and then dropped, because of local opposition, and then Sandy Island was identified. Every other village supported this idea, if only to prevent the dump coming their way. 'It moss be Sandy Island.' Vices argued in Angel Beach. 'Consider de name. The place call green cas it gwine green.' But Dr Bury, who owned the land in Sandy Island, and who negotiated a lucrative rent for the site, had his yard surrounded by furious villagers and was forced to drop the project for his own safety.

The next place they picked was Angel Beach, but at dawn, the day after the rumour swept through the village, Flossie and Miss Dahlia formed a roadblock on the Main with the eight picknee from their yards. The roadblock was considered the basic democratic right in Beach, more basic than voting, which only people who could read and write got to do. But anybody could form a roadblock, and many did, because only if you stopped the traffic did the big people dem listen. Although Miss Dahlia and Flossie and Trouble tipped over trash cans, and burned tyres on the road, stopping all the traffic, they were only actually after one car, a black Toyota Landcruiser which came through every morning at seven twenty, driven by Mr Dunbar McFarlane, a member of the Negril Chamber of Commerce.

When Kermit ran down the line of cars to the barricade shouting, 'Mumma, him a com, him a com,' the two women whose combined weight was thirty-seven stones, or 518 pounds, bore down on the poor man, who quickly pushed down the lock on his car door when he saw them. Half the crowd didn't know what the issue was about, and the other probably wouldn't have minded the domp anyway, but after a swift discussion with the two women, Councillor McFarlane agreed to keep it out of Beach all the same.

Beach had no official council, or instrument of local government with any influence whatsoever. Village government was undertaken entirely unofficially only when it was needed, by anybody who could be bothered to do it – like Flossie and Miss Dahlia with the roadblock. In Firefly Bay things were run differently. They had a parish council, with a sub-committee for economic development, and they had an active Rotary Club and Kiwanis Club, all of which had the main aim of developing Firefly Bay, because Firefly Bay was determined to go places. This is how, against the wishes of de mijarity av de likker people, Firefly Bay made a formal request to the Negril Chamber of Commerce for the domp. The terms were straightforward: in return for a mile of tarmac road up into the hills, the electrification of thirty houses above the Main, and a rent of thirty thousand J a year, they were prepared to fill up a long undisturbed gully half a mile long and three hundred yards deep, thick with mighty cotton trees, and harbouring a clear-water stream, with the hotel rubbish from Negril.

Councillor Harold Hoyte (chairman of Rotary Club, Kiwanis Club and the Firefly Bay Masonic Chapter), with the deputy chairman of the Firefly Bay Parish Council, The Honourable Mrs Shirley Hoyte, resident magistrate, proudly made the announcement of the successful bid for the domp, at a specially convened meeting in the Firefly Bay Primary School.

'This development is a major step forward for our community,' said the Councillor, to a round of appreciative applause from the seated, and hatted, burghers of Firefly Bay. But at that, from the back of the hall a bare-chested rastaman with long locks and sleepy eyes called out, 'Dis one fool ting. Ya nah fill de land av Jah wid pollution fram de white man, or Jah com down and seek retribution wid one tundebult or eart quake or orricane dat will smite ya dead.'

''Top ya noise, Yami,' somebody shouted. 'We want corrent in fi we yard for teevee and fridge. We want our village to get rich. If ya nah like i', den bwai, gwaan fram ere.'

'Ya man!' a few people yelled, laughing. 'Ya want to poor al ya life ya eedit dread?'

'Money is not my richness,' Yami declaimed at the voices railing against him. 'My richness is to live and walk pon the earth barefoot.' This brought a gale of derision from the baldead standing around him. At that, he picked up the rod he was never without, hoisted his bag onto his shoulder, and with his head held proudly high, he started his walk back to his yard, high in the hills, overlooking the gully which the Parish Council were going to fill to the brim with giarbage.

The majority of land in Beach was owned by Mr Webster, who had a family of children whom he loved, but who, it turned out when he died, inexplicably left all his lands to the lawyer who made his will, a man of Asian extraction who resided in Canada. When squatters, led by Miss Dahlia, became recalcitrant, he sold it in a job lot to a white man whom Sandra cleverly brought to Beach from the beach in Negril. He had little idea of the political powder keg he was buying.

Only one section of the coast wasn't owned by Mr Webster, and that was an exquisitely beautiful strip of land on the western side of the cove, across the creek from Flossie's shed and Sandra's yard. When you walked through the woods to the sea you came upon a lagoon perfect for swimming, flashing with tropical fish that darted into caves hollowed by the crystal sea out of limestone cliffs. This plot fell into the hands of a Chinese-Jamaican businessman called Mister Ronny. Everybody in Beach had big plans, and Mister Ronny was no exception. People hoped he was going to build a sky-scraper hotel with one big car park, but he went one better than that: he was going to flatten the forest to build a container port, complete with warehousing and cranes, and dynamite the coral reef at the mouth of the cove to form a deep water harbour for freight shipping. For days they bragged about their luck up and down the Main. Even Trouble, who had relocated to Negril, and had lately been scorning Beach whenever he returned on a visit, had to admit the plan was wickid.

Beach engendered great plans, schemes big enough to lift the place out of the ranks of other sleepy fishing villages and transform it into a top resort, where tourists milled about in hundreds, carelessly throwing bucks around. Hopton's Rock Top Cave was planned to be a Dunn's River Falls, but no-one ever came to the smelly dank cave and the sign went mouldy and fell off the tree. A German called Hojan built and opened a huge and ugly restaurant called The Poseidon, but its massive car park grassed over with disuse and the place closed down. If only half the plans came off, Beach would be like Negril, or Ochi, but unfortunately none did, and the cafes, sheds and bars remained determinedly empty, the fry fish and bammy and bon and cheese in the glass showcases consumed only by the people who made them and their friends, while all day and all night hissing coaches full of tourists roared by on their way to and from the airport.

Mister Ronny's surveyor and builder spent two days surrounded by picknee on Mister Ronny's land, planning the container port. They discovered the sea had undermined the rock and made it unsuitable to build heavy structures on, so the whole scheme was scrapped. Mister Ronny put the land up for sale and began to look elsewhere to locate his container port. Shepherd Bush George was going to offer him fifty acres he owned, until it was pointed out that land without sea frontage wasn't very useful for a port.

Mister Crooks, who had hoped to be a subcontractor on the wharf, said, 'Seem like nottin never gwine big up Beach now,' and talked of leaving the village where he was born and raised fifty years earlier. Only the two German men who netted little tropical fish from the reef for exports to pet shops in Germany, and who had built a big house on the hill on the proceeds of the business, were happy that the project had fallen through.

Mister Ronny's land was finally sold in 1987 to a tax attorney from New York called Brian who wanted to quit the city and start a new life. Brian was a tall, slender man of fifty who wore a bandana, combat fatigues and had an abiding interest in guerilla warfare and the art of survival in the jungle. He cut a clearing in the forest and erected a palisade of sharply pointed staves, as if at any moment he was going to be attacked. Behind the staves he lived a manly existence amongst his tools, bedding down in a hammock slung across the inside of a camouflaged tent.

One day, while sawing down trees on the edge of his property he came upon a small encampent made by Yami, the dreadlock who had fled the domp in Firefly Bay. There was a rough bed made of old sugar sacks under a cane trash lean-to, and a wooden bench by a fire that burned on a mound of ash two feet high. Yami looked up from the fire and saw Brian crashing through the undergrowth with a machete in his hand and a combat knife strapped to his shin.

'What the hell are you doing here? This is my property. Get off it.'

Yami took a long pull on the brown paper spliff he held in his hand, and then passed it to Brian, bidding him sit down.

'No way man,' Brian snapped angrily. 'I gotta sort this situation out. You're squatting on my property.'

'Den mi will pick up mi bag and rod and go. Bot first let we smoke a spliff of ganje, far de Lard say "He causeth the grass to grow far de cakkle, an' herb far de service of man, that he may bring forth food pon dis eart'"'.'

'That's the Bible, right?'

'Ya man,' smiled Yami, holding out the spliff, 'so let we give tanks and do de Lard's work.'

Brian took the spliff and settled beside the fire, watching the thin plume of blue smoke rise up into the jungle canopy.

'You got too much ash on that fire. It's gonna clog the flames. You wanna clear it out, or better still construct a concrete incinerator. Then you'll get an efficient fire without any heat wastage. Plus you can throw trash on it.'

'Dis flame never out, day and night dis fire burn for Jah. An' mi never put no trash on i', only logwood and can be ganja ash, not cigarette or no plastic or nottin unrighteous. Dem tings Babylarn. Den de ground and de bush and de air, and maybe de people,' here he gave Brian a distant, but winning smile, 'take good vibes from de fire. Mi ave one vision from Jah, and Jah tell mi fi com down a sea an' burn logwood trough de day and night, and ya haffi live ya vision.' His head then disappeared from view behind a huge white cloud of exhaled ganja smoke.

'This herb tastes good,' Brian remarked.

'Yah man, herb is the healing av de nation, ya know? Herb like fruit. Keep you healty, mind clear, a true.'

'Ya man,' agreed Brian.

'The more people smoke, the more Babylarn fall.'

They sat in silent contented contemplation for an hour and three quarters, which was a short while by Yami's standards. Brian's stoned head spun with a vortex of non-sequential thoughts along with the sight of the shirtless dreadlock beside him, his matted brown hair cascading down his muscled brown back. High above them, a flock of green parrots screeched amongst the shards of sunlight in the dark canopy. Brian had planned to 'drop' these trees with one of his buzz saws, for 'security reasons'. They impeded 'clarity of vision'. But sitting with Yami by the fragrant hardwood fire he felt that perhaps he would put off the job till another day. It was the first time in two weeks he had stopped strutting about with a weapon of some sort in his hand, and contemplated where he was.

Later, Yami explained to Brian that Jah had sent him a second command in another vision: to build a tourist bar on Brian's plot of land. Incredibly, Brian listened carefully, and said, 'Well I guess if Jah told you to, we'd better get on and build it.'

Brian loved construction, but it was obvious from the beginning that he hated tourists – he wasn't that keen on people; the palisade of sharpened stakes was hardly a welcome mat, after all, but he was charmed by Yami, whose rastaman ways cast a spell over him. The tourist coaches, which were audible from his property, got on his nerves. Like a lot of foreign white people in Jamaica, Brian felt he wasn't a tourist, and thought that the presence of other tourists devalued his own experience, which he considered authentic, while theirs of course was phoney and commercialised.

He imported a lot of expensive woodworking machines from the States, like computerised lathes and turning machines, and Yami brought down some dread bredren from inna de hills to work them. Within a couple of months all the machines were broken, but by then a large circular bar had been built, full of hardwood chairs and tables, at which the dreads lounged comfortably for most of the day.

In addition to the heavy machinery and tools, Brian imported a stencil set, with which he set to work making a lot of off-putting signs for his customers. There was a fine tradition of signage in Angel Beach. Every one of Beach's tourist attractions and businesses was signed on the Main; indeed, the sign was the most important part of the enterprise in Beach. For some, a bar or some other flimsy attraction was merely an excuse to design, commission and erect a sign. There were twelve signs on either side of the Main in Angel Beach Bottom Side. Coming from Mo-Bay, the first was Hojan, the German's sign for The Poseidon Bar Restaurant and Grill. The bar went bust within three months of opening – a real success story for Beach, but the sign lived on for years, its rather deformed porpoise flapping in the breeze for months before finally being recycled as a table top by Gucci. His MOONRISE GUESTHOUSE sign, in bright red with black writing, was the next sign. From then on, they came thick and fast. HOPTON'S ROCK TOP CAVE started off quite small, but when the business failed to attract tourists, instead of examining the disgusting state of the cave, which was used by all Hopton's staff as a latrine, he did what every struggling business in Beach did: increase the size and claims of his sign. His new one was two metres square, and read STOP AT WORLD FAMOUS HOPTON'S ROCK-

TOP CAVE TOURIST SPOT COACHES WELCOME. It drew in no more customers, but was much admired by the village, and did big up Hopton's status. The next sign, a few hundred yards on, was opposite Gaddaffi's shed. It was a small metal government one on a pole that had read NARROW BRIDGE, but was painted over by Gaddaffi to read COOL BEER. It goes without saying that in Gaddaffi's shed there was no beer cooler than the tropical climate, but nevertheless the sign did make tourists stop in Beach because it dramatically increased the number of collisions on the river bridge, so it was considered a tremendous success. Busta's Coffee Shop had three signs, advertising fresh orange juice, fried fish and coffee, at various points over the next fifty yards, and then beyond him, as the road rose and began to leave Angel Beach Bottom Side there was a criss black and white sign for Flossie's Shed, that read PLEASE REPLACE ALL DIVOTS, which Wordswort had found floating in the sea near the big Tryall Hotel golf course in St James, and another, past Sandra's yard, which Trevor and Mooney put up which said ONE STOP COOL DRINK FISH LUCKY STRIKE TOURIST VIEW POINT. This sign represented a new development in the Beach business community: it was a stand alone sign, with no business of any kind attached to it. Much admired, it gave its owners all the kudos and fun of having a sign without any of the hard work, worry and of course cost, of actually running a commercial enterprise.

To these signs Brian added many more. Yami wanted to open the bar before it was finished, but Brian said, in an early indication of disinterest in actually serving any customers, that nobody should be allowed in until all the building and landscaping was completed. This dumbfounded Yami, who could see how adequate the facilities were and how beautiful the gardens were looking. Often, if the palisade gate was left open accidentally, passing tourists, seeing the delightful location, pulled over and wandered in asking if it were possible to get a drink and have a swim in the lagoon. Brian always chased them out rudely. There was another problem attached to waiting until the building was completed, as far as Yami was concerned: no building project in Angel Beach had ever been completed, by anybody.

A name for Yami and Brian's bar, One Love Café, came to Yami in another vision from Jah. Brian produced a huge six-colour sign to hang outside the pallisade, as well as many smaller ones for erection within. Four, on the Main, read DO NOT PARK HERE, and one over the doorway read WATCH YOUR STEP. It might have been meant figuratively, but there was actually a small and undangerous step down on the path below it. Inside, were many more: DO NOT PASS THIS POINT. NO LITTER. NO IDLERS. NO FOOD OR DRINK IN THIS AREA. NO CHILDREN. Had Yami been able to read them, he would have been dismayed, but as he couldn't, he loved them. Encouraged, Brian made more signs: when Yami built a handsome mahoe and cedar bench overlooking the lagoon, a flex spot to sit and watch the sun drop into the sea at sunset, Brian added the final touch: a painted sign saying DO NOT SIT.

Yami managed eventually to persuade Brian to open the gates to customers, if only for limited periods. Brian tried to close the place between the months of November and May, i.e. the tourist season, 'for maintenance', but Yami played his trump card, and said Jah had sent him a vision in which One Love Café was open all year round. Brian then tried to restrict the hours of opening, 'for security reasons', but could only enforce them while he was present. When tourists did turn up, he couldn't deny they were open and resorted to other off-putting techniques. He'd hand out menus saying things like, 'Oh, by the way, everything's off,' or 'I don't advise the fish, the chef got food poisoning from it last night. Well, we think it was the fish, it could have been the chicken or the vegetarian dish.'

Outside the palisade, where the likker people dem of Beach group up inna de shade of de guango fi watch proceeding, a debate about Yami was well advanced. People had seen him arrive with his rod and shoulder bag from Firefly Bay and set up camp beside the sea, and presumed he was a rental dread trying to capture land from Mr Ronny. Except there was something special about him: he had cursed Firefly Bay, a whole village. Even if the curse was empty, it was impressive enough, for words really meant something in Beach.

Maxwell, who had spent time staring at the logwood fire with Yami before Brian turned up, was the only inhabitant of Beach to admit to liking Yami. Idling with Gaddaffi in the shade of the long-armed guango tree, he said, 'Nuh mock de dread,' when Gaddaffi dis Yami.

'Ya man,' said Gaddaffi. 'Mi like all colours. We all de same. Black, white, whatever. Cept rastafarians, wid dem lang hair and beard. Me don't like dem, man. Dem wortless. For sure.'

'No man, rental dread wortless, who take coke and tief white wooman monny,' argued Trevor. 'But Yami not rental. Him bongo dread. Him nyam only ital food and burn logwood fire all trough de night. Ya haffi respec Yami. Serious man. Him ave one vision from Jah dat tell him fi build one tourist bar in Beach.'

Gaddaffi laughed at that.

'Nuh laugh, man,' warned Trevor. 'Nuh mock de dread. Him cast spell pon Firefly Bay.'

'And what happen to Firefly Bay after him cast him spell?'

Gaddaffi spat. 'Eh? Mi tell ya what. Nottin. Jah don't send no rental dread no vision. Him just tell Brian dat fi get one job.'

'No man. Him say monny is nat him richness.'

That made Gaddaffi laugh, long and loud, and all the other people who were listening, Vash, Squeecher his brother, Sophia and Mooney, laughed too.

Brian had to make a trip back to the States for a hair transplant to cure his baldness, about which, you could tell from the bandana, scarves and large assortment of hats he sported, he was tortuously self-conscious. Of all his problems, it was the one he need not have worried about: in Jamaica there was no distinction made between short hair and pattern baldness. Both are called bald 'ead. Brian could not have picked a country where baldness had less of a stigma attached to it. To many Jamaicans baldness had a cachet; it meant you could afford fi trim at de barber. One entertainer even boasted about it, calling himself Shinehead. So many people shaved their heads nobody even noticed who couldn't grow hair, and certainly nobody cared. There was not even a word for baldness, it was so inconsequential. Still, Brian went to the States for his hair transplant, dreaming perhaps of returning two weeks later with locks like Yami's.

While he was away, the gates of One Love Café were thrown open, and the place filled with curious, slightly nervous tourists, who swam, drank, and just chill out with Yami. He loved working as a waiter. He had difficulty understanding the whities' English but that didn't matter. Dreads did not need to know English; it only diminished their mystery and exposed them to difficult and searching questions about their religion and lifestyle. Yami just laugh an' chill an say ya man, ya man, until it was obvious he'd said the wrong thing, and then he say nor man, nor man. Seduction of tourists by rastas more often than not turned on some kind of misunderstanding, and had both sides been able to understand each other fully, would never have occurred so frequently. The fact is, and this was what vex bald 'ead bud, de white gal dem love de rastafarian.

Rasta is a religion for the twenty-first century. It has all the ingredients for huge growth in post-Christian times. With no written rules or formal church structure anybody could define what it involved without fear of being wrong. From the start, it was the perfect religion for people who no longer wanted to be in a flock. All of its adherents were archbishops in the matters of liturgy and theology. Yet in addition to this, Rastafarianism had all the conventional components of a world religion, starting with a magnetic and charismatic messiah, Emperor Haile Selassie, the coolest black man in sixteen centuries, who stared out of his portraits with a lot of attitude, wrapped in a leopard-skin stole. The religion's St Paul was Marcus Mosiah Garvey, the man who roared, 'Rise up you mighty people!' and inspired black people all over the world, before the white man jailed him, and as hymnographer there was Bob Marley, the man whose blood was made of equal parts of riddim an' love. He was the only musician, black or white, who had not made one bad record. On top of this, Rastafarianism had a few additional features suited to the modern era – it was a religion that had its own haircut: dreadlocks, the first black hairstyle white people were really jealous of, and incapable of having themselves. And of course, uniquely, it had its own drug: ganja. And it was a good drug, the best drug; probably the only drug in the world, pharmaceutical or recreational, whose reputation was improving with time.

When the tourists came into One Love Café, Yami moved

amongst them bare-chested, his sun-drenched locks cascading down his slender back. Sometimes he would get high and kick back with a nice white girl beside the lagoon. There was one beauty who kept returning to One Love Café called Julia, for whom it was particularly wicked to play hookey and lie beside a semi-naked rasta while the rest of her class were back at her private school in Connecticut. Yami once spent an hour and a half with her watching the green parrots in the forest canopy, and would have spent longer except he suddenly remembered he had taken a food order from a table of eight tourists and had forgotten to go by the kitchen to inform the chef.

When Brian came back after the operation, Yami showed him the tin of bank notes he had collected in his absence, but Brian was vex. He took particular exception to Julia, whom Yami had installed in his rastaman hut on the cliff edge above the lagoon.

'She godda go. Today,' he told Yami. 'I mean, you never said anything about having strangers hanging round the property day and night. I'd never have agreed to that. Never.'

'She nuh stranger, Brian. She cool. She cook and wash and help wid every likkle ting. Come and meet her. You like her.'

'I don't even want to say hello. I know her type. Just get her ouda here, okay? And close the gates. We don't open for another six minutes.'

Brian brooded alone in his bunkhouse with his mirror, appalled by the unnatural furrows of hair planted on his scalp. On the third day he emerged from the toolshed with the largest of his three buzz saws and, strapped ten feet up the big guango tree, began to sever the upper branches of the beautiful, noble tree. It was a tree old enough to have given shade to resting slaves; its generous crown spread not only over the customers at the bar and restaurant, but also out over the palisade to the Main where they gave cool shade to anyone idling on the Main between eleven and three-thirty. Yami woke when he heard the sound of the chain biting into the wood and came out to ask what was going on.

'Brian. Com dung man from up der. Nuh chop down dat tree. It give shade for we fi live in. It Jah tree. Ya kiant kill dat, man.'

'Don't you listen to the radio? There's a hurricane forecast. Hurricane Frederick. When a hurricane comes it's standard procedure to pollard the biggest trees so they don't get uprooted, that way they grow back after the storm has passed. It's standard US Army procedure. It's in the US Army field survival manual.'

'Dat one fool ting, Brian. Mi never hear nobody do dat.'

'Sure. The US Army's wrong, of course it is, Yami. I mean what do they know compared to you? I mean they only have the most advanced data and technology, not to say experience, in the whole world. But they are wrong. Of course. That must be it,' he said, yanking the cord on the saw.

'Bot Brian. Everytime dey say horrican come on de radio it alway turn back. Alway, an' it never com to Jamaica.'

'This wasn't a local news item. This was a report from the Caribbean hurricane tracking centre,' he shouted over the idling buzz saw.

'Ya kiant believe dat man pon de radio. Nobady know where a horrican go. Only Jah know dat, man.'

Brian laughed sarcastically. 'The hurricane tracking centre is in Miami. That's the US. They use a satellite. I don't mean to mean to be rude about Jah, but when it comes to the prediction of hurricane movements, he don't know shit compared to a twenty million buck satellite.'

'Dat Babylarn, dat satellite, dat spy biznis. Nobody can know de wedder bot Jah.'

'Yeh, sure, well don't believe it if you don't want to. You're the one who's gonna get killed by a falling tree in a hurricane, not me, thanks. Haven't you ever heard of your own Minister for Disaster Preparedness?' It was a portfolio in the Jamaican Cabinet that Brian approved of. 'I just heard him on the radio, man. He was on RJR half an hour ago warning the whole island about Frederick.'

'It never gonna com, man. It alway turn back ...'

But Brian pulled the ear protectors round his head and proceeded to slide the screaming chain into the trunk of the mighty tree. After half an hour's cutting, and another twenty minutes of hammering wedges into the incision, the top of the old tree gave a horrible groan, and then a cry, before crashing down into the undergrowth behind the bar. Brian ran over to the felled timber, climbed up on it, like a hunter on a rhino, his buzz saw in his right hand, wiping sweat from his big brow with the back of his left hand before resting it on the machete in his belt. To some frightened tourists who came up from the lagoon to see what the commotion was, he explained about dropping trees: 'You drop something big like this, you don't feel like doing it again in a hurry, you know? It's like every time I kill a fish scuba-diving. I don't feel like killing for a few days after. I mean like you do all the butchering, tearing out the guts and vital organs, and so forth, and you're, you're ... I'll tell you one thing, you really get to know a fish when you kill it, and you really get to know a tree when you drop it ...'

The tourists were soon driven back to the lagoon, and Brian walked bow-leggedly to the bar looking for some shade to drink a beer in, as the place where he normally sat was

now blasted by the brightness of the mid-morning sunlight.
While gulping his Heineken, the radio on the counter broadcast an update on hurricane Frederick: the alert was
downgraded as Frederick was blowing itself out west of the
Caymans, and was now no longer a threat to Jamaica.

Yami refused to burn any of the felled wood on the sacred
fire because it was against his religion.

'Where does it say that in the Bible?'

Yami took a long toke on his spliff, and blew out the
bluey-grey smoke in twin horns from his nostrils. 'It written,
Nuh cast unrighteousness pon de eart or pon de flame, for
de lard Jah will cast ya inna de bottomless pit,' he said,
proving himself to be, by the standards of his religion, a
Biblical scholar.

'Look Yami,' Brian said, 'I think it would be better for
both of us if you thought about moving on from here. Okay?'

But the very next day, Brian told Yami he could stay.

Some tourists came in that afternoon and asked Yami
what had happened to the decapitated guango tree.

'Dat orrican damage,' Yami answered.

'Really?' they answered. 'Wow! We never heard you had
a hurricane.'

'Orrican Frederick,' Yami said. He could see Brian listening while changing a tyre on his jeep.

'Did it do a lot of damage on the island?'

'None at all, man,' said Yami shaking his head. 'Dis only
damage it do.'

Brian threw down a spanner and stomped off into the
bunkhouse.

Later, coming up behind Yami as he meditated pon de
sunset Brian said, 'I changed my mind. You better go. You
better leave. I mean if you like to make jokes about me to
customers on my own property, you know. It's not cool any

more. You can stay tonight, okay, but put that fire out and be gone by tomorrow night.'

Yami replied to Brian, 'Ya kiant order mi fram dis land. Dis land a fi mi now. Mi work pon it and live pon it and sweat pon it and dat mek it mine. Ya kiant mek mi go. Only Jah can mek mi go.'

When word of this exchange got to the street, Gaddaffi said to Maxwell, 'Yami try fi get monny fram Brian. Just like mi say. Didn't mi say dat?' He turned and appealed to Wilbert, who heard nothing but said, 'Ya man.'

Trevor said, 'Yami tell mi dat monny nat him richness. Him one bongo dreadlocks man, believe mi.'

Yami refused to leave One Love Café. A few weeks later, to break the deadlock, Brian offered Yami money. He said he could have 50 US if he went, but Yami said, 'Mi nuh one prostitute, Brian. Dis ting wort more dan money.'

'Well whadya want?' asked Brian, touching the top of his head to check the implants.

'Mi nah want monny. Mi want fi stay where Jah tell mi fi stay.'

But nobody except Maxwell believed Yami, because people wanted rastamen to be hypocrites, and people said, when they talked about it, which was often because everyone was interested, 'Yami believe him can get more dan fifty US fram Brian.' And whether or not they were right, Brian raised his offer, in units of 40 US, to 170 US. Everytime Yami walk pon de street the people would hail him up and say, 'Yo, dread. Dat ole eap o monny Brian a give ya. Tek it while ya can, ya know?'

'Mi know it plenty dollar. Bot what need mi av US? All mi need is air fi breathe and food and water fi live. Jah a tell mi a build One Love Café. Ongle Jah can mek mi go.'

On the day he raised his offer to 200 US, there was another

hurricane warning on the radio. Brian heard that there were some whities over at Sandra's taking elaborate precautions, as per the Minister for Disaster Preparedness's instructions on RJR. At the edge of Sandra's yard a crowd grouped up to laugh at the whities taping windows, packing their clothes and filling all the water receptacles. Brian pushed his way through the crowd to set the whities right, but by the time he got back to One Love Café he had to admit the weather looked unusual. There was the warmest, most humid wind he'd ever known, and the sea looked unusually predatory.

Brian tuned in to the Minister for Disaster Preparedness, but the one disaster the Minister hadn't prepared for, a direct hit on the Ministry by a hurricane, had occurred. The antennae, telephone and power lines were swept off the Ministry's roof, and nothing more was heard of the Minister for Disaster Preparedness for three days, by which time Hurricane Gilbert had struck the island and long since left.

Hurricane Gilbert stalked along the spine of the island, taking only six hours to decimate the entire country. After it passed, Vices estimated that it left only nine unbroken panes of glass in the whole of Jamaica. It arrived in Beach at about sunset, though the winds had been ferocious for a few hours before then, bending trees back and forth and making the fronds of coconut palms resemble hair under-water. Brian left the corner of the creaking, moaning bunkhouse to see if it looked like any trees were going to crash down onto the roof. He saw bits of corrugated zinc, torn from the roof of Blender's shed, fly at sixty-five miles an hour in the gloom down the road towards some children who were still out having fun in the gusts. He looked at his enormous guango tree stump, and made a mental note to point out to Yami how well it fared in the storm.

A few hours after dark, the wind doubled and then trebled

again in ferocity. The bunkhouse squealed and groaned, the walls puffing out and squeezing in. Up on the hill, Mr Crooks, seeing his roof coming loose, tied one end of a thick rope to a rafter, the other round his waist, and braced himself in a doorway to hold it down. With an almighty scraping and ripping sound the roof came away and lifted Mr Crooks, his legs kicking madly, up into the air. He landed thirty yards away from the house and was dragged seventy yards more through mud and brush before the rope finally snapped. He scrabbled away to safety, and his roof flew up into the sky twisting and turning like burnt paper over a bonfire.

Miss Dahlia was old enough to have seen and remembered Hurricane Charlie in 1951, so she knew the correct form. You had to do three things: first, she prayed to the Lard Gad almighty far deliverance; second, without delay, she escorted her six dependant picknee to Beach Primary School, and third, she immediately set off on foot with Trouble to Sandy Island to loot a fridge freezer from Wing Ho Sing's hardware store.

Brian left the bunkhouse at four a.m. for an inspection. He stood in his doorway, terrified. The wind by now was absolutely non-negotiable; outside if it didn't kill you it was only because you were lucky. The guango stump he had so carefully pollarded was flattened. Beside it, the circular bar and restaurant was blasted into a thousand splinters, most of which were travelling at speeds over one hundred and ten miles an hour to Negril. The wind was so implacable it even bent the government road sign (the one that said COOL BEER) that was made of steel and offered almost no wind resistance.

The pounding eased back at dawn, and as the light grew, stunned and dishevelled people came out to see the damage.

Many wept to see their houses vanished and their yards flattened.

Mr Crooks and Miss Myrtle stood, stunned, in front of the pile of splintered timber strewn across their yard.

'De lard send dis fi ponish we far our sin dem,' Mr Crooks declared.

Miss Myrtle, looking at the devastation, thought, 'Mi never sin dis moch. Why de Lard ponish mi? And why de Lard let Rayon house stand but blow our house to West-morland? Rayon sin plenty. Plenty.'

All over Jamaica, millions and millions of tears were shed, but in Beach at least, there was also some laughter.

Miss Dahlia failed to loot a fridge freezer from Ho Sing's, but got a microwave instead. She staggered back to her yard, where Nerine was picking up splinters of house.

'Momma, de house mash op.'

'No worry bout dat, gal. Look what mi get wid Trouble. One teevee.'

An animated group of Seventh Day Adventists group up in front of the Jehovah's Witnesses' Kingdom Hall, which, before Gilbert, was a huge proud structure forty feet tall, and after, an L-shaped fence three foot high.

'De Kingdam all mash op, man,' they said to each other, all laughing. 'De lard com and dash i' away.' More laughter. 'Dem nah gonna build back dat for monts. Look a' i', it al brok dung, every board and every zinc is gone. Mi kiant believe i'.'

'Ya haffi laugh!' screeched a big fat lady, a pillar of Seventh Day Adventism. 'Ya haffi laugh.'

Some places were inexplicably spared, and left completely untouched, as though the storm had a sick sense of humour. Flossie's bamboo shed stood exactly as it had before the hurricane, with even the half consumed saff drink that Amoy put down to pick up her most valued possessions, her school books, before her flight to Beach Primary, still standing on a windowsill no wider then two inches.

The worst hit village was Firefly Bay. So there was something to cheer up the likker people dem of Angel Beach. The hills above and around Firefly Bay were stripped of every square inch of vegetation. Every single wooden house was shredded or flipped over and left in the mud, and those which were concrete were flooded by the overflowing river and filled with mud and pulped vegetation. Of the newly installed electricity poles nothing remained except odd lengths of high voltage cable tangled around the legs of broken goats and cattle.

In Beach it looked bad enough, as though a war had blown through, not a storm; and in the days that followed, displaced refugees, feeding stations, and queues for food and water became commonplace. Brian loved it. He strutted around topless with his chainsaw in one hand, a dagger strapped to his shin and a machete in his belt. For a brief few days he forgot about the mess on his scalp.

Low-flying aircraft dropped food by parachute which was distributed to the villages. Angel Beach Bottom Side got a pallet of 144 tins of French snails well past their sell-by date. Vinton hungrily opened them up and nyam one.

'Can go on,' he told Mooney and Trevor, nodding.

'No sah,' Mooney said. 'Mi nah eat slug. Me rather hungry den dat.'

Trevor went to look for Yami. He felt the bushman would know what to do. At Brian's a group of people were talking.

'It just lucky nobady dead, dat what mi say,' said Miss Myrtle, sent out by Mr Crooks on a search and rescue mission for bits of missing roof. All over Beach fights were breaking out as people disputed the ownership of twisted pieces of zinc and splintered siding boards. She had in her arms one three-foot length of snapped 4 by 2, clearly identifiable as Crooks's house by its brown paint.

'No man, two people dead in Firefly Bay,' said Vash.

Trevor looked at Yami.

'One landslide of giarbage mash op Councillor Hoyte house and yard, and kill him an' him wife. Dem say de goverment should not have put de domp uppa Firefly Bay, and now it gonna move again.'

'Dem dead like de Dread say dem will dead,' Trevor said.

'Ya man,' said Vash. 'De Dread set one curse pon Firefly Bay. De Dread kill two people in Firefly Bay.'

Yami said, 'Mi nah do nottin. Mi ongly prophet. Jah kill dem cas dem sin gainst de air and de water and de eart wid pollution and giarbage.'

'Rispec, Dread,' laughed Trevor, vindicated. 'Rispec to the max.'

Yami went silently to collect his few belongings. At his fire he closed his eyes and looked up at the sky. 'Mi give tanks to Jah, far deliverance,' he intoned. 'Irie vibes.' Then he wrapped a burning ember in some silver foil, tied it with wire to his rod, picked up his shoulder bag and walked towards the gate.

'Where you going, Yami?' asked Brian.

'Mi go a home, Jah a tell mi de time is ready fi start anudder logwood fire inna mi old yard a' Firefly Bay. Jah have clear de way far mi.' He squared his shoulders and prepared to leave.

'Hey wait,' Brian said, coming up close to him and lowering his voice. The group of onlookers bent forward to listen. 'Look, about the money, what with all the rebuilding costs, loss of business etcetera, I don't think I can give you the full two hundred bucks. How about eighty?'

'Mi nah want no monny.'

'Hold on, Yami, take some at least. Look, I got five bucks in the bunkhouse. Take it or I'll feel bad, seriously.'

The assembled group watched in awe as Yami shook his head and hoisted his bag onto his shoulder.

'Goodbye Brian,' he said and walked back to restart his old logwood fire in his old yard above the valley behind Firefly Bay. And all the people, when they heard about it, dem haffi respec de dread.

After Gilbert, Brian lost heart and his old life as a tax attorney began to seem attractive again. In 1989 he put his land up for sale and moved back to New York City.

SAYING GOODBYE

Sandra run out of her yard all her boyfriends because she
decide to marry Rupert. He lazy and one idiot and he beat
her and burst her head couple time but he have Canada
passport so she moss marry him. But when, after they wed,
Sandra applied for her visa to go and live in Toronto they
aks her if she have one Police recard. Sandra have one and
she know dem nah want nobady fi go up inna foreign wid
no recard. To get a Police record clean cost five hundred US
so Sandra decided to sell Mr Poole's house to pay for wiping
her Police record. She meant to sell the house in the traditional Swing family manner; that is, take the money and then
refuse to move out, and threaten the vendor until he gave
up trying to get the house, but the whitey who bought it was
careful, and took her to his liar and made her sign a paper
which he said he'd show to the Police if she tried to stop him
moving in, or attempted to move back in herself. Since she
stop friend wid ole heap o police, dem vex wid Sandra and
nah help her gainst de white man. But she didn't care, she
got two thousand US for the house – easily enough to clean
her Police record and catch a flight inna foreign.

The day Sandra left the house to the whities, Vinton, who
had lived in, and under, her house, on round-the-clock call
as dogsbody, cook, gardener, child minder and cleaner for
five years, had nowhere to go.

'Tek up mi bag,' Sandra snapped at Vinton, who lugged them to the taxi, into which Rupert and Sandra were squeezed to bursting point, bickering over a tube of candy. With the last overflowing lada bag pushed inside, Vinton said, 'Bye, Sandra,' drawing their five years together to a close.

'Driva! C'mon,' she shouted.

'Next time,' said Vinton, walking slowly backwards.

'Move!' Sandra shouted at the driver, who had been flirting in the shade with Bubbles, a comely sixteen year old who'd joined the last crowd ever to assemble at Sandra's yard to see what she was up to. As the car drew off Vinton turned away.

'Hol' on!'

He heard Sandra shout and the car stop.

'Tan tan!' she called.

'Ya man?' answered Vinton.

'Tanks. Ya hear?'

'Ya man. Rispec, Sandra. Every time. Ya have a good time up a Canada.'

'For sure,' she replied, giving him the smile he had longed for. He waved her goodbye and picked up his possessions: a rusty machete, one shorts, one ganzi, couple cassette, broken scissor, and a National Geographic with some photographs of Canada which he had pored over whenever he could to imagine where Sandra was going without him.

His immediate problem was where to stay. No girl would take him in; they weren't interested unless you had your own place, and he couldn't go back to Miss Liza because he'd dis her since living at Sandra's. Flossie, his momma, was out of the question – she already had seven sleeping in two rooms, and anyway he dis her too. If only he had a father, or knew who his father was, but Flossie would not tell him. If he knew, he'd ask him for shelter or a couple bucks at least. He couldn't stay with Mooney because of his father, Mr Crooks, and he couldn't stay with Trevor because his father beat boys terrible for nothing.

While waiting at the edge of Sandra's yard to make his next move, a taxi drew up with the wife of the white man who bought the house, who had been shopping in Content. Cleaning equipment spilled from her arms as she walked across the yard, and Vinton instinctively got up to help her. As soon as she got in the house she let out an appalling scream. Vinton rushed in to see what the matter was, but it was only one of Sandra's rats running up and down the lounge because its nest in Sandra's suite had been removed. The white lady stood on a table screaming, while the white man held a shoe in his hand and shouted, 'Don't worry darling, I'll get it, I'll get it.' But Vinton could see he was too slow for Sandra's rat, so he grabbed his machete and dashed after the rat to kill it. When he skewered it on the point, he held its wriggling body up to the white lady, but that made her scream more.

'Thanks,' the white man said. Then he added to his wife, 'I doubt very much there'll be any more. Will there?'

'No man,' Vinton corrected him. 'Just maybe him wife and four or six picknee.'

'What?'

'Mi deal wid dat. No problem.'

'It's quite all right, thank you very much,' the white man said.

But the lady said, 'Would you? We'll pay you if you get them all.'

So that day and the next Vinton killed five rats, twelve teenager cockroaches, and numerous assorted bugs. The whities wanted to kill moths, because they had no idea they were the spirits of dead people come back to visit the living, but when Vinton explained how bad it was to kill them, they learnt to leave them alone.

The whities were scared of a whole heap o ting: not just bog and roach and rat, but dog, people dem not know, specially if dem carry machette, power cut, and so many other things dem aks Vinton fi sleep inna de back room, like Sandra did.

With his sleeping quarters fixed, for a few nights at least, and a few J in his fist (as both pockets had holes), Vinton could constentrate on the thing that he really cared about: girl dem.

After a month, the whities went back to their own yard inna foreign. They asked Vinton to stay as caretaker in the yard, but locked every room in the house except for Vinton's, left clear instructions that nobody was to enter them in their absence, and took the key away with them.

'It is really important to me that no-one enters our rooms while we're away, do you understand?' the white man said.

'Come on, darling, I'm sure Vinton understands,' the white lady said.

'No, I want to make it clear. Vinton, don't let anybody into our rooms, on any account, while we're away. I'll be more than very angry if I find you've disobeyed me. If you let us down on this, you will lose your job. Understand?'

They gave him an immense sum for bills, and departed with tears in their eyes for the airport, leaving him to his own devices.

There were three people in Beach who looked after whitey tourist yards. Vash kept an eye on Jim and Nolene's place called High Trees, though he soon lost his job because every time Jim and Nolene went back to Boston, Vash forced an entry into their locked cupboards and sold their possessions.

Across the cove from Vinton, Volley, a bredren of Vinton, was caretaker of a house a couple of white men bought with drog biznis money. It was a good job, caretaking, but it could go wrong: when one day Volley's whities were nailed with eight kilos of Angel Beach ganja in the Bahamas and given twelve years in jail, Volley was left to handle things back a yard for a decade on 43 US dollars.

There were ways to keep the bills down: Vinton got Mooney to dig up the road at night to by-pass the water meter, and got Vices to by-pass the corrent meter, though he got hurled across the yard when, saying, 'Mi know how it run, no problem,' he put the screwdriver on the wrong wire. With this done, Vinton then spend down all de bills money in couple days on Red Stripe for de boys, domino, clothes, a trim, and gal dem.

Vinton friend with five girls, or as he called them, likker beans: Sophia, Dawn, Jacqueline, Angie and Opal. He invited them one by one to the yard, helped them in through the window and showed them the whities' magazines and books, and let them try on the white lady's clothes and make up, while listening to cassettes on their stereo and running down the batteries in their flashlight. When they were bored of that he showed them his back room, with its chair, broken mirror and bed, which he swiftly fucked them on before bundling them out the back door and trotting off down the Main to look for the next likker bean.

These were glory days for Vinton Wellington. Pay landed magically in his savings account at the bank, wafted invisibly across the sea from foreign to the National Commercial Bank in the new shopping mall in Content. The 20 US a month made him by far the highest paid yout in Angel Beach, or at least in Angel Beach Bottom Side. When Vinton got a large sum of money, which meant anything over 3 US, a marathon gambling session ensued, either poker or dominoes, because that was the most entertaining way of distributing his pay around his best friends, Mooney, Trevor and Vices, who had none themselves. At the beginning of each month the soft nights were rent with laughter, derision, accusations, and screeches of triumph, and little children lying in bed in Angel Beach Bottom Side went to sleep listening to the smack and crack of dominoes hurled onto the polished surface of the white lady's dressing table, which Vinton, Mooney, Trevor and Vices heaved out through the whities' window to gamble on beside the Main.

One night, two or three years after the whities started employing Vinton, a tourist coach, instead of roaring by at fifty miles an hour, ten inches behind Vices' chair, drew up with groaning brakes and a door that hissed open. Hopton, the driver, called out, 'Tan tan, mi just see ya whities at de airport.'

'Jeezus,' exclaimed Vinton, who was wearing an amber necklace he'd found under the whities' bed. 'Tank ya, Hopton. Respec. Vices, Mooney, get de table back in a house fass.'

'No sah!' shouted Vices, who was winning the game of dominoes.

'Ya man. Dis a serious ting.'

'Cho!' complained Vices, sulkily. But he stood up, ruefully studying the dominoes in his big hand, and allowed Mooney and Vinton to pick up the dressing table, which was now polished from years of dominoes, and battered from countless entries and exits through the bedroom window.

Trevor ran across the road to repossess the white lady's sunbed from Miss Dahlia's yard where Kermit, Nakissia and Najia were slumbering on it in their bedroom, and Vices, as soon as he'd finished racing up Vinton and Mooney for scratching the table on the window frame, when a little help from him could have prevented it, dashed to his yard on the back street for the white man's flashlight and cassette player, both of which Vinton had lent to him in return for a rhinestone buttoned shirt. Vinton set about cutting the lawn with his machete in the darkness.

Everything was more or less in place when the airport taxi pulled up and the whities emerged blinking and confused after their long journey from foreign.

'Everything all right, Vinton?' the white man always asked, after saying hello.

'Ya man. Everyting criss,' Vinton replied.

'Thought I'd surprise you just for once to see what's really going on when my back is turned,' the white man said.

'Vinton! My necklace! You found it! Where was it?' exclaimed the white lady.

Vinton's hand clutched at his throat. 'Mi find it 'bout de place,' he laughed.

'D'you see that, darling? Vinton's found my amber necklace. You are brilliant Vinton.'

The white man, who was searching for a key on a big bunch, muttered something to himself. Inside his rooms he turned on the light and looked around. The floor was speckled with the dried leaves of the dogwood tree that had wafted under the corrugated iron eaves on the sea breeze during his absence. He noticed that Vinton had been using the dressing table, cassette machine and a few other things, again. The crisp new pack of cards were now fat and furry from abuse. But in the three years the white man had been coming to Beach he had learnt that nobody could have possessions in Angel Beach Bottom Side without sharing them, so said nothing, and went outside to sit on the porch, smoke a spliff with the guys and catch up on some gossip.

* * *

So life go on, an' life sweet far Vinton. He have gal
dem, monny, and a yard fi live in. And to top it all, for his
eighteenth birthday present the whities wrote Vinton a letter
inviting him on holiday inna foreign, with them. Amoy,
Vinton's fourteen year old sister, the best reader in the
village, read out the letter under the single gloomy bulb of
Flossie's shed crammed with fifteen people sheltering from
a rainstorm. There was Mooney, Maxwell, Vices, Vera, Miss
Dahlia, Nerine, Kermit, Nakissia, Najia, Trouble, Opal,
Bubbles, Vash and Rayon U-Roy who was wet up from the
downpour.

'Dear Vintan,' she said, constentrating hard. 'Since men-
tioning to you that we were thinking of having you over
here for a week or two in return for the three years of
wonderful holidays you've given us in Angel Beach, I have
now made the arrrangements ...'

One breezy warm spring morning the white man, swinging in his hammock, had offered the trip to Vinton, but
Vinton thought he was just saying it to make the two of
them feel good for half an hour. But he really meant it.

'... Here is the ticket I promised to send you.'

'Talk loud,' someone shouted, because the white man's
CD player was on volume 9 on the counter.

'Ya man, loud,' Kermit shouted. Nobody suggested turning down the CD.

'Don't lose it,' Amoy continued, raising her voice. The
additional noise of the rain on the corrugated zinc roof, only
inches above her head, made it harder to be heard. It sounded
like the ecstatic applause at the end of a show, designed to
bring the DJ back on for more. Drips of water began to form

under the light bulb and fall onto Kermit's upturned face. 'Your flight leaves Montego Bay on Saturday, September de third, at twenty thirty.' Here, Amoy paused. 'That's half past eight post meridian, in the night,' she explained.

'Mi know dat,' snapped Vash, twitching with jealousy. He had worked as caretaker for Jim and Nolene, before they run him outa de yard cas him tief Ken Walkman an' brief, but they never asked him to go to Boston. Why did Vinton's whities ask Vinton? Vash was glad he tief Jim and Nolene tings.

'You ony have two months to get a passport, so apply straight away. I enclose a letter of invitation and financial reference for you to give to the Immigration officer at Gatwick airport, so they'll let you into Britain.' Amoy had to pause here while the rain redoubled its efforts and the applauding crowd rose to their feet and punished their palms to salute the return to the stage of the star for a final encore. When it began to fade, Amoy continued: 'We will meet you at the airport. Ring transfer charge if you have any problems.'

Amoy handed the letter back to Vinton proudly, for he was the first member of the noble house of Wellington to leave the island. He was to be a tourist. Nobody from Angel Beach was ever a tourist. It thrilled Amoy. Everybody talked, and then shouted, at once, congratulating Vinton, who was more surprised than most to see the ticket, and had been quite happy with the promise of travel, even if it was subsequently broken, for in Angel Beach Bottom Side even a broken promise of something fine was a thing to be treasured.

Vash grabbed the ticket from Vinton. 'Dis nat real ticket,' he jeered.

'Ya man. Dat real,' said Vices in his deep voice. He was

always the expert on everything, and so big and so argument-
ative that nobody doubted his authority. But at that moment
Hopton's huge Blue Danube bus drew up inches from the
bamboo shed, and with a hiss of brakes and a clatter of
doors, Hopton emerged, shouting, 'Flossie! Fetch mi one
hot Red Stripe. Mi kiant drive no more widout a drink fi
clear mi brain.'

'Hopton,' said Rayon U-Roy, 'you see ole 'eap o airplane
ticket wid tourists. Dis one fraud?' It was passed to Hopton
while Flossie levered the top off the bottle on the two rusty
nails that Mooney had hammered into the bar the day she
tore out two teeth opening a Dragon Stout for a customer.
Hopton looked at the ticket, his skin glistening with the
sweat of the hot and humid night, and drained the liquid
from the bottle in one pull. 'Dat look real,' he announced.
'Dat ticket can fly. For sure.' He handed it back. 'Flossie give
mi nudder Red Stripe. Dis plane kiant lift aff pon one engine.'
He grabbed the second bottle, and wiping the rusty sediment
from around its mouth with his shirt, ducked back outside,
where forty-three tourists waited patiently in his coach to
be driven to their flight home from Donald Sangster International Airport in Mo-Bay.

'Carry mi dung one Walkman fram a foreign,' Amoy
begged her brother.

'An' one shorts and jeans shirt,' barked Vices.

'An' one Bally shoes far mi,' added Trevor.

'Bring mi one mattress, ya hear?' shouted Miss Dahlia.

'An' Vinton, carry dung one .38 semi-automatic pistol,'
piped Trouble, 'cas dat mi need inna Negril. Bud.'

Vinton laughed in their faces and forced his way through
the crush to the door. Outside, the rain clouds had moved off
towards Firefly Bay, and late afternoon sun was shafting in
under them. Gullies and culverts burbled as the flood water

subsided, and ponderous waves of steam rolled off the tarmac road.

'Yo. Tan-tan,' Vinton heard Rayon U-Roy call behind him. 'One ting. Com ere.'

Vinton halted. 'What ya want mi fi carry dung? One BMW?'

'No man,' laughed Rayon, as his thin legs conveyed him up the slope.

'Look like everybady want someting.'

'Ya nah haffi worry bout dat Vinton,' Rayon said.

'Yes sah. Mi com back dung wid nottin, dem race mi up. Believe mi.'

'Com back? Ya nah gonna com back a Beach, Vinton.'

'Mi nah gonna what?'

'Ya kiant go a foreign and com back a Angel Beach. Dis one big chance ya have. It never gonna repeat. Tek it and get outa here while ya can.'

Vinton's face lit up at the idea. But then he said, 'An' never com back?'

'Sure ya com back dung. In couple year when ya one big man wid Benz and house and plenty o' gift for we sufferers.'

Vinton stood still and looked over the pasture. Kermit waded through the long grass carrying a bucket of water to a tethered cow in the dusk.

'Dem have job and monny and plenty car up a foreign. And can be white gal dem. White gal love up de yardy inna foreign. Everytime.'

But Vinton had heard the white man and lady talking, and it didn't sound easy to make your way inna foreign if you were a yardy. 'It nat easy fi get job inna London,' he said.

'Job? Ya nah need job, man!' Rayon laughed, putting his stringy arm around Vinton's shoulders and guiding him into

Vinton's yard. 'Government pay ya fi live der. And if ya have haccident, like get bounce by car, dem pay ya million a dallar.'

'Dat so?'

'Ya man. It call surance.'

'Bot mi nah have no paper fi stay.'

'Nuh worry bout dat. Boydie have no paper but him live inna Peckham since tree year.' Boydie was a bad boy from Angel Beach Top Side. He did drugs biznis and even kill one man inna Police shootout. It was someone from his own gang, accidentally, but it still earned him the respect of a proper murderer. He'd fled inna foreign on a false passport.

'De whities say Police inna Englund always ketch ya,' Vinton said.

'Police inna Englund? Ya nah need worry bout whitey Police.'

'Why?'

'Whitey Police inna Englund nuh carry gon. Boydie tell mi.' Rayon chuckled to himself at the very thought of a cop without a gun. 'So if dem trouble ya, ya just lick dem down. It easy.'

'Dem nuh carry gon?'

'Nuh sah,' said Rayon, almost crying with happiness. 'No gon! Boydie tell mi. Everybady know.'

'If dem nuh ave no gon, why everybady nuh turn tief and robber and bad boy?'

'Cas dem idle. Bot dat tief biznis easy inna Englund. If de Police ketch ya tief, ya just lick dem down and ron way inna de bush fi hide.'

'Bot der is nuh bush inna London. De white lady and man tell mi. Dat why dem like i' here.'

'Well dem liards, cas Shepherd Bush George live ole 'eap o year in Shepherd Bush.' Vinton had to admit that this was true. 'Ya whities nuh tell you de trut' bout Englund cas dem want fi you a stay here, in Beach, fi cut dem yard an' pick up dem giarbage.'

'If mi run off inna London mi gonna need monny.'

'Dat mi already tink bout. Cas ya mi friend, and mi want fi help ya get start inna foreign. Let we go inna ya room fi talk biznis.'

Indoors, Vinton put on the radio to give them privacy. Rayon smiled his lupine smile and sweated profusely, occasionally wiping his face and head with a hand towel he always carried with him. 'Ow much monny ya ave?'

'Twenty-one US.'

'Twenty-one dallar. Dat can work. Show mi de white man letter.'

Vinton pulled it out of his pocket. Rayon read the letter and closely inspected the communication with the immigrations officer. 'Dis good,' he said. It was typewritten on crisp pale yellow paper with an embossed letterhead. 'Wid dis ya gonna walk right inna Englund. No problem. Dem nah gonna trouble ya wid dis. No sah. Mi can give ya twenty-one US of ganja for ya bag which can sell for two tousand dallar inna London.'

'Ya man. Dat would be cool.'

'For sure,' said Rayon, 'it mi idea. Dem alway cool. Every time. Tek de ganje to Boydie, and him help ya sell i'. Boydie can show ya how ting run inna London. Ya can move wid him posse if ya want.'

'Dat sound cool. Mi link op wid Boydie,' said Vinton, glowing with anticipation.

'Gi' mi de monny, den,' said Rayon.

Vinton laughed. 'Mi nuh need fi buy ganje from you, Rayon. Wordswort ave ole 'eap him will gi' mi.'

'Bot do him know how fi smuggle i' in suitcase? How fi

hide i' so dog dem nah sniff i' out? Mi know cas mi bredren inna Kinston tell mi. Ya nuh want fi go a jail, do you?'

'No man.'

Rayon put out his hand. 'Den dis de best way,' and Vinton opened his billfold and handed over all his meagre savings.

When Rayon went, Vinton kick back pon him bed, wid him hand behind him head, his thoughts fixed on the gangsta life in London. On the radio Bob Marley sang 'When you bend a new corner, feel like sweepstake winner', and Vinton thought, mi know what ya say, Bob.

When news broke of Vinton's plan to turn into a drugs dealer, stay in London illegally and join a gangsta mob, opinions were divided. Most people said they were right behind Vinton. His bredren, Mooney, Trevor, Vices and Trouble, were sad to see him go, but never showed it. 'When mi get set up nice,' he told them, 'mi call for ya and carry you up. Tross mi.'

'How long will that tek?' asked Trevor adoringly.

'Mi nah know, bot soon. Tree or seven monts or maybe two year. Soon as mi can. Believe mi. Ya tink mi want fi be inna foreign widout mi bredren?'

Only Amoy was dead against the plan. 'Ya one idiot Vinton Wellington. Ya know what happens to drogs dealers? Look at Perry and Minto. Dem inna jail far ole heap o years. And what if you get to London? Ya kiant read or write, you have no trade and no relations to help you. All your family is here. Dis de place you born and raise. Ya kiant stay up dere.' Then she added, quietly, 'ya family need ya, ya know?'

'Ya jealous, gal. Mi fed up wid dis likker place. It too smallish for a big man like mi.'

But there were still some pleasures to be extracted from his last weeks in Beach. His elevation in life to drugs dealer and London bad boy deeply impressed his friends, and drew girls like magnet draw nail. Just the sight of an airticket made the Beach girls weak at the knees, and he missed no opportunity to push them back on his bed the moment they looked unsteady.

The passport application defeated Vinton, so he asked Amoy to help him, she being the only person he knew up to the task and the owner of the only functioning biro in Beach that week. She filled it in on the counter of Flossie's shed, tears in her eyes. Meanwhile Vinton borrowed a shirt from Vices and went to Content to get a passport photograph. The trip did not go well. Before mounting the wooden stairs to the studio he had one flex trim with the words BAD BOY razored above his right temple, but the picture nuh look too nice. For a start you couldn't see the words at all, but more importantly he looked too black.

'Dat one black bwoy!' Vices shouted with laughter when Vinton nervously showed it outside Flossie's shed. 'Photographer moss have plug out de light cas ya is pure black.' Mooney, Trevor and everybody else who was high colour laughed loud, while Vinton, Amoy and Flossie kept quiet, feeling small.

'Give dat back,' Vinton shouted over the hoots and screams of laughter. 'Mi can be black, bot it a mi a go a foreign, nat you – country boys,' he laughed back. But Amoy offered him some money she'd saved for a geography text book, and he went to Mo-Bay the next day to a better photographer who always gave you high colour. When he passed the photo around, Vices said, 'Dat cool. Nice phota.'

'Alright, brown boy,' said Trevor, though Tanya-Kay, one of Vinton's likker beans, looked at the photo and said, 'Who dat? Dat nuh look like nobady mi know.'

But Tanya-Kay had ole 'eap o lyrics.

It was an historic day when the passport came, for Vinton was the first little person in Angel Beach Bottom Side to possess one. In the privacy of his room he held the slim royal blue book in his big gnarled hands, and felt a lump in his throat. When mi was one picknee mi nah have nuttin. No shoe no yard no monny no farder, and mi mudder run mi outa de yard. Bot now mi have de first passport inna de community and mi one big man. His birth certificate, which he had never seen before, slipped out and slid with a faint hiss across the floorboards. He picked it up and looked at it. Out of the indecipherable jumble of letters sprang a recognisable word: FATHER. In the box beside it was written: Walter Carvel.

There was a man of that very name in the Back Street. Maas Aubrey, they called him. Maas Aubrey? His father? Vinton always pictured his father miles and miles away from Beach, but he had walked past Maas Aubrey's yard, where he lived with his wife Miss Norma Linton and two picknee, thousands of times. Maas Aubrey was cool. Everybody said it. He lent the cricket club his lawnmower and didn't get vex when Vices ran it over a rake buried in the long grass and it mash op.

Vinton decided to take a walk. He left his yard, crossed the Main after letting a tourist coach thunder by, and took the track up past the symmetry to the Back Street. Two nude picknee soaped themselves at the standpipe on the corner. He passed on either side of him the wooden houses set back in their yards, until he came to one with a much admired burgundy and cream concrete extension, and a lawn with a clipped hibiscus hedge. For many years Vinton had thought about meeting his father. He planned to step up to him, introduce himself, and maybe buy the man couple cold Red Stripe and chat bout tings. He had actually daydreamed about telling him he was going up a Englund. Make him proud to have him as a son.

A large, jolly man was playing cricket with two little boys, using a mango tree as a wicket. Maas Aubrey stood behind the bowler and held his arm as he made the delivery. The ball struck the tree and the bowler swivelled round to Maas Aubrey, who shouted, 'Owzat! Well bowl!'

The other boy fling down him bat, narrowly missing his brother. Maas Aubrey looked towards the street and noticed Vinton, standing there watching over the hedge, and laughed, saying, 'Picknee nah like him likker brudder to out him.' Miss Norma emerged onto the porch wiping her hands on her apron. Behind her he glimpsed a television. 'Food ready!' she called, and the two boys and their father trooped in, chatting to each other happily. Vinton was left staring at the empty yard. Ya kiant bitter bout de past, he told himself. Dat man nat mi farder. It too late for any man to be mi farder. Dat man Maas Aubrey. Him cool. De past finish. It de future now. Mi bend a new corner now.

The night before Vinton left, his friend dem com an' check him, and make gift dem for his journey and new life inna foreign. They came from all over Beach: Vices with a T-shirt that said JAMAICA NO PROBLEM, and 60 J. Mooney gave him his baseball cap and the 200 J he had saved for a wood plane. His brother Trevor gave him 63 J in coins and some barely used Walkman batteries, and his sister Amoy gave him the 200 J she'd spent five months saving for a geography text book. Shepherd Bush George came to shake his hand and give him a London Underground map. Miss Dahlia gave him some fry fish in foil, and Flossie brought round two lada bag of mango, bammy, fry fish, poff, buller and bon an cheese.

Rayon crept round with the ganja hidden in two dry coconuts, which had been resealed so well you could hardly see the join.

'Dat com to a likker more dan what us agree.'

'Why dat?'

'Cas dem big, man. Mi get maybe couple pound of ganje in dem.'

'Ya?'

'Ya man. Dat gonna cost anudder four ondred dallar.'

'Far ondred J?'

'Ya man,' laughed Rayon. 'Bot tink. Dat one investment. Dat four ondred gonna grow to can be couple tousand J inna Englund. And Boydie and de crew gonna love ya.'

Vinton sighed. He only had 520 J.

'Dis kiant wrong, Vinton, serious.'

Vinton pulled out all the money he'd been given and handed over 400 J to Rayon.

'For real,' said Rayon, beads of sweat covering his forehead. 'Mi gotta go now. Later. Bes of luck, man.'

He was too excited to sleep. The night was sweet: the big moon rose over the hill and burned like a slender flame on the water of the cove. The comforting slap and hiss of the sea on the sandy shore mingled with the chirruping cicadas and tree frogs, and the night jasmine poured its scent over Vinton where he lay restlessly under the open window, thinking of fast cars, shopping malls, underground trains and McDonalds cheeseburgers.

'Tan-tan,' he heard whispered in a girl's voice.

'Ooodat?' he answered, sitting up.

'Tanya-Kay.' Tanya-Kay, the cutest and most beloved of all his likker beans. For that week, at least. Vinton opened his door, and saw the fifteen year old bathed in dappled moonlight. Small, with flashing almond eyes, a beautiful, defiant face, and breasts which were talked about from Grange Hill to Mo-Bay.

'Gal. How ya get here?'

'Mi climb outa mi window and walk trough de bush. Vinton, mi got someting fi tell ya.'

He came down the wooden step and took her arm. 'Talk can wait. C'min side.'

'No.' She shook his hand off. 'Listen. Mi pregnant. Mi gonna have ya baby.'

'Na.'

'Ya man. Serious.'

'Jezus,' Vinton sighed, scratching his head. 'Ya try fi dash i' away?'

'Ya man. Tree time. Mi try fi wash i' out wi Pepsi and baking powda, mi try fi hook i out, mi try everyting, but it stick, an i' too late now.'

'Why ya nah tell mi?'

'Cas mi nah want fi bodder ya.'

'It is mine?'

'Ya man. Mi swear. Mi swear.'

Vinton sighed again. 'Jezus. Dis mi nuh need now. Ya know mi ketch one airplane inna foreign in de marning?'

'Ya man. Dat why mi com. Can ya give mi couple dallar far baby bottle and baby clothes?'

Vinton went into his room and reappeared. 'Mi only hav dis,' he said, 'bot tek i'.'

She held the notes up to the moonlight and counted them. 'One ondred and twenty J? Ya kiant buy nottin wid dat. Give mi more.'

'Mi nuh have no more. Mi haffi give i' all to one guy. Mi swear.'

'Ya liard, Vinton. Ya go pon airplane tomorrer, sure ya have monny.' She turned away and stuck out her bottom lip.

'Mi swear, Tanya-Kay. Tross mi.' He touched her smooth brown forearm. She jerked it away.

'Give mi mo' monny.'

'Mi nuh have none.'

'Den mi go back a yard. Mi farder vex wid mi far get pregnant and him beat mi bud if mi nah get back a yard before him wake up.'

'Com inna mi room for one minute.'

'No Vinton.'

'Mi nah gonna forget ya, Tanya-Kay. Ya now mi baby mudder. An' mi nah gonna forget mi baby. Tross mi. Mi go a Englund, but mi send down monny and tings for de baby and one day can be bring ya op wid de picknee. Mi want fi be a good farder.'

'Liard. Ya chatt noff Vinton. Good farder. Ya go pon plane tomorrer an' mi and de baby never gonna hear from ya again.'

'Yes ya will, believe mi.'

'Sure. Ya can say it easy, Vinton, bot mi know mi never will. No yout never com back fram a-foreign. Everybady know dat. Goodbye.'

He called her back, but she kept walking through the gleaming leaves of the moonlit trees. Vinton said, 'Raas claat,' and lay back down on his bed to wait for dawn.

For centuries, the people of Angel Beach Bottom Side had been forced into bidding goodbye to their friends and relatives. Torn from their mothers, brothers, sisters and children in Africa, and then sold and dispersed around the Caribbean as slaves, they knew that all relationships could end at any time without warning through forced separation or sudden death.

Vinton's friends group up at his yard, all dressed in their finest travelling clothes, even though they were going nowhere, to say goodbye. All of them knew that they would probably never meet again, for people who went up young inna foreign, turn English or American, and never made it back to a place like Angel Beach Bottom Side. To make the pain of separation bearable, everybody pretended Vinton was coming back.

'Likker more,' said Mooney, handing his holdall through the minibus window. He tried to lock hands with his friend, but the angle of the seat to the window made it impossible, so he just held his fist up and smiled.

'Later,' said Trevor, looking miserable.

Amoy was in the shed hiding her tears from everyone.

'Bye Vinton!' she called to her brother. Some of his likker bean dem lined the side of the road looking forlorn, though not, he noticed, Tanya-Kay.

'Ya man, seen,' said Vinton. And the minibus drew out of Beach with everyone watching it.

When Vinton disembarked at London Gatwick airport, he had difficulty establishing when exactly he was off the air-plane and on English soil. When finally he saw through a window what he thought was dawn breaking over London, but was in fact midday on a cloudy November day near Crawley, he told himself: 'Dis fi mi new country. Now mi turn Englishman.'

There were so many signs, and whenever he stopped and put down his bag to read them, people bumped into him. At a high desk, a cooly wuman looked at his passport, his return ticket, the whitey's letter, asked a few questions, and then stamped his passport and waved him on. There were now so many more signs, he gave up trying to read them and just followed the passengers from his flight. When he picked his bag off the carousel he followed a man to an exit, and was just reaching the automatic doors at the far end of the customs hall when a white man in a uniform hail im up.

'Have you got something to declare, sir?'

'Uh?'

'You are in the red channel. You wish to declare something? Are you carrying more than two litres of spirits or four of wine? Cigarettes? Gifts of any kind?'

'No sah. Nuttin.'

'So why are you in the red channel?'

'Dat mi kiant answer, cas mi nah know what is de red channel,' Vinton smiled.

'Can't you read?' asked the Customs officer, rhetorically.

'Well, mi can read, but mainly certain word. Nat every one, ya see ...'

'Where have you come from?'

'De airplane.'

'No, where did your journey start?'

'Angel Beach.'

'Which country?'

'Jamaica.'

'How much money do you have on you?'

'Nuttin,' said Vinton openly.

'Please put your bag on the bench, sir.'

Vinton placed it on the steel surface. The customs officer unzipped it, and began to empty it. Up until that moment Vinton had forgotten all about the coconuts. But even when he suddenly remembered them, his external demeanour

didn't betray the fact. Many times he'd seen Police miss
ganja or knives at roadblocks near Angel Beach.

'Do you have any firearms? Ammunition? Drugs of any
kind?'

'No sah,' answered Vinton with innocent surprise. The
man's hands delved in the bag and withdrew one, and then
the other, coconut. Vinton thought about Trouble's eldest
brother, Boom Stepper, who was doing a seven-year stretch in
a Cayman Island lock-up for swallowing condoms full of coke
for Barry Man, a notorious thief, liar and coke dealer. The
white man inspected the coconuts. Vinton remained cool.
He, Mooney, Trevor, Vices, Nerine, Trouble and Flossie had
looked closely at them in his room, and couldn't see the join.

The white man looked across the hall to a man with his
feet crossed on a table in a side office.

'Les,' he called. 'You busy? Bring me the hammer and
chisel, will you?'

'Ang about.' Les appeared holding the tools. Vinton swallowed and smiled weakly. The chisel was placed on the hairy
coconut and struck with the hammer. At the first blow it
sheered off, but for the second attempt Les held it while the
hammer fell again. With a sharp crack the nut fell in half
revealing two equal cups of white coconut, and nothing else.
A miracle. Tank ya, Jah, Vinton mouthed. Respec. The chisel
was placed on the second coconut and the same thing happened: it too was empty. Rayon U-Roy Fairfax, ya jinall, ya
crook, mouthed Vinton this time, smiling from ear to ear
as the white man, most surprisingly, repacked his bag and
zipped it up for him.

He planned to get in touch with Boydie and the crew and

link op as soon as possible, but it took a little longer than he thought to get his bearings, and the white man and lady had laid on a programme of sightseeing and events which he couldn't get out of.

They took him down to the bottom of their street to buy a coat and jeans and shirt and brief and sweater in a shop called Emporio Armani, which was criss but not as good as some shops he'd seen on the drive in from the airport in a more central part of the city called, he was told by the white man, Lewisham High Street. He was then walked around the corner to buy one shoes and belt at a shop called Gucci. Many of his friends in Jamaica bought Gucci T-shirts in the market in Content, so that was cool.

He rang the telephone number Rayon gave him for Boydie, but he never got an answer. On the third day he asked the white lady to try it.

'That's out of order,' she told Vinton. 'Either there's something wrong with the phone or the number's wrong. How long have you been trying?'

'Tree day.'

'It must be a wrong number. It looks a bit odd. Do you have an address?'

Vinton passed the piece of paper to the white lady.

'It says care of the Duke of Percy, Peckham,' she said to her husband.

'The pub, I assume, rather than the person,' he said.

'Ha ha. Let's see if it's in the book.'

Vinton rang the pub when she got the number, but couldn't understand the lady who answered, so he passed the receiver to the white lady.

'I'm trying to trace someone called Boydie. I have a friend of his from Jamaica staying, who wants to meet up ... Does he have another name, Vinton?'

'Ya man. Him name Sherlock Allen. Boydie one alias.'

'He might be called Sherlock Allen. Yes. You know him? Right. Can you give him a message to ring Vinton Wellington?' She gave the number and rang off. 'He's the cleaner there. Comes in at six a.m. each day for three hours.'

The whitey's yard was well set up. Ole 'eap o room on four floor, wid step all the way to de top. Even de picknee have one room fi sleep, one fi play call nursery, and one bartroom, which she share only wid de nanny. Vinton room have tree big window wid fancy curtain and him own bartroom trough one door wid one bard and two tilet, one big an' one small. Downstairs dem ave big kitchen and two lounge full of TV, hi-fi, video, CD, everyting. It nice the way people live inna Englund.

He tried to make himself useful around the house before he turn gangsta. He played with the picknee, called Ella. She was coming up to her second birthday and had blonde hair, blue eyes and looked like an angel in the Bible. Often the white man and lady went to meetings. Vinton didn't know what they did at them, but knew they must be in shops because they always returned with big bags full of new things. One time, when the nanny was at the gym, Vinton baby-sat Ella.

The two of them sat on the sofa in the nursery watching Thomas the Tank Engine when Ella start fi bawl. He took her on his knee and made faces till she begin fi laugh.

'You look so sweet!' the white lady said, surprising Vinton. She threw off her coat and put down her handbag. 'Thank you,' she said, 'you're so good with her.'

'Mi like picknee, cept if dem bad and craven like Kermit, den mi haffi beat him bud.'

'Look at her, she's so happy.'

Vinton blushed with pride. Then he said, 'Mi gonna have one baby.' He didn't mean to say it, and as soon as he said it, he wished he hadn't.

'You are? Really. Who with?'

'Tanya-Kay.'

'Darling,' the white lady called to the man, 'Vinton's going to have a baby.'

'Just one?' the white man answered. 'Which of the harem have you selected for the honour?'

'Tanya-Kay.'

'Congratulations, Vinton. At least the mother is beautiful,' he laughed.

'Cho,' said Vinton.

'I can see why you'd roger her, but why on earth she wants to do it with you beats me completely.'

'Cas she love mi up. All de gal dem love mi,' laughed Vinton. 'Mi mash down every gal mi meet!'

'You can take all of Ella's baby stuff when you go.'

'Darling,' said the white man, 'some of it's really expensive.'

'... There's the basinette, bottles, bath, nappies, nighties, the travel cot ...' The white man shot her a look. '... Stop being so mean. If we ever need more we can easily get that stuff here. It's impossible in Jamaica.'

'Ya can carry it dung when ya go nex a Beach?' Vinton blurted.

'No way,' said the white man. 'I'm not taking that lot on the plane. You take it when you go. It's your baby.'

'Ya man,' said Vinton, 'for sure. Sorry.'

At night, Vinton merged into the London scene. His hosts took him to gallery openings in the West End, drinks parties in Chelsea, dinner at Quaglinos, Mezzo, the Soho House and other fashionable restaurants, and late-night dancing at nightclubs or parties in Notting Hill Gate. Vinton drank plenty, but ate little until he got home to Moma's fry fish, bammy and poff. Afterwards he lay down under the goose-down duvet on pure linen sheets, gazed about the softly carpeted bedroom with its silk curtains and thought This the life far mi.

Boydie didn't ring, but Vinton wasn't worried. He rang the Duke of Percy couple times bot de lady vex and cuss and use bad word. He didn't need Boydie to run away; after a week in the city Vinton knew how dem ron tings. He needed a job. No problem. There was one shop call Affice Angels where dem give out job. The white lady had told him when he'd asked what it was, and alone he'd located a shop where they rent and sell house, apartment and yard. Life inna London was criss and easy, smooth an' cool. You could pick any yard you liked from photographs in the big window.

Most days the white man and lady took him out. They went to the cinema – though always to films with too much chat and not enough gon and naked wuman. They went to ole 'eap o' art gallery and museum. One time they took him to an exhibition about Slavery Days. There were ole 'eap o' old picture dem of slaves and slavery days, and ball and chain and manacle and torture tool. The exhibits made the whities sad and solemn, and at one moment standing in the gloom in front of a set of handcuffs designed for a child, Vinton thought he saw the white lady wipe a tear from her eye, but it was dark and he wasn't sure. He nuh fancy that museum too much. The whities loved the past: they had old furniture, old pictures, and even drank old wine, when the shop sold new wine cheaper! Vinton wanted the future. Not the past. He found it at the Trocadero Centre, a huge build-ing in Piccadilly Circus devoted to electronic games and an exhibition about rock 'n' roll.

After only two and a half hours playing on the machines

the white man said, 'C'mon Vinton, let's get out of this hell hole.'

'No man. It criss. Dem would love i' inna Angel Beach. Love i'.'

That night they went to a party at the White Cube Gallery for Damien Hirst, then to the Groucho Club where Vinton sat on the sofa drinking vintage champagne squeezed between Jarvis Cocker and Damien Hirst. Later, him vamit into Damien Hirst's mother's handbag. When he got home he lay in bed thinking about the girls he had seen that night. Then he thought of Tanya-Kay, then Sophie, Claudette, Dawn, Marjorie and the others. In the Groucho there was a man dressed as woman. She, he, looked good, and give Vinton a wink and hold his hand. Mooney and the guys would laugh about that. He thought about them. Wondered what they were doing. He was happy inna foreign but missed certain things: bon an cheese, fry fish, Red Stripe brewed in Mo-Bay, doing do-do inna de bush, the big hot sun, which was shrivel and perish inna London, the warm day, for him stuff up wid cold, and the moon, which never come out inna London. Bot most of all him miss Mooney, Maxwell, Vices and the other likker people dem. And he miss Tanya-Kay, too, just a likker bit, and him tink bout her.

Sometimes, Vinton ventured out on his own. The white lady always checked how many layers he had on before he left the house, and the white man pressed bank notes into his hand, saying, 'Take this. Have a good time. Remember to leave enough for a taxi home. Have you got the address and phone number? Good. Let me give you a little bit more. Here. Take it. You look after us in Beach, so we'll look after you in London.' This way Vinton accumulated some money for when he ran away.

One afternoon Boydie got in touch.

'It a Vinton,' Vinton explained into the phone.

'Who?' Boydie's low voice asked.

'Vinton Wellington. Flossie Son. Busta nephew, and Wordswort nephew. Fram Cousin Beach, Bottom Side. Rayon Fairfax mi bredren.'

'U-Roy?'

'Ya man, U-Roy!' laughed Vinton with relief.

'How U-Roy?'

'Im cool. Im send him best wishes and regards.'

'So. Ya inna London?' Boydie asked.

'Ya man.' Vinton looked around to check no-one was listening, but the white lady had left the room and closed the door. 'Mi com a London fi live.'

'Wishart ya stay?'

'Mi stay right now wid som whitey friends inna Knights-bridge.'

'Dem have room or bed for me?' Boydie asked quickly.

'No, man, mi gotta leave ere. Mi hope fi link up wid ya.'

'Sure, man. Com an' see me. Let we have couple beers an' talk. Com dung a Duke o' Percy at nine o'clock inna morning.'

In the taxi to Peckham, he counted his money. He had forty-two pounds. It seemed a lot until he got to Peckham and the driver asked for seven pounds. That was 250 J. You could go to Kingston and back on that.

There was trash on the broken pavement and ply-wood over many of the windows in Peckham. Three black pedestrians bowed their heads into the gusty wind to cross the road. Vinton got out of the taxi and shivered before going into the pub. At the bar there was a big white man

on the telephone, with some papers on the bar beside him.
He put his hand over the phone the moment he saw Vinton.

'Whadder you want?'

'Mi am looking for somebady call Sherlock Allen.'

'C'min. Oi. Eddie Murphy. There's a mate here for you.'

Boydie came out of the ladies' toilet holding a mop. He
wore a thick polo neck jumper with a tight T-shirt pulled
down over it, a filthy pair of grey slacks and wellington
boots. He peeled off a rubber glove and met Vinton's
knuckles with his. Both men looked very happy, as if the
other one was the answer to their prayers.

'Let me finish up ere and then we'll take a walk up the
street.'

Boydie took Vinton to a house quite unlike the whities'.
It was dark, damp and fiercely cold. The front and back
gardens were filled with garbage, and many windows were
broken. Boydie kicked at the door and called out a name.
A big dog started to bark somewhere. A man downstairs
grunted, and they went into the basement where he let them
into a cold wet room and locked the door behind them.
Vinton shivered and sniffed. Under a naked bulb the white
man put a little plastic bag of crack on a formica table.
Boydie felt in his pocket for his pay.

'Ya wan' some?' he asked Vinton.

Vinton shook his head. 'Mi nah lick shit,' he said sheepishly.

'C'mon!' Boydie laughed. 'This is ow you keep the cold
out, innit? Smoke a pipe and I'll take you up to meet the
crew. C'mon. Ow much bread you got?'

Vinton put his hand in his pocket and pulled out his
money.

'The boy got some money!' Boydie beamed. 'Gimme
nother. Eel pay.'

Vinton took a pull on the pipe while Boydie held the flame to the crack. He felt great, not at all cold or nervous.

'All right!' he exclaimed. 'Let we meet de posse now!'

'Ya man,' said Boydie, now sweating, 'let we meet de boss.'

They headed up the street, their heads bowed into the cruel wind. 'You come on the right day, man,' Boydie explained. 'Tonight there's gonna be some action. We taken all we gonna take, you know? So tonight we gonna start the street war.'

'Ya man,' shouted Vinton. 'De street war!' This was the kind of talk he'd been waiting for.

'We been taking a lo' o' punishment, you know, but now we gonna sekkle the score.'

'Ya man. Now the yardy here, it time fi sekkle the scar.'

'Ya man!' exclaimed Boydie.

In a large council estate Boydie knocked on a door. A good-looking black girl opened it. Vinton smiled as sweetly as he knew, but the woman, when she saw Boydie, shouted, 'What the bleedin ell you doing ere again? Ow many times I told you get lost. I don't want you or your friends round ere, right?'

Boydie laughed, saying, 'Alright girl, take i' easy man.' To Vinton he said, 'C'mon.'

At another house on the other side of the project they gained entry. They went down a thin corridor into a room with four yout sitting around smoking cigarettes and looking bored. The teevee was on but nobody watched it, except Vinton.

'Boydie,' one of them called. 'Where's me ten pounds?'

'Old on, give me a minute. Hey, Vinton, me beg you ten pounds.'

'Lend it to him,' the first youth ordered Vinton.

'Respec,' said Boydie, as he took it. That left Vinton with

seventeen pounds. 'This is Vinton. He's just come in from Jamaica.'

'Where d'you come from?' asked the first youth. He was lean, with a trimmed beard and glasses.

'Angel Beach,' Vinton said proudly, adding, 'St John,' when there didn't seem to be any recognition.

'Never eard of it,' the first youth said, and the others laughed. A pretty girl of about seventeen came in the room. She was tall with a cornrow hairstyle. Vinton gave her an openly admiring look, and a big welcoming smile.

'What the fuck are you looking at?' she asked.

'The pretty gal who just walk inna de room,' Vinton answered.

'Nigger, fuck yuself,' she spat. Everybody laughed at that. Especially Boydie.

An older man of about twenty-two, good and fat, with a bald head and a big gold chain around his greasy neck came in. 'All right,' he said, commanding everybody's attention. 'We gonna move on them tonight. Everybody ready? Rahim? Kiddy? Sizla? Mucky? Who're you?'

'Mi name Vinton.'

'He just got in from Jamaica.'

'You wanna do some work tonight?'

'Ya man.'

'Cos we gonna need back-up tonight.'

'Yeh.'

'Yeh.'

'You godda gun?'

'Gun?' Vinton swallowed. 'No sah. Mi nah ave no gun.' Then after a moment he added, 'Mi leave dat back a yard.'

'You'll need one tonight,' laughed Sizla.

'We all gonna need one tonight,' said Mucky.

'Ya man.'

'For sure,' they all added.

Vinton was beginning to relax. Talking about guns with his new London crew was his idea of living. Then something terrifying happened: first Mucky and then Sizla reached under their T-shirts and took out pistols, real guns. Sizla slapped his from palm to palm as he bragged about what he was going to do that night, and Mucky kept aiming his at things around the room, pretending to fire.

'They think they got power,' Mucky said. 'But we got power. Right? Fuck them. We got power too.'

'And we gonna sekkle the score tonight,' said Boydie.

'Yeh,' said the others menacingly.

Vinton joined in, but wanted to say, 'Can't we settle the score widout gun? Ongle wid chat and curses and bad words?' Because the guns made Vinton tremble.

The big man said, 'I'll be back bout eight with Gambino. So be ready, okay? I'll see what I can do about a heater for you. Later.'

He left. Vinton was hoping he wouldn't get a gun when Boydie said to him, 'Gambino's the don. He'll get you a heater, no problem.'

Vinton started feeling not too good.

'Boy. You. Country boy.'

'Ya man,' answered Vinton.

'You got money?'

'Ya man,' Vinton answered.

'Go out and buy some cigarettes and gum. We need some.'

Vinton stood up. But when he got to the door, the one called Sizla said, 'Someone go with him.'

'I'm not going,' said Mucky. 'Freeze my ass off. No fuckin' way man.'

'He don't know nuttin. Relax,' said Boydie.

So Vinton went out on his own.

At eight o'clock on the dot two big cars drew up and double-parked outside the house. Vinton, Boydie and the other four soldier dem tucked their guns into their belts and trooped out into the cars. Vinton was shown into the back of a BMW with blacked-out windows and gold hub caps and radiator grill. Gambino was in the driver's seat. All Vinton could see of him was a big head with close-cropped bleached white hair, a massive jaw and a heavy gold and diamond earring that dangled down to a thick and violent neck. Beside him sat a light-coloured, wiry MC of some repute. Gambino turned to Vinton.

'You the rookie?'

'Ya man.'

'Take this.' He slapped a semi-automatic pistol into his hands. It felt heavy and dangerous. 'Load it up.' He passed back a clip of .32 shells. Vinton fed the bullets one by one into the hungry gun. 'Acquaint yourself with the safety,' Gambino ordered. Vinton clicked the little silver switch back and forth. 'Good.'

Without any sound from the engine, the car leapt forward, pressing Vinton into the black leather upholstery. They sped through wet streets gleaming with reflected neon and street lights. Gambino paid no particular attention to traffic signals.

'What about his initiation ceremony?' the MC asked, indicating Vinton. 'If he's gonna ride with the crew he gotta do the initiation ceremony.'

'Yeh,' agreed Rahim and Kiddy on either side of Vinton, cruel enjoyment in their voices. Vinton swallowed.

'This is his initiation ceremony,' laughed Gambino. The

speakers thumped out Coolio rapping "Gangsta's Paradise":
THOUGH I WALK THROUGH THE SHADOW OF THE
VALLEY OF DEATH ...

Gambino suddenly slowed down. They crawled through
a quiet street. Rahim looked behind them.

'Where's Mustapha?'

'Gone to deal with shit-face's wife and kids,' smiled
Gambino. 'Right. We're nearly there. Rahim, Boom Stepper,
Kiddy. In the building. Rookie, you stay with me to deal
with any witnesses and anybody they flush out.' The car
drew to a halt outside a minicab office in a three-storey
building. 'Right. Move! Go! Now!'

Vinton was just thinking that he had had all the fun he
wanted, cruising streets in a BMW with a posse, and was
ready to pack it in for the evening and go for a beer with
the guys or try to pick up some girls. But he was swept
along.

The car doors flew open and the youths rushed the building. There were cries of surprise and then gunshots, some
rapid, followed by screams and moans of the wounded and
dying. Vinton stood with Gambino, their backs to the car,
scanning the building and the street. A top-floor window
flew open; shouts could be heard from within, followed by
at least a dozen gun shots. A man with blood all over him
climbed out of the window onto the sill and tried to reach
for a handhold to get himself onto the roof, but a hand from
inside caught hold of his ankle and tugged until he fell, his
limbs flailing, his mouth twisted and screaming, down
towards where Vinton stood. He hit the pavement with a
horrible thud. But it didn't kill him, because he started
moaning, and tried to crawl forward.

Vinton wanted to say, 'Right. Mi gotta go now, guys. Mi
forget mi haffi check one person. See ya. Cool. Bye.'

Kiddy, at the window above, shouted, 'Gambino! They're at the door here. Get them from behind, man.'

Gambino ran into the building giving Vinton the order: 'Finish him off.'

Vinton thought he'd wait to see if the man died of his own accord before doing anything he might regret later. So far, he reminded himself, he hadn't done anything too bad. But the night was beginning to make him panic.

More shots, in quick succession, indicated that Gambino had come up behind his enemy on the stairs. A minute later Vinton heard Gambino roar and then stagger from the building holding his left thigh, which was soaking in blood. Vinton looked at him and thought: dat too bad. Dem trousers was cool. At that moment a young girl, no older than Nakissia, six or seven, darted out of an alley to see what the commotion was. She stood on the pavement, her hands held up to her face as she absorbed the horror of Gambino and the dying man on the pavement. Gambino levelled his gun at her and pulled the trigger, but it just went click.

'Kill her, kill her, before she gets away!' Gambino yelled at Vinton.

Vinton wanted to say, 'Bot she just one likker picknee,' but decided that it wasn't quite in keeping with the ethos of the Gambino posse. He felt in deep. Very deep. Too deep. The girl turned to run, Vinton raised his gun, closed his eyes as the sight on the barrel came up between her slender shoulders, and pulled the trigger. Nothing happened. The safety catch was on. By the time he fumbled with it and got it off she had disappeared.

The wail of a Police siren got louder and louder.

'The Beast,' Gambino cried. 'Get in the car and drive, arsehole,' he shouted at Vinton, staggering to the passenger seat.

'Mi kiant drive,' Vinton stuttered.

'You want me to drive with three bullets in my leg? Get in. It's automatic. Anyone can drive it.'

Vinton found himself behind the wheel with Gambino breathing stertorously beside him.

'Where's de udders?' he asked.

'Dead. It was a set-up. Someone talked. They knew we were coming. When I find out who it is ... aargh,' he moaned as he tried to reposition his leg. Vinton tried to recall the single driving lesson he'd had in Bessie, Devon's ancient Hillman, in the Back Street. The Back Street suddenly felt a long, long way away. 'Step on it.'

They lurched off, but Vinton soon got the hang of it. Gambino reloaded his gun beside him. 'Give me your gun,' he croaked.

'Dat cool, tanks. Mi ave plenty o' bullet,' Vinton replied.

'Don't be stupid, punk ass. You never know how many you have to kill.'

A Police car got onto their tail.

'Shall I slow down?' Vinton asked, thinking, maybe he could get off with just a speeding ticket.

'No. Faster.' Gambino ran down his window and started shooting back at the Police car. A minute later there was a squeal of brakes and the shattering crunch of a bad collision right behind them as the Police car hit another vehicle.

'All right!' Gambino laughed. 'That's one problem solved.' He leant back and raised the window.

The chopping sound of helicopter blades in the night air became steadily more audible, and a spotlight hit the car from above.

'Blue thunder,' said Gambino. 'Take a right at the top, then next left. Fast.'

They drew into some disused warehousing near the river.

Gambino directed Vinton through a maze of turns with the helicopter hanging overhead. Finally they came to a cul de sac blocked by a tall wire fence with more warehouses and the river beyond.

'Get out. Come on. Fast. If we can get over that fence we're in the clear. There's a tunnel on the other side.'

Vinton looked at the twenty-two foot link fence. He doubted he could climb it, and Gambino would have trouble getting over a bench.

'Open the boot of the car.'

Vinton went round to the back of the car, pressed the button and when the boot sprung open saw a dead man curled up around a holdall.

'Get the bag,' Gambino barked at him.

The bag was open enough to reveal its contents: four sub machine guns and eight bags of white powder. Sixteen kilos of coke.

'Put that on your shoulder and help me up.'

With the heavy bag on his left shoulder, and his right arm around Gambino's wide back, his hand under his wet, warm armpit, Vinton began to scale the fence one handed. The chopper alerted more patrol cars, because the sound of sirens once again rang in the cold damp night air, and soon head-lights panned across the graffitied warehouse walls.

'Faster,' urged Gambino.

A Police car skidded into sight and squealed to a halt. Two cops got out and ran towards the fence, which Vinton, despite holding a 215 pound wounded man and 48 pounds or armaments and drugs, was near the top of.

'Freeze! Police!' one of them called.

Vinton began to think of an excuse to explain away his predicament. It was not easy, even for a Beach man.

'Shoot them, for Christ sake,' Gambino gurgled.

'They're cops. You get life for that,' Vinton said.

'What's wrong with you, punk? Shoot them, arsehole.'

So Vinton, steadying himself by holding onto the fence with his teeth, reached for his gun. He turned, clicked off the safety, aimed and pulled the trigger, again and again and again. Boom Boom Boom Boom. They must have shot back because he felt a warm wet patch spreading all over his thighs. Sweet Jezus, he thought to himself, so much blood, I must be hit bad.

At that moment he woke up. He was bumping along in a minibus from the Donald Sangster International Airport at Mo-Bay on the winding coast road to Angel Beach. On his lap a mother had placed a sleeping toddler who had pee pee all over Vinton's lap. Outside, in the early evening gloaming, the familiar and comforting landscape of Firefly Bay passed by.

It was on the way to buy the gangstas' cigarettes in Peckham that Vinton decided things looked and sounded a bit too serious for his liking. He was all for violence and gangstas – so long as no-one got hurt. When he saw a taxi with FOR HIRE lit on it, he put out his arm and took it back to the warmth, safety, and yes, boredom, of the whities' house, where he stayed for two days before flying back to Jamaica.

Dusk at Flossie's shed. Mooney, Trevor, Vices and Trouble were playing dominoes on the roadside. Opposite, on a hammock, Rayon swung to and fro drinking one hot Dragon Stout. Inside the bamboo shed, Amoy was carefully pinning up the bad passport photograph of Vinton. Behind the shed Flossie was cooking puddin on a charcoal cooker, the smoke and sweet scent of which was wafting across the yard where some picknee played in the dust before bed. Tanya-Kay crouched on her haunches close to Flossie, helping her out in return for being allowed to stay in the yard, for she'd been run outa her yard by her father. Across the cove, the setting sun was reddening the cliffs, and the water was quickly darkening. Above, the deep blue sky was merging with the shadowy hills that encircled the village.

For a few minutes everybody but the picknee were quiet while they listened to a Bob Marley song on Irie FM, all their thoughts trained momentarily in the same general direction.

'Well I remember when we used to sit,' sang Bob,

'In the government yard in Trenchtown.

Hubba hubba servin the hypocrites

Mingle with the good people we meet.

Good friends we ave, and good friends we last ... (at that, Mooney looked away and took a long swig of his saff drink).

Along the way.

In this bright future you can forget your past

So dry your tears I say (here, Tanya-Kay looked out to sea)

No woman no cry.

No woman no cry.'

A minibus, Pomp Action, pulled up across the road from the shed, and the door on the far side slid back. It remained there for some time while the passenger, whom nobody could see, disembarked. The crash of the shutting door, and the gunning of the engine heralded the departure of the bus, on its way to Byng River, Sandy Island, Lemon Grove and Negril, revealing, after it left, Vinton Wellington standing with his voluminous luggage on the roadside.

The guys noticed him straight away, but carried on slapping dominoes on the table. Vinton, passing by them on the way to the shed said, simply, 'Yes.'

And they answered, 'Yes, Vinton.'

Inside the shed Amoy shouted, 'Tan-Tan!' joyously, bringing Flossie in the back door, her face almost breaking with happiness. Behind the shed, Tanya-Kay stopped grating coconut for a moment, and smiled, hearing his voice, before starting again. Rayon, on the other side of the road, slipped off the hammock and disappeared into the hills.

That night far up and down the line, people said to each other, where they gathered by the water pipe or on a porch or under a street light or in a shed, 'Vinton a back – ya hear? Ya man. Him a com back dung a yard. Ya man. Him com back dung.'

ACKNOWLEDGEMENTS

While writing *One People* I drew heavily on the following books: *Acts of Identity: Creole Based Approaches to Language and Ethnicity* by R. B. Lepage and A. Tabouret Keller (Cambridge University Press, 1985), *Jamaica Talk* by F. G. Cassidy (Macmillan, 1961), *West Indians and their Language* by P. A. Roberts (Cambridge University Press, 1988), and all of the incomparable works of Louise Bennet. Anyone interested in the Jamaican language will really enjoy these books. I would like to express my gratitude to Hawthornden Castle for giving me space and time when I needed both. The publication of this second edition gives me the opportunity to clarify something about the book. Angel Beach is a fictional village, it does not exist, and the characters and stories in *One People* are my invention. However, if you are lucky enough to visit Jamaica, you will find the same warmth of welcome and generosity of spirit that I hope pervades Angel Beach in any one of the hundreds of little fishing communities dotted around the island's gorgeous coastline. I must also thank Sian Austin and Julia Murray Scott for their early encouragement, and Emily Dewhurst and Amoy Williams for her help later on. Finally, my greatest thanks must go to my wife Portia, without whose generosity and brilliance I would never have been able to write *One People*.

If you would like to contact the author please email him at the following address:

guy.kennaway@virgin.net